D0126939

The Christmas Village

ALSO BY ANNIE RAINS

Sweetwater Springs

Christmas on Mistletoe Lane

A Wedding on Lavender Hill (short story)

Springtime at Hope Cottage

Kiss Me in Sweetwater Springs (short story)

Snowfall on Cedar Trail

Starting Over at Blueberry Creek

Sunshine on Silver Lake

Season of Joy

Reunited on Dragonfly Lane

Somerset Lake

The Summer Cottage

The Christmas Village

A Forever Home (short story)

The True Love Bookshop

THE CHRISTMAS VILLAGE

ANNIE RAINS

FOREVER
New York Boston

This book is a work of fiction. Names, characters, places, and incidents are the product of the author's imagination or are used fictitiously. Any resemblance to actual events, locales, or persons, living or dead, is coincidental.

Copyright © 2022 by Annie Rains

Cover design by Daniela Medina
Cover illustration by Allan Davey/Shannon Associates
Cover images © Shutterstock
Cover copyright © 2021 by Hachette Book Group, Inc.

Hachette Book Group supports the right to free expression and the value of copyright. The purpose of copyright is to encourage writers and artists to produce the creative works that enrich our culture.

The scanning, uploading, and distribution of this book without permission is a theft of the author's intellectual property. If you would like permission to use material from the book (other than for review purposes), please contact permissions@hbgusa.com. Thank you for your support of the author's rights.

Forever
Hachette Book Group
1290 Avenue of the Americas, New York, NY 10104
read-forever.com
twitter.com/readforeverpub

Originally published in trade paperback and ebook by Grand Central Publishing in October 2021
First Mass Market Edition: September 2022

Forever is an imprint of Grand Central Publishing. The Forever name and logo are trademarks of Hachette Book Group, Inc.

The publisher is not responsible for websites (or their content) that are not owned by the publisher.

The Hachette Speakers Bureau provides a wide range of authors for speaking events. To find out more, go to www.hachettespeakersbureau.com or call (866) 376-6591.

ISBN: 9781538703472 (trade paperback), 9781538703465 (ebook), 9781538723791 (mass market)

Printed in the United States of America

OPM

10 9 8 7 6 5 4 3 2 1

ATTENTION CORPORATIONS AND ORGANIZATIONS:

Most Hachette Book Group books are available at quantity discounts with bulk purchase for educational, business, or sales promotional use.
For information, please call or write:

Special Markets Department, Hachette Book Group
1290 Avenue of the Americas, New York, NY 10104
Telephone: 1-800-222-6747 Fax: 1-800-477-5925

For Ralphie. Christmas became magical again when you were born. Even though you're growing far too fast, I hope you'll always hear Santa's bell.

The Christmas Village

Chapter One

A noise woke Lucy Hannigan. She peered into the darkness of her bedroom, heart thumping beneath her heavy quilt, and waited to hear it again.

Or hopefully *not* hear it again.

Another loud bang had her body shooting upright in bed. It sounded like something had been knocked over outside. Was someone at her back door?

Lucy grabbed her iPhone on the bedside table and looked at the time. Five a.m. wasn't the hour for friendly visitors. But if this was just a friendly guest, then whoever was making the ruckus would ring the doorbell. From the back side of the house, someone would need to open Lucy's fence, which was secured by a lock.

Lucy eyed her French bulldog, Bella, who was snoring soundly in the corner of the room. "Some guard dog you are," she whispered, standing on shaky legs, her ears tuned to anything that went bump in the night—*er*, early morning.

Lucy had been out late, helping to deliver a baby at Maria Fernandez's house. Being a midwife, she was used to keeping late hours, but she'd hoped to sleep in this morning. Now she was wide awake with adrenaline pumping through her veins.

Something scraped against Lucy's back porch. She stood frozen for a moment. This time, Bella opened her eyes and lifted her head.

"Bella, bark," Lucy whisper-shouted. Perhaps the sound of a ferocious canine would frighten the intruder away. "Bark!"

Lucy had inherited her mom's old French bulldog along with this excessively large home in The Village, the oldest neighborhood in Somerset Lake, North Carolina. The house had belonged in her family for generations along with half the businesses in town. Along the way, families had grown smaller, businesses had been sold off, and all that was left in the Hannigan family now was Lucy and this pink house.

"Bella, bark!" she ordered again.

Instead, Bella lowered her head, closed her eyes, and huffed softly. Once upon a time, Bella had been trained to be a watchdog. Now she could barely hear or see. She could still catch a scent though. That wasn't helpful at this moment.

Lucy stepped out of her bedroom. It was the only one downstairs. She did everything on the first floor because Bella couldn't climb the stairs anymore. For the most part, Lucy just pretended that the second level of the house didn't exist. This house was big enough for two large families to live comfortably. It felt a bit wasteful to have so much unused space.

She shuffled quietly down the hall in socked feet, her heart pumping as she clutched her cell phone in her hand.

What did she really think she was going to do if she ran into a burglar? Invite him in for coffee?

The noise happened again. Lucy gasped. Then

she simultaneously pressed the Power button and the Volume button on her iPhone four times in quick succession—the shortcut to dial 911. The phone immediately began to sound an alarm that punctured the darkness. This time, Bella scurried out of the bedroom with a few loud barks.

Lucy held the phone to her ear, her hand shaking so hard she could barely keep from dropping it.

"Nine-one-one, what's your emergency?" a familiar woman's voice asked.

"Moira?" Lucy whispered. Moira was one of Lucy's best friends, and she worked as an emergency services dispatcher in town.

"Lucy?" Moira asked. "Why are you calling me here? This line is for emergencies only."

Lucy leaned against the wall in the hallway, one hand pressed to her chest. Her heartbeat forcefully thumped the pads of her fingers. "This *is* an emergency. I think someone is breaking into my home. There are noises on the back porch. Can you send a deputy? Or the whole sheriff's department?"

Moira asked a few more questions and kept Lucy on the line. She was so professional that Lucy almost forgot that the woman helping was her sarcastic best friend. Minutes felt like hours and then someone rang her front doorbell.

Bella ran ahead of Lucy, stopping behind the front door and barking in a deep, misleading baritone.

Lucy followed and went up on her tiptoes to look out the peephole. A Somerset Lake sheriff's deputy was standing on her porch. She wobbled on her toes until she could also see the man's face. Black hair, dark eyes.

"Is that a deputy?" Moira asked, her tone continuing to exude calm professionalism.

"Yes." Lucy returned to flat feet. Her heart was racing for a whole other reason now.

"So you're safe to disconnect this call?" Moira asked.

"Yes. Thank you. We'll have coffee later?" Lucy asked.

Moira audibly sighed. "These calls are recorded, Luce. Just text my cell."

"Right." Lucy tapped End on her phone's screen, reached for the doorknob, but hesitated. Of all the deputies at the Somerset Lake Sheriff's Department, why was Miles Bruno the one who responded to the call?

The doorbell chimed again.

This time, Lucy sucked in a breath and turned the knob. She opened the door and peered back at Miles, almost forgetting that she was terrified of whatever was making the noises on her back porch. This man still had a hold over her, even twelve years after he'd broken off their brief engagement.

"What's going on?" he asked, his tone just as professional as Moira's had been.

Lucy pointed in the opposite direction. "The back porch. There's a noise." She hugged her arms around her chest, realizing that she was wearing a too-thin cotton pajama top and pants. It was late November, and the chilly air zipped right past Miles, through her door, and penetrated her clothing.

Another noise had Lucy whirling in the direction of her kitchen, which led to the back door. "Did you hear that?" she asked breathlessly.

Without answering, he stepped over the threshold and walked past her.

What kind of egotistical burglar continued to break in once a sheriff's car had pulled into the driveway?

Lucy locked the front door behind Miles, just in case the burglar decided to run around to the other side of the house. She heard Miles open the back door and braced herself for a fight. Good guy versus the bad one. What if the bad guy won? What if he had a weapon?

I should hide.

Lucy looked around the living room, which still housed her parents' furniture. Everything she owned had belonged to her mom. Her father had passed away when she was in college. One morning, he'd had a heart attack in his sleep and never woke up. Lucy had been devastated at the time but losing her mom last year hurt even more.

Lucy hurried over to the couch and squatted down, sandwiching herself between it and the end table. She'd always been horrible at hide-and-seek as a child. Anyone with two good eyes would find her, especially since her breathing was so shallow that her lungs were making a scraping sound. She momentarily tried to stop breathing but that only resulted in an audible gasp a minute later and more shallow breaths.

She listened for what felt like an eternity. Then she heard heavy footsteps approaching.

Please be Miles. Please be Miles.

She squeezed her eyes shut and then jumped as Miles called her name.

"Lucy? I've dealt with your burglar. It's safe to come out now."

The breath whooshed out of her lungs. The good guy had won. Miles had always been one of the good guys, even when her broken heart had told her he was one of the bad.

∞

As soon as Miles heard the address, he'd known whose house he was en route to. Lucy Hannigan had lived in the pink house on Christmas Lane since she was a kid. And since they were teenagers all tangled up in the thrill of first love.

Lucy peered up at him from her hiding place behind the couch.

"There was never a burglar," he said. "But if there was, that would be an awful hiding spot."

Lucy frowned up at him. "Well, I didn't have a lot of time to find a better one."

He chuckled and offered his hand to help her stand.

She hesitated, and he knew she was just stubborn enough not to take it. Lucy was independent—that's something he'd always admired about her. All the women in his life had that in common. His mom, his sister, Ava. His aunt Ruth. Not that Lucy was a woman in Miles's life anymore. She was more of a friend who kept him at an arm's length. He couldn't say he blamed her.

Lucy surprised him by extending her arm and slipping her hand in his, palm to palm. He tugged gently, and she came up fast and close, her green eyes narrowing in. Her soft pink lips puckered and made a small O of surprise. "Thank you," she said a little breathlessly—probably because she was still calming down from the scare.

"You're welcome." He didn't release her hand immediately. She didn't let go either. Instead, they looked at each other for a long moment. Once upon a time, Miles could swear he saw forever in those eyes of hers, reaching across time to old age. He'd been able to imagine Lucy's red-toned hair turning a soft white and her sitting on a front porch swing still holding his hand somewhere.

Lucy pulled her hand away and dropped it down by her side. Her gaze flitted past him, a look of uncertainty crossing her expression. "If it wasn't a burglar," she said, "what was making all that noise?"

"An opossum. The little guy had his head stuck in a mason jar on your back porch. Want to see?"

Lucy looked horrified. She shook her head quickly. "No, that's okay. The mason jar is for harvesting rainwater," she explained. "My mom used it to—"

"Wash her face and hair." He nodded. "I know."

It was a Hannigan family beauty secret. That beauty secret had been common knowledge since Reva Dawson had put it up on her town blog a couple years ago, boasting something about pH levels and minerals and referencing the Hannigan beauty. Miles had seen a lot of rainwater jars out on folks' back porches since then. The Hannigan name had always been able to sell anything in this town. Even an old wives' tale.

"The creature is still in my jar?" Lucy folded her arms in front of her. Either because she was cold—the house was a little drafty—or because she was protecting herself, and not from a burglar this time.

"Yes. You had a plastic bin on your porch. I contained it inside to make sure it didn't run off while I talked to you." Miles grimaced. "I'll try not to break the jar but I wanted to make sure you won't be upset if I do."

Her arms loosened and dropped by her side. Lucy

looked from him to the back door and the critter beyond. "Those jars cost less than a dollar. The thing needs to breathe."

"He's getting enough to stay alive right now."

"No. You should free him." She shook her head. "It's just a jar. I can get another at the store—really."

But Miles suspected the jar held sentimental value. It was her mother's, just like the house and her dog. He'd been worried about Lucy since her mother passed. He saw something sad when he looked into her eyes. He'd wanted to reach out to her many times over the last twelve months but he'd always hesitated. She had close friends, and he doubted she wanted to hear from him.

"Go. I don't want that thing to die on my watch." Lucy gave his shoulder a little shove, the unexpected touch shooting unexpected warmth through him.

Miles started walking toward the back door, sending up a little prayer that he could save the opossum, the jar, and Lucy's heart. He stepped outside with Bella at his heels. She hurried over and sniffed the thing with its head in the jar. When it swung wildly toward her, she took off, running back inside.

Miles chuckled to himself. "Don't worry, little guy. I got you. You're creating quite the commotion this morning, you know," he told the opossum. It was gray with a white face and bright pink nose. Kind of cute, maybe, but this wasn't the first opossum Miles had come in contact with. He knew they had teeth like razor blades, and he didn't really want those teeth to come anywhere near him. The last thing he needed this holiday season was rabies.

"Okay, you grab the jar. I'll grab the opossum,"

he told Lucy, whose eyes grew wide. "Unless you'd rather touch the critter," he said, knowing full well she wouldn't.

She shook her head quickly, making him chuckle.

He grabbed the opossum's backside first. Then Lucy bent and secured the jar. They both straightened and looked at one another. Of all the ways Miles imagined he might get close to Lucy Hannigan again, having an opossum in a rainwater jar between them wasn't one of them. "On my count," he said.

She nodded, her green eyes still locked on his. She stepped away from the jar now, holding it far away from her body as if the creature might escape and launch itself at her.

They both lowered back to the ground and prepared to pull in opposite directions.

Miles's fingers tightened just enough around the creature to keep it still. As soon as its head was free, he was going to let go and let it scurry off this porch. "One. Two. Three." He pulled the critter. Lucy pulled the jar. The opossum was free with a quick pop of its head. Miles's fingers flung open, almost tossing the creature in the direction of the steps so that Lucy didn't freak out. From his peripheral vision, he could see that she was dancing on her feet, freaking out anyway as she watched the scene unfold.

Miles smiled to himself. It took all of five seconds for the opossum to disappear into the night.

Miles looked over at Lucy. "You okay?"

She looked a bit shell-shocked. "Yes. That was certainly an adventure for one night."

"Well, it's kind of already morning." He tipped his head at the scattering of light rising behind the mountain skyline. The mountains of North Carolina were softer than those on the West Coast. These rolled like a lazy river along the clouds. Any which way you turned in Somerset Lake, the view was the same—all sky and Blue Ridge peaks.

"I guess it is," Lucy said. She hugged the mason jar to her body. "And I will be wide awake for the rest of the morning. I was hoping to sleep in."

"Late night?" he asked.

"Nine hours of labor and delivery," Lucy confirmed. "But at the end of it, there was a healthy baby and two very exhausted and happy parents."

"A tired midwife too," Miles added.

"Yes." Lucy broke into a yawn. "But after all this excitement, there's no hope of going back to bed now."

Miles couldn't take his eyes off her as she fidgeted with the strings of her pajama pants and patted down her long auburn hair. "The bright side is you can enjoy your coffee while watching the sunrise."

Lucy noticeably stiffened. No, he hadn't been referring to the time they'd done that when they were eighteen—hers had been decaf because of the baby. Judging by her face, however, that's exactly what she was thinking about.

Time to leave.

Miles walked past Lucy and back inside the house. "I'm still on duty," he said as if to explain his rush. Not that she'd invited him to stay and catch up or enjoy a cup of coffee with her. "Do you mind if I wash my hands at your sink?"

"Of course. After rescuing me from my burglar, that's the least I can do," she said, following him inside the kitchen.

"You didn't need rescuing," he called behind him. "Although, I guess you would still be crouched between the wall and the couch right now if not for me," he teased. He turned on the faucet and pumped some soap from the dispenser into his palm.

After getting cleaned up, he headed toward the front of the house. He opened the door and stepped out onto the porch. "See you later, Lucy," he called over his shoulder.

"Goodbye. And Miles?"

He stopped walking and turned back. "Yeah?"

"Thank you."

"Just doing my job. And I'm glad I was the one who got the call. It's good to see you, Luce. Have a good day." He headed down the steps and made quick strides to his cruiser.

Once he was inside his car, he blew out a breath and flicked his gaze to Lucy, who was still standing in her open doorway. After a second, she turned back and closed the door behind her. Miles reversed out of her driveway to finish his shift. After that, he'd be going straight to the Youth Center, where he volunteered regularly.

With Thanksgiving coming next Thursday, the kids at the center were finishing up charity meal baskets. Once upon a time, Miles's family had been the one in need. These days, the Bruno family was doing all right, even if they'd never lived in a fancy mansion-size house like Lucy's in The Village. Miles had a good job with a stable income. Next on his list was to purchase a house of his own. Maybe after that, he'd finally be ready to settle down.

The problem was that he'd ruined any chances with

the only person he'd ever been interested in spending his life with. It was kind of hard to take back telling your ex-fiancée that the reason you'd proposed was because you'd felt obligated.

Ouch.

But telling Lucy the truth would sting a whole lot more—which was why he never would.

Chapter Two

Lucy stepped into Sweetie's Bake Shop later that morning, dragging her feet and in desperate need of a double espresso. She'd just left a client's home and really wanted something stiffer than her usual French roast brew.

The mother-to-be that Lucy had just visited didn't respect Lucy's time. The TV in her living room had been blaring, and the future mom was doing laundry in between Lucy's midwifery services, making what should have been a thirty-minute house call last well over an hour. This was one of those times, rare as they were, when Lucy missed being an obstetric nurse in a hospital setting.

"Hey, sweetie." The café's owner, Darla, waved from behind the counter. Never one to mince words, she said, "You look rough. Are you meeting my daughter here this morning?"

"Yes. Moira said she'd stop by after her shift." The shift where Moira had answered Lucy's 911 call. *How embarrassing.* Lucy was never going to live this down with her best friend. "Can I get a double espresso please?"

"Of course, you can. And I'll go ahead and make Moira's coffee too."

Lucy had no doubt that Darla knew exactly how her daughter drank her brew. Moira had always been an old soul, drinking black coffee since she was seven and reading the newspaper before she'd ever reached double digits.

"And what'll you have to eat?" Darla wanted to know. "How about a Sweetie Pastry?" Instead of naming the bakery after herself, Darla had titled it in honor of the Sweetheart Tree on the edge of Somerset Lake where lovers sometimes carved their initials.

Lucy looked at the food in the display longingly. Everything looked as good as it tasted. Lucy knew this firsthand because she'd sampled every cookie, pastry, and muffin on the menu. "A pastry sounds delicious but I think today I'll have a French baguette."

"You got it." Darla took Lucy's debit card, ran it through the scanner, and handed it back. Then she prepared Lucy's espresso and slid it across the counter along with the baguette wrapped in a square of parchment paper. "I'll bring Moira's breakfast over in just a sec."

Lucy thanked her and then found a seat along the wall of the bakery, which was decorated in soft pastel colors. Lucy settled at her table and took a sip of her espresso, looking up when someone called her name.

"Morning, Lucy," Mayor Gil Ryan said as he walked toward the counter.

"Hey, Gil." Lucy didn't harass the poor guy by calling him Gilbert the way that the guys in town did, knowing how much he hated that. Lucy thought it was a nice name though. It brought back memories of her teenage years reading *Anne of Green Gables* and falling hopelessly and helplessly for the character Gilbert Blythe.

Lucy pulled a piece off her baguette and popped it into her mouth, almost sighing at the cottony texture of the bread that practically dissolved when it hit her tongue. She hoped Gil would get his breakfast and move on quickly before Moira arrived. Moira always got a little frustrated with Gil's attention. He wasn't flirty or inappropriate in any way. He was just nice. And he was *extra* nice to Moira.

Darla, knowing her daughter and probably thinking the same thing, was quick in giving the good mayor his coffee and Danish. As Gil headed out with his breakfast in hand, he waved to Lucy. "See you later."

"Bye, Mayor Gil," she called back.

A moment later, Moira strolled in with their friend Tess at her side. Tess owned Lakeside Books and led the book club they attended every Thursday night.

"Thank goodness Gil is gone," Moira huffed as she laid her purse on the chair across from Lucy's. She sat down, and Tess took the seat right next to Lucy.

"I saw Somerset's friendly mayor come in and waited around the corner to avoid him," Moira explained.

Tess rolled her eyes and shook her head. "And I caught her in the act on my way here."

Lucy giggled, nearly choking on another bite of her baguette. "Gil is nice. Handsome." She ticked off the mayor's positive qualities on her right hand. "He's smart. Rich. A genuinely good person. What am I missing?"

"You're missing the fact that I'm not romantically interested in him."

Darla stepped over with Moira's coffee, bagel, and a kiss on the cheek for her only daughter, leaving a bright pink lipstick print in her wake. She also placed a coffee and bagel in front of Tess. "Morning, Tess. I'm assuming you want your usual?"

Tess reached for the drink. "Thank you, Darla."

"Of course." Darla looked at Moira. "How was the night shift?"

She blew out a breath as her bottom lip poked out. "Awful. I can't wait for Celia to get back from her honeymoon so I can return to working days."

"She's a newlywed. They should be up all night for entirely different reasons," Darla said with a snicker.

Moira reached for her coffee. "Thank you for this, Mom. I need it." She sipped it gratefully.

"Of course. Let me know if you three ladies need anything else." Darla turned and headed back to the counter.

"So..." Moira said. Judging by the grin on her face, she knew what had happened with Lucy's burglar. "An opossum, huh? Did he steal anything valuable?"

"Only my pride." Lucy rolled her eyes and sipped her espresso. "I'm guessing Moira told you what happened this morning?" she asked Tess.

Tess nodded. "I never knew you were so jumpy."

"The opossum was loud, okay? Very loud. And I live alone in a huge house with a ton of things that someone might want to take. How was I supposed to know it was an animal?"

Moira cackled and bit into her bagel with a loud crunch. "And Miles was the one who responded," she said after chewing and swallowing. "How did that go?" She waggled her eyebrows.

Lucy was beginning to regret asking Moira to meet her here. "He saved the creature and left."

Tess looked disappointed. "That's it? I thought there

might be something juicier to that story." Although a widow, Tess was the romantic of the group. All the books she chose for book club always had a happy ending. She wouldn't hear of it otherwise. Lucy guessed it was because Tess's own love story hadn't ended happily.

"Like what?" Lucy asked.

"I don't know." Tess shrugged. "Like a brush of the hand or better yet a kiss."

Lucy's mouth dropped even though she wasn't a bit surprised. "I hate to break it to you two, but Miles and I are friends."

"Boring." Moira took another bite of her bagel, hazel eyes rolling upward.

"If you want exciting, find a book in Tess's store," Lucy muttered.

After a quiet minute of eating, the conversation moved to other things.

"So, any leads on renting out your garage apartment?" Tess asked.

Lucy shook her head. "I've had that sign for renting my garage apartment out in the yard forever. Not one person has inquired. I was hoping the extra money would help me pay the last of my mother's bills."

"Bummer," Moira said. "I've heard of inheriting valuables after a loved one passes but never their debt too."

In Lucy's case, the bills were all related to the house. It was so unlike her mom to be irresponsible with finances. For Lucy's entire life, her mom had been frugal. In her last few years though, her mother had hired several contractors before she'd gotten sick and had failed to pay half of them. Funny, they'd all come collecting when Lucy was still grieving this time last year.

There was a roofer. A plumber. A painter who'd painted the entire house in a fresh shade of pink. There were so many unpaid bills for Lucy to take care of along with that of her mother's funeral.

Lucy had promised herself that she'd wipe them all out by the New Year, which by her calculation was only six weeks away. And for the most part, she had. There was only one outstanding bill left on Lucy's radar. "I really should sell the house. That would give me plenty of money to pay off the last debt my mom owes. But..." She trailed off for a moment. "Giving up the house feels like I'd be saying goodbye to my mom completely. And there's Bella. That's her house."

"Bella is a dog," Moira pointed out, eyes rolling again. "She'd adjust to a change of scenery just fine."

There was also the fact that Lucy loved living in the pink house. Even as a little girl, being there felt like having her own, life-size doll house. It had felt magical to her, and in some ways, it still did. Every corner of the house was special in some way, from the abalone shell backsplash of the downstairs sink to the antique oak stair baluster to the expansive upper level. Even the attic felt special with its stained glass windows that streamed in jewel-colored light on stored-away things.

"It's too bad no one's biting on the garage apartment," Tess said. "The passive income would be great."

Lucy leaned back in her chair and folded her arms in front of her. "And a couple months' rent would take care of the hot tub bill that my mom left me." She'd never even seen her mom use the hot tub. When Lucy had come home to be a nurse to her ailing mother, she'd just assumed it was paid for. Like everything else. Her mother's health had gone from bad to worse so quickly that there'd been no time to talk about frivolous things like bills and finances. Lucy's mom had barely been able to talk at all as the throat cancer metastasized through her body. One month her mom had been bustling with the energy of a dozen five-year-olds. The next, she'd struggled to open her eyes.

"Just be careful who you do decide to rent to." Moira popped the last of her breakfast in her mouth and chewed. "Getting a terrible tenant could make your life miserable. They might blare music at all hours, have parties, or have a dog that poops all over your property."

Lucy felt her eyebrows raise.

Moira dabbed her mouth with a crisp white napkin. "Trust me, I've heard it all on the dispatch."

"I'm sure you have," Lucy said, sharing a look with Tess.

"You could ask Reva to spread the word about the rental," Tess suggested. Reva Dawson ran a blog online about the town. She spread all the news she could get her hands on, which was why everyone in Somerset Lake read it as faithfully as they would any newspaper.

"That's not a bad idea," Lucy said. *Geesh. I must really be desperate to consider spreading the word on Reva's blog.* "Now that it's the holidays, it might be hard to find someone. People don't usually make big life changes this time of year."

Moira looked at her seriously. "It's a hard time of year for some people. The call center gets more calls than usual."

Lucy narrowed her eyes. "I know where this is coming from, and you don't need to worry about me. I'm fine."

"Great." As if to prove a point, Moira asked, "So what are you doing for Thanksgiving next week then?"

Lucy hugged her arms around herself even tighter. "Bella and I are, um, planning to stay home for a quiet day of reading. I have a huge stack of books that I've been meaning to get to."

"As much as I promote reading, doing so while home alone on Thanksgiving isn't the best idea," Tess said.

"Not home alone. I have Bella." Lucy understood that her argument was weak.

Moira gave her a serious look. "Just know that my offer for you to come to my family's home still stands. My mom owns a bakery. There'll be lots of breaded things."

"You can also feel free to join me at my parents' home," Tess offered. "I'm the only single person there so bringing an ally would be a good thing."

These weren't Lucy's first invitations. She knew her friends meant well. But it was somehow sadder to sit around everyone else's dinner table and pretend to be having a good time—when all you really wanted was to be alone to count your losses, which for Lucy, felt immeasurable in the last year.

∞

Miles had worked all day, starting early at Lucy's house. Now his shift was over, but instead of going home, he was in the next best place. In his mind, at least.

He stood at the head of one of three long tables

with kids of various ages. The kids were bused from the school to the Youth Center every afternoon, where they completed homework, played games, and worked on projects that taught them team-building skills while also benefiting the community.

Right now, they were working hard on making Thanksgiving cards to accompany the food baskets that they'd put together for the holiday delivery that always happened the weekend before the big day.

Miles walked between two of the tables, commenting on the colorful drawings as he passed through. The children on this side of the room were mostly younger, except for Charlie Bates. Charlie was thirteen but he liked to help out with the younger kids.

"Hey, Charlie. How're you doing?" Miles stepped over to where the boy was seated.

Charlie looked up, lifting his lanky shoulders to the ears he hadn't quite grown into yet. "Just hanging out, Deputy Bruno."

"Is your sister here?" Miles asked. Charlie's sister, Brittney, was fifteen and had the attitude of three teenaged girls.

"Nah. Mom doesn't make her ride the bus here anymore. She gets to hang out with her boyfriend," Charlie said.

"Boyfriend? Already?" Miles shook his head. "Well, thanks for helping out, bud. It's appreciated. How's your mom and dad?"

Charlie's eyes dulled. His father had been laid off last month, and from what Miles had heard, they were struggling. Even so, he hadn't seen the Bates family on the list of homes that would be receiving holiday food baskets this weekend.

"They're good," Charlie said in a less-than-convincing tone of voice.

"Glad to hear that. Let me know if I can help, okay? Don't hesitate to ask for anything you need."

"Sure." Charlie wasn't looking at him anymore. Instead, he was back to drawing bubble letters on a piece of paper for the little girl beside him.

Miles patted a hand on his shoulder and kept walking. "Keep working on the cards. We need them to be finished by this weekend," he said as he walked back down the aisle to join the other adult volunteers, one of whom was Jake Fletcher.

Miles had gone to school with Jake. They hadn't exactly been friends, but since Jake had moved back to town this past summer, they had gotten closer. Jake worked as a lawyer in Magnolia Falls, and he also helped his fiancée, Trisha Langly, run the Somerset Cottages down on the south side of the lake.

"How's Charlie?" Jake asked.

Miles's gaze moved to the boy sitting at the table with the younger kids. "He seems to be doing okay, considering."

"His dad is having a hard time finding work. I spoke to him the other day," Jake said.

Miles couldn't help thinking about his own childhood and father. "I wish the sheriff's department was hiring."

"Lack of jobs can be a drawback of such a small town. Hopefully something will turn up soon."

Hopefully before the family got into dire straits. When Miles was growing up and his own father had lost his job, it had a domino effect that ended with his father walking out on Miles, his sister, and their mother. After that, hard times had gotten even tougher.

Miles glanced over at Jake. "So, have you and Trisha set a date for the wedding yet?"

Jake grinned from one ear to the other. "New Year's."

"This coming one?" Miles raised his eyes. "That's fast."

"When you know, you know," Jake said. "And Trisha and I don't need anything big or fancy."

Miles listened to Jake go into a few details. He and Lucy had decided the same thing when they were briefly engaged. They didn't need a big church filled to the brim with people. They'd wanted to do things simply. Lucy had said she wanted to get married at dusk in the gazebo in the backyard of the pink house "with fairy lights everywhere." And she'd wanted to wear a white dress trimmed in lavender ribbon because, at eighteen, that had been her favorite color.

Miles smiled to himself, wondering for a moment if it still was.

"I was thinking..." Jake said, pulling Miles from his memories, "maybe you would agree to be one of my groomsmen."

Miles felt his jaw drop. "You hated me in high school."

"True. But I like you now."

Miles chuckled. "I'd love to stand up there with you, buddy."

Jake offered his hand for Miles to shake. "Thanks. I would appreciate it."

"Well, I'm honored." Miles smiled back at his friend, even if something inside his chest felt a little achy.

Miles had seen a lot of his friends settle down in the last couple years. He didn't buy into the whole biological clock; all he knew was that he liked the idea of spending his life with someone. But not until he was 100 percent certain he could support them. He didn't want to take any chances that he'd let a family down the way his own father had. That's why he'd hesitated about dating seriously until this point in his life.

Miles had the stable job and income now. The last thing on his list of criteria was a house that he owned instead of rented. His dad was always delinquent on rent. Miles's family had been kicked out of three homes before his dad left their family. It was always his mom's dream to own a house. A place that no one could take from them. Miles had adopted that goal for himself. He'd been saving money for a down payment, and he was gearing up to make it happen. Not today, but maybe next year.

For the next couple hours, Miles encouraged, played with, and joked with the youngest members of his community. At six p.m., when the Youth Center closed, Miles headed out to his truck. His cell phone rang as he slid behind the steering wheel. He pulled it out of his pocket and read the caller's name.

Tony Blake.

It was so infrequent that Miles's landlord ever called that he picked it up and answered right away, worried that maybe the older man was sick or needed help. "Hello, Mr. Blake. How are you?"

"Good. And yourself?" Mr. Blake asked.

"I can't complain. I have all my needs met, including a roof over my head." Miles laughed because it was supposed to be a joke.

Mr. Blake remained quiet. "About that," his landlord finally said, clearing his throat, "your lease is up at the end of the month." That wasn't news to Miles. For the last several years, he'd re-upped his lease every November after Thanksgiving. "The thing is, I'm downsizing my life, and I've decided that I won't be leasing out that house anymore. I'm going to move into it myself."

Miles took a moment to process what Mr. Blake was telling him. "I'm being kicked out?"

"I'm sorry, Miles. You've been a great tenant. But I'm afraid to say, I need you to move out. As soon as possible."

∞

The next day, Lucy woke to her alarm clock instead of a frisky opossum with its head in her rainwater jar. She had her coffee first and then showered and dressed for the day. After that, she went to the counter of Sweetie's Bake Shop for another cup of brew and a bite to eat before sitting alone at a table along the wall and pulling out her laptop.

She took a huge bite of her bagel as she pulled up Reva Dawson's blog for the town. Reva liked to use bullet points to list the town's goings-on. That way you could read it more easily, digesting the gossip in small increments so that you were sure to remember it all and pass it on.

It wasn't all gossip, of course. Listed today, for example, was that Lakeside Books was having a sale on children's titles, Choco-Lovers was having a chocolate tasting on Thanksgiving weekend, and the Youth Center was helping with the Thanksgiving meal baskets that were handed out every year. And...

Lucy nearly choked on her bite of bagel. It lodged at the back of her throat before she could swallow effectively. She slapped a hand on her breastbone, helping it along, and reached for her coffee to wash it completely down. The coffee was too hot though, and it burned the roof of her mouth. She supposed that was better than choking.

When she could breathe again, she reread the bullet point with her name.

- Lucy Hannigan had a break-in on Thursday morning. Deputy Miles Bruno was called to the scene and he handled the little rascal who turned out to be a raccoon.

"It was an opossum!" Lucy practically yelled at her computer screen.

Darla set a glass of water in front of Lucy. "Here you go, sweetie. Don't want you to keel over in my bakery. That's bad for business."

"And then it would make a bullet point in Reva's blog," Lucy said sarcastically. "Thank you." She reached for the glass of water and drank half before setting it down. Darla was still standing there.

"Can I get you something else?" she asked.

Lucy checked the time on her phone. "I have a client appointment in fifteen minutes." Lucy looked at Darla. "Can I get another one of these? For my client."

"Sure you can." Darla headed behind the counter, talking behind her. "Pregnant women love baked items. Who is this for?"

"Mandy Elks."

Darla glanced back, her mouth forming an exaggerated O. "She's ready to pop any day, isn't she?"

"Not soon enough," Lucy muttered under her breath. Mandy was sweet but pregnancy had made her a bit demanding. She was high-maintenance, which meant that Lucy was making daily house visits to check on her now. And to bring her breakfast.

Lucy paid Darla for the extra bagel, grabbed the bag, and headed out. Ten minutes later, she pulled into the driveway of Mandy Elks's house. After doting on Mandy just enough to maintain a pleasant relationship, she headed back to her car. Then she headed home for a small break. She noticed that the FOR RENT sign in the front yard had fallen—again. She walked over, picked it up, and drove it back into the ground, using the force of all her weight.

As she was struggling to get the stake deeper into the dirt, she was vaguely aware of a vehicle approaching, slowing, and stopping.

Lucy turned toward the deputy cruiser now parked on her curb. She straightened at the sight of Miles getting out, her heart betraying her with an extra beat or two. She supposed Miles would always have that effect on her. "Everything okay?" she asked.

"That's my line." He stepped toward her, all tall, dark, and handsome.

"I came by to check on you after yesterday's scare."

Lucy straightened. "I'm fine. Just a little embarrassed, that's all."

"I also came to ask about that sign in your yard. I saw it when I was here."

"Yeah. I'm trying to rent out the garage apartment," she said. "I've had this sign up for a while but no one is biting."

"Mind if I ask how much the rent is?" Miles asked.

Chapter Three

Lucy straightened as the implications of that question circulated in her mind. "Why do you want to know how much I'm charging?"

Miles shrugged. "Well, it appears that I'm about to be homeless. At least temporarily. Mr. Blake is downsizing and wants to move back into the house that I've been living in for the last seven years."

"When?" Lucy asked, trying not to notice how Miles's uniform hugged his shoulders and biceps just right.

"He wants to move in on Thanksgiving weekend."

Lucy gasped. "That's not even a two-week notice. Can he do that?"

"I guess I could fight it but it sounds like Mr. Blake needs the place more than me. He's had two knee operations this year, and he can't climb stairs anymore." Miles shoved his hands in his pockets. "I can get my stuff out and store it temporarily at my mom's place. I guess she'd let me stay on her couch for a while." His gaze dropped to the sign.

Lucy really wished he didn't know about her garage apartment. She didn't want him living so close by. That would be awkward, right? An ex-fiancé living on the same property? "I haven't decided how much to charge yet," she said. "I think there might be vacancies at the Somerset Cottages. Trisha fixed them up over the summer. That would be a nice place to live."

"They're all full," Miles said. "I called as soon as I got off the phone with Mr. Blake." He looked at her for a long moment. Then he pulled his hands from his pockets and presented open palms. "I just need a temporary place while I look for something else. I'm thinking it might be time for me to buy a small house of my own. I've been saving money with that in mind."

"Wow. Buying a house is a big decision."

"It is. I was going to start my search in the new year but I guess my timeline has sped up... I'm a great tenant. Mr. Blake can vouch for me."

This is so awkward.

"It would be handy to have a deputy sheriff living on your property. In case of break-ins," he said in a teasing tone.

"That's true. It's just..." Lucy trailed off.

Miles narrowed his dark brown eyes as his expression turned serious. "Because we used to date? Because we were engaged?"

"That was a long time ago," Lucy said, maybe a little too quickly.

"Right," Miles agreed. "And we're friends now. So it shouldn't be weird at all."

"Right." She didn't have this tightly coiled tension in her chest with anyone else though.

Miles held up his hands. "But we'll still be friends if you tell me no. I promise."

"Can I think about it?" Lucy asked. "I mean, I haven't even decided how much I want to charge or if I'm really even doing this."

They both knew that was a lie. The sign had been out for a month.

"Sure. Think about it. And in the meantime, I'll keep looking for a place to avoid sleeping on my mom's couch. I love my mother but she loves to get into my business a little too much, always asking who I'm dating, why I'm not dating so-and-so, and when I'm going to settle down with a nice woman."

Just that little bit of information was enough to make Lucy feel awkward. Seeing Miles all the time would definitely be weird.

Miles's radio buzzed to life at his hip.

"Shoplifting at Hannigan's Market."

He took a few retreating steps toward his vehicle at the end of her driveway. "I need to go. I'll talk to you later?"

"Yeah." Later. And hopefully by then she'd have a different renter in place and a reason to tell Miles he couldn't live here.

He paused before getting into his car. "Hey, Luce?"

"Hmm?"

"You know my mother makes enough food at Thanksgiving to feed the entire lake. She insists that I invite friends. I've already invited the other volunteers at the Youth Center. Jake Fletcher is bringing Trisha. Reese Whitaker said maybe. What do you say? Want to join us on Thursday at two o'clock?"

Lucy hesitated. "Um."

"Do you already have plans? Because Thanksgiving Day is not the time to stay home alone."

Lucy wondered if he'd been talking to Moira or Tess. Or maybe Reva had broadcast in her blog that Lucy was orphaned this year.

- Someone please adopt lonely Lucy Hannigan for the holidays.

Miles opened his car door and stood behind it. “Mom has this challenge,” he continued before she could argue with him. “Whoever invites the most people to Thanksgiving dinner gets an entire pumpkin pie to bring home.”

Lucy laughed softly. “I remember that challenge.”

“And agreeing to dinner doesn’t mean agreeing to renting the apartment to me. It’s two separate things.”

“Thanks for the invitation, Miles. The truth is, I actually already have plans.”

His eyebrows drew up on his forehead. “Oh. Okay.”

That was two small fibs she’d told Miles this visit. She was definitely not landing herself on Santa’s good list this year. Once Miles was gone though, she’d go inside her house and make plans. Then what she’d just told Miles would be true.

His radio buzzed again.

“You better go,” she said.

Miles glanced at his radio. “Yeah, shoplifting in Somerset Lake is a rarity.”

“Thank goodness for that. I’ll let you know about the apartment,” she promised—already knowing her answer would be no.

Miles flipped on the sirens of his car, which he rarely ever did, and sped to the scene. Shoplifting wasn’t necessarily an emergency and he suspected it was more of a misunderstanding than anything. He couldn’t remember the last time he'd truly caught someone stealing.

Within minutes, he pulled up to the curb in front of Hannigan's Market and cut the engine. He quickly got out and strode inside to meet the manager, Sandy Dunkin. She was sitting at a little counter along the store wall, separate from the cash registers.

Miles's heart sank when he saw who was sitting alongside her.

"Hey, Sandy." He stepped up to the counter and glanced over at Charlie Bates, the thirteen-year-old boy who helped the younger kids at the Youth Center. What had Charlie done? Now Miles was even more sure that this whole incident was a misunderstanding.

"Thank you for coming, Deputy Bruno." Sandy's expression was regretful as she glanced over at the teenager. "Charlie here had some store items in his pockets as he tried to head out. I caught him last week and had a talk with him already. I told him, if I caught him again, I'd have to call the law. He promised he wouldn't lift again, but..." She trailed off. "So, this time I called you. I had to keep my word."

Miles folded his arms in front of him. "Keeping your word is important. Hey, Charlie," he said, addressing the boy whose chin was tipped down, nearly touching his chest.

Charlie mumbled something that Miles thought might be a hello.

"I'll give him a ride to the station, and then I'll have him call his parents," Miles told Sandy.

Now Charlie's face whipped up to meet Miles's eyes. "No! You can't do that!"

Miles faced the boy. "Why not?"

Charlie looked at Sandy and back at him. Miles took the hint. They needed to talk privately.

"I'll take him from here, Sandy. Thanks for calling," Miles said.

"Thanks for getting here so quickly. I'm sorry, Charlie," Sandy said regretfully. "You left me no choice."

"Let's keep this just between us, can we?" Miles asked Sandy as an afterthought. Sandy wasn't one to gossip but sometimes word got out to the folks who were. Gossip wouldn't help Charlie or his family.

Sandy nodded solemnly. "I won't say a word."

"Thanks." Miles walked alongside Charlie out of the store and to his cruiser. The chilly late November air made him fold into his coat deeper as they walked. They didn't talk until they were both seated inside the warmth of his vehicle. "All right, Charlie. What's going on?"

Charlie's chin was resting on his chest again. "Please don't call my parents," Charlie pleaded.

Miles thought that maybe he heard tears in the boy's voice. "Give me one good reason."

"Because...because my mom lost her job a couple days ago too. My dad was supposed to be looking for work but the truth is he took off last week. My mom said he'll be back and we'll be okay, if we can just get through this rough patch."

"Rough patch," Miles repeated. That was an understatement.

"If I cause trouble for my family, I'll just make things worse."

"Then why were you shoplifting?" Miles asked. He still hadn't started his car yet.

"Because we don't have snacks. My sister and I just

get peanut butter sandwiches and ramen noodles right now. I wanted to get something else, just so Brittney would stop frowning so hard. I was going to pay for it later, I promise."

The story felt so similar to Miles's own. His family had struggled, and his dad had finally broken under the pressure and left. Miles had been older than Charlie at the time though. He'd been able to get a job, at least. "Stealing is a crime."

Charlie was pale. "Yes, sir."

Miles suspected the poor kid was envisioning himself going to jail from now until next January. "I'll make you a deal. I'll buy your family a little bit of food right now. But you have to do something for me."

Charlie's eyes widened as he looked over. "What?"

"I haven't figured that out just yet," Miles said. "No more stealing though. If that happens again, I will call your mom."

Charlie's gaze slid over to meet Miles's. "Yes, sir."

"Okay." Miles pushed the car door back open. "Let's go inside the market and get some snacks and maybe a box of mac and cheese for you and your family tonight. Then I'll drive you home."

"What'll you tell my mom? She'll wonder why you're buying us food."

"I'll tell her that you and I have struck a deal. I'm delivering food baskets this weekend. Think your mom will be okay with you helping? I can pick you up."

"Yeah. She won't mind."

"Good."

They went back inside the store, Miles waved at Sandy, and they perused the aisles, putting several items in a cart before checking out and leaving the store with a couple of bags of groceries. Then Miles drove Charlie home and walked him to the door.

"What's all this?" Mrs. Bates asked with a surprised smile.

"Well, I asked Charlie to help me with a few things. I hope that's okay. In exchange, he wanted to buy food. This is a good kid you got here."

The mother turned to her son. "That's very generous, Charlie."

"It is," Miles agreed, rubbing his chin thoughtfully. "I was wondering if you could spare Charlie tomorrow to help me deliver food baskets in the community."

Mrs. Bates looked between Miles and her son. "Well, he's babysitting a friend's six-year-old at one thirty. But he can help you in the morning, I suppose. This is a lot of groceries just for a few hours of work though." She gestured for Miles to follow her inside.

Miles walked through the living room and into the kitchen, where he laid the bags on the table. "I've been needing help here and there. I'm sure I'll find something else for Charlie to help me with."

Mrs. Bates nodded again. "Of course I can spare Charlie if you need him."

Miles turned to leave.

Charlie followed him to the door. "Thanks, Deputy Bruno," the boy said a bit shyly.

"You're welcome. You might regret this arrangement though, kid. I'm gonna make you work for it."

"I don't mind," Charlie said, a small smile touching the corners of his mouth. "I just want to help my family until my dad gets back."

"All right. I'll see you at the Youth Center at nine o'clock tomorrow morning, Charlie." Miles turned and headed back to his cruiser. When he got inside, he checked his cell phone before pulling back onto the road. He still hadn't heard from Lucy about that garage apartment. If she didn't call back, it looked like he might be sleeping on his mom's couch for Thanksgiving and maybe Christmas too. How was that for motivation to go ahead and make his dream of being a homeowner come true?

Ashley Herring should have been a movie star. She was a high-maintenance diva misplaced in a small-town void of all the extravagancies she seemed to think she was due. Lucy kind of felt bad for Ashley's husband, Allen, who was doting on his pregnant wife the best he could, and yet he seemed to keep falling short of Ashley's expectations.

"You want me to take a birthing class?" Ashley asked Lucy as if the idea was a foreign concept.

"Like Lamaze?" Allen asked.

"Kind of," Lucy said. "I teach the expectant mother's class over at The Village's community building on Tuesday nights. It's more than just breathing lessons. It's how to eat healthy for the baby and what to expect during the various stages of pregnancy. It's so important that an expectant mother take good care of herself. The father too."

"Can't you just teach me that stuff during our appointments?"

Lucy maintained her smile, despite her fraying patience. "This is more in-depth. The information I provide at the community building is on top of what

I'm already teaching you during our home visits. You don't have to come, of course. I'm just letting you know that it's an option."

Allen put his hand on Ashley's shoulders. "It'll be fun. Kind of like a date night."

Ashley's face scrunched up. "Date night is a nice dinner over candlelight. It's not commiserating with other swollen-ankled moms-to-be over acid reflux and Braxton Hicks pains."

Lucy's smile wobbled just a touch. "That's not what this is. Allen, you are free to come on your own if you'd like. It's good for husbands to be involved in everything going on during this special time."

"Well, he's not going without me," Ashley whined, her hands flattened over the mound of her belly, roughly the size of a basketball. Was Ashley like this before she'd gotten pregnant? Lucy wasn't sure because they'd only been acquaintances before Ashley had become her client.

"Great, then you two can come together. Tuesday nights at seven."

"What if I go into labor on a Tuesday night?" Ashley asked. "You'll be teaching a class. Who will help me?"

Lucy took a breath, drawing it deep into her lungs before answering. "If you go into labor on a Tuesday night," she explained, "then I will, of course, cancel or reschedule the class and meet you at the birthing center. The participants are all pregnant. They understand that labor is unpredictable."

"Thank you, Dr. Hannigan," Allen said.

Lucy had already told Allen several times over but it was worth repeating. "I'm not a doctor. I'm a nurse practitioner. If a real doctor hears you call me that, they might get offended. I didn't go to school as long as they did."

"Got it," Allen said, a small grimace lining his lips. "Sorry. We'll see you on Tuesday night."

Ashley didn't look happy about this new plan, which she was treating like an inconvenience. Lucy suspected that Ashley would be happy to have the knowledge as she progressed into her pregnancy though.

After leaving the Herring house, Lucy went by Hannigan's Market for groceries before going home. Hannigan's used to be owned by her family, but like everything else in Somerset Lake, it now belonged to someone else. Except for the pink house on Christmas Lane and Bella.

Note to self: Bella needs more treats.

Lucy pushed her buggy down the market aisles, heading toward the pet section. Groceries for one was quick and easy. That was the upside to being a single woman. The downside was that she shopped alone and ate alone. Everything she did, for the most part, was in solitude. She was the very image of an independent woman, which she was proud of, but sometimes she took it to such an extreme that she felt a bit lonely.

This close to the holidays, the aisles were extra crowded, and folks were chattier than usual. Lucy managed to make it out with just a few waves and hellos. Then she loaded the bags in her backseat and got into the driver's seat. She cranked the car and made a mental to-do list for the remainder of the day. One of the items gave her a pang of guilt. She still hadn't called Miles back about the apartment above her garage because she didn't have a good excuse to say no.

But she did have two good reasons *not* to say no. First, saying no implied that she wasn't comfortable with Miles. That there was still sexual attraction between them. That maybe she still harbored feelings for the man who had once broken her heart. He didn't just break one tiny little piece. He'd shattered it with all the gentleness of a sledgehammer.

Secondly, if she didn't say yes, she'd be carrying her mom's debt into the new year, which she'd promised herself, no matter what, she wouldn't do. She needed to move on from the heavy weight of it. Somehow, staying in her mother's debt kept her stuck in her grief as well. She couldn't fully move on until the last bill was paid.

Lucy reached for her phone, took a breath, and started to call Miles. She hesitated. Just the thought of holding a conversation with him made her anxious.

This is silly. They'd dated a million years ago. They were friends now. Just friends. Even so, instead of calling, she tapped out a text.

> ***Lucy:*** I've decided to charge $850 for rent through the end of the year.
>
> ***Lucy:*** Not sure if you're interested.

The rent Lucy was asking was fair, in her opinion. The garage apartment was complete with an open kitchen, living area, bedroom, and a bathroom. Lucy had lived there after high school and when she'd come back and forth during college.

The dots on her screen started bouncing.

She held her breath, part of her hoping that Miles wasn't interested. The other part needed him to say yes.

> ***Miles:*** That sounds good. I'll take it.

Lucy swallowed. Her mouth was suddenly parched. She was also shaking a little bit. Her ex-fiancé was moving in next door. This was probably an epically bad idea.

> ***Lucy:*** Okay then. When do you think you'll start moving in?
> ***Miles:*** I'm delivering holiday food baskets tomorrow for the Youth Center. I'll be there Sunday, if that's okay.

Sunday. As in two days from now. Two days from now, Miles Bruno would be living next door.

Lucy texted back.

> ***Lucy:*** Perfect. Sunday sounds good.

Chapter Four

On Saturday morning, Miles got up and quickly changed into a pair of jeans and a long-sleeved tee. Then he combed his hair, brushed his teeth, and headed into the kitchen. He drank half a glass of water and grabbed an apple for the drive to Charlie's house. That was one of the things that had him most excited for the day. Helping to deliver the food baskets with Charlie would be good for the kid. Sometimes when you were stuck in a hard time, seeing others in similar conditions made you feel less alone.

A short drive later, Miles pulled into the Bateses' driveway. Charlie was already sitting on the front porch, dressed in jeans and an oversize gray hoodie. He stood and paused for a long, drawn-out yawn and then continued walking toward Miles's truck.

"Your mom woke you up, didn't she?" Miles said in lieu of hello.

"I usually sleep in on the weekends," Charlie confirmed. "But it's all good. I don't mind," Charlie said with a shrug and another exaggerated yawn.

"Great. We're going to have an amazing day. You'll see." He glanced over. "Hungry?"

Charlie smiled for the first time this morning. "Yeah."

"How about we go to Sweetie's first and grab a little something to eat on the way? My treat."

Charlie looked a bit more enthusiastic. "Yeah. Mrs. Darla's chocolate muffins are the best."

"That's not breakfast. That's cake," Miles teased. "But whatever you want this morning, you get."

"Coffee too?" Charlie asked.

Miles side-eyed him. "Are you allowed to drink coffee?"

"My mom says I'm old beyond my years."

No doubt because life had dealt him a hard deck of cards thus far. "Half caff," Miles agreed.

Charlie was grinning now, boyish dimples carving deep holes in his cheeks.

After stopping at the bakery and loading up on carbs and coffee, Miles and Charlie went to the Youth Center to load the baskets into the back of his truck. Miles noted that the baskets looked disturbed as he picked the first one up. The contents were shifted around and laying unnaturally in some. He kneeled beside one basket and inspected it for a moment, taking stock of what was inside.

"What's wrong?" Charlie asked, standing behind him.

"I'm not sure yet," Miles said.

"What's in all the baskets?" Charlie asked.

Miles rattled off the list as he continued to assess what was off about the situation. "A couple cans of vegetables, a bag of rice. A box of mashed potatoes, a pie crust and a can of pumpkin filling, ingredients for string bean casserole—my personal favorite—and a gift card to the market for a turkey."

"Wow. That's a lot," Charlie said.

"It is." Miles realized that the bags of homemade cookies weren't there. He looked at the next basket and the ones near that. "The cookies are missing," he told Charlie. "All the bags of cookies that the women's group at the church made and donated are gone."

"Who would steal cookies from the baskets?"

Miles shook his head. "Exactly. Stealing Christmas cookies is pretty low." He blew out a breath. The baskets were still deliverable. They still had all the necessary ingredients for a nice holiday meal minus the special touch of something homemade. He'd deal with the missing cookies later. "All right," he said, looking at Charlie over his shoulder, "cookies or not, we have a lot of baskets to deliver this morning. We better get started."

They loaded the truck bed and then drove to the first address. Miles pulled onto a road and slowed to read the house numbers. "We're looking for house number two-eleven," he told Charlie.

Charlie peered out the passenger side. Then he pointed a finger into the window. "There it is."

"Great job." Miles turned in and parked. "All right. You wanna do the honors?"

Charlie blanched a little. "What do I have to do?"

"Grab a basket from the back, carry it to the door, ring the bell, and when someone answers, say, 'Happy Thanksgiving.'"

"That's it?" Charlie asked.

"Pretty much. Easy, right?"

"Sounds like it. What if they ask who the basket's from?" Charlie asked.

"Tell them it's from the Youth Center and the

community. Go for it, bud." Miles sat behind the steering wheel and watched as Charlie delivered the first basket and then the next ten after that. It didn't take long to hand out the first haul.

"Fun, right?" Miles asked.

"Better than the skate park," Charlie said, more enthusiastic than usual.

At nearly noon, they loaded the truck with more baskets and headed to the next house on the list.

"I'll get this basket," Miles told Charlie. "I know the people who live here."

Kimberly and Chris Evans kept to themselves for the most part. Miles hadn't even known they were struggling financially although, come to think of it, Chris was laid off last year. He'd been working odd jobs around town as far as Miles could tell. Miles wasn't sure what Kim did for a living.

Charlie leaned back into the truck seat, prepared to sit this one out. Miles got out of the truck, grabbed a basket from the back, and walked it up to the front porch. He rang the doorbell and waited. When no one came to the door, Miles rang the bell again. This time, he heard someone call from the other side. Miles leaned in and listened more closely. Were they calling for help?

He twisted the doorknob, and the door opened. "Hello?" he called out, searching for someone.

"In here!" a woman's voice answered.

Miles followed Kim's voice to the back bedroom and found the young woman bent over with her hand on her very pregnant belly. "Kim, are you okay?"

Her face was scrunched in evident pain. "I'm having... a contraction."

Miles set the basket down on the floor and pulled out his cell phone. He dialed 911 and held the phone to his ear.

Moira's voice answered. "Nine-one-one. What's your emergency?"

"Moira?" Miles asked.

Moira sighed. "What's your emergency?" she repeated.

"I'm at Kimberly Evans's home, and she's having contractions. I'm not sure if she's in labor or not. She might need to go to the hospital."

"Or," Moira said, "we can just send Lucy there to check her out first. Lucy is a friend of Kim's, and she's been giving her a little advice on the side."

"I see." He looked at Kim. "Would you like us to call Lucy Hannigan?"

Kim nodded quickly and then moaned through another contraction. "Yes, thank you. I don't want to go to the hospital before I'm ready. It's too expensive."

"I'm on it," Moira said on the other line. "I'm texting Lucy right now. And for the record," she told Miles, "a pregnant woman having contractions is not an emergency."

It felt like one to Miles. "Sorry," he said.

Moira laughed quietly. "Lucy just texted back. She says she'll be there ASAP."

"Lucy Hannigan is on her way," Miles told Kim.

Kim moaned through what Miles suspected was another contraction.

"Where's Chris?" Moira asked on the other line.

Good question. "What about Chris?" Miles asked Kim. "Where is he?"

"Out of town. For a job interview. I can't mess that

up—" Kim moaned again. "I just need Lucy. Please tell her to get here quickly!"

"Hear that, Moira? Tell Lucy we need her," Miles said. And he didn't misspeak. It wasn't just Kim Evans who needed Lucy. He was out of his element right now, and Lucy couldn't get here fast enough.

ᘓ

Lucy got to Kim Evans's house as quickly as she could. She bypassed Miles's truck in the driveway, noting that the bed was full of food baskets. Charlie Bates was waiting on the front porch, waving Lucy in that direction.

What is Charlie doing here?

Charlie was the thirteen-year-old son of Maria Bates. There was no time to ask questions though. Kim needed her. Lucy stepped inside the house and followed the painful sounds toward the back bedroom where Miles appeared to be trying to make himself useful, fluffing pillows and putting them down by Kim's feet.

"What's going on, Kim?" Lucy stepped quickly toward the bed.

"Oh, thank goodness you're here! I'm...having contractions," Kim said through a grimace. "They're pretty bad."

Lucy could see that clearly by Kim's scrunched expression. "How far apart?" she asked.

"A few minutes," Miles answered. "I've been timing them."

Lucy's gaze hung too long on Miles, who was not the patient. She looked at Kim. "Your water isn't broken?"

Kim shook her head. "No."

"Any bleeding?" Lucy asked, scanning Kim's body for anything alarming.

"No."

"Good. Okay, I need to examine you to see what's going on." Lucy turned back to Miles and gave him a pointed look. When he didn't move, she asked, "Can you give us some privacy?"

"Oh. Yeah. Of course." He looked embarrassed and maybe a little shell-shocked for the brave deputy who always seemed to have his act together. He hurried out of the room and closed the door behind him.

Lucy returned her focus to her friend. Kim's current contraction seemed to be letting up. Her face relaxed, and her eyes opened fully. "You know Chris and I don't have insurance. We can't afford for me to go to the doctor's office any more than I need to."

Lucy sat on the edge of the bed. "I know." And she'd agreed to check on Kim for nonurgent situations if the mother-to-be was also getting cared for at the free pregnancy center in Magnolia Falls.

Lucy pulled a pair of sterile gloves from the medical kit she'd brought with her and went through a short exam. The Braxton Hicks contractions were easing up, which was a good sign.

"You're not in labor," Lucy finally said. "You're not even dilated. Did you overwork yourself today somehow?"

Kim was lying back on her bed, her hands resting on her swollen belly. "Maybe a little. I decided that the house needed cleaning, and I couldn't seem to stop."

"That's called nesting," Lucy said. "You're preparing for the baby, who doesn't appear to be coming today."

That was good news since Kim's due date wasn't until next month, closer to Christmas.

"Thank you for coming over so quickly. And on a Saturday too."

"You're welcome. And you can feel free to call me about anything. You know if the situation is urgent. Medical insurance or not, you go to the hospital if you have contractions that don't ease up, your water breaks, or if you have bleeding." Lucy narrowed her eyes to make a point.

Kim nodded solemnly. "I know. I will, I promise."

"Good."

Kim shifted back and forth to bring her body to a sitting position. Then Lucy walked to the bathroom directly off the bedroom to dispose of the gloves and wash her hands. Miles and Charlie were waiting in the living room when Lucy walked back out.

"She's resting. There won't be a baby today or any need to go to the hospital," she informed them.

Miles looked so nervous that it was almost adorable. He turned back to Charlie. "I promised to have you home by one o'clock." He pulled out his cell phone to check the time. "It's ten minutes till."

Charlie stood from the couch. "Right. I'm kid-sitting to earn extra cash."

"At least you got to deliver the first round of baskets with me. I really appreciate the help," Miles said.

"It was actually kind of fun. You don't have to drive me home. I just live at the end of the road, and the kid lives across from me."

"You sure?" Miles asked.

"Yeah." Charlie shrugged lanky shoulders as if to say, *No big deal.*

Miles gestured outside. "Grab a basket off the truck bed and bring it home to your mom."

Charlie hesitated. "Really?"

"Of course. We have plenty." And Charlie's family needed the food as much as the rest of the folks who'd be getting a basket today.

"I will. Thanks. See you later, Deputy Bruno."

"I'm volunteering at the Youth Center next week," Miles called to him. "I'm gonna need help setting up and breaking down a few activities."

"I can lend a hand," Charlie said on his way out.

Lucy watched the two and wondered about the arrangement they seemed to have. Why would a thirteen-year-old boy be helping Miles? She didn't think it was out of the goodness of Charlie's heart, although she'd always considered the teen and his older sister, Brittney, to be nice.

Charlie stepped out of the house, leaving Lucy and Miles alone in the front room.

"So she's okay?" Miles confirmed.

"If she wasn't, I'd drive her to the hospital myself," Lucy assured him. "It's just Braxton Hicks contractions."

Miles's gaze clung to Lucy. "Thanks for getting here so fast. Pregnant women make me nervous."

This made Lucy laugh. "Why is that?"

"I had to deliver a baby once. A neighbor called about a disturbance, and I responded to the call. There was no time for an ambulance to arrive. It was just me and the mother, and within minutes, baby made three."

"Sounds scary. But I'd also say you were lucky," Lucy said. "Seeing that miracle of life is the most amazing feeling in the world."

Miles looked down at his feet for a moment. "It was. It also made me feel pretty helpless. I was glad to have you on speed dial today."

"Well, if that's all, I'll return to my previously scheduled Saturday." Lucy stepped past Miles onto the porch and watched as he locked Kim's front door and pulled it shut.

"What were you doing on your previously scheduled Saturday?" he asked, walking beside her as they descended the porch steps.

Lucy didn't want to tell Miles the full truth, that she was bored out of her mind and dwelling on the fact that he was moving into her garage apartment tomorrow. "I was thinking about cleaning the apartment so that it's nice and shiny for you when you arrive in the morning."

"No need to do that. I'll clean it." Miles shoved his hands into his pockets. "Instead, why don't you join me in delivering the rest of the food baskets? I have about fifteen left."

Lucy looked at his truck, weighing her answer. She kind of wanted to say yes but that would mean spending all afternoon with Miles while riding shotgun.

She turned back to him ready to say no because she didn't need to encourage the attraction between them. And part of her suspected that he was only asking because he was worried about her being alone as the holidays drew near. That seemed to be a theme among the people she knew. "Are you going to try to make me say yes to your mom's invitation to Thanksgiving dinner too?" she asked, folding her arms over her chest.

Miles chuckled quietly. "No. But the invitation still

stands. It's up to you if you decide to accept it or not. You'd be doing me a favor by coming and helping me win my mom's guest challenge."

Lucy really wanted to help deliver the baskets with him. Focusing on others was always a good way to forget your own problems. Or the fact that Lucy was missing her mom right now. "Okay," she finally said. "I'll help."

∞

Miles's palms were sweaty against his steering wheel. Pregnant women unnerved him but so did Lucy Hannigan. "What's the street number?" he asked as he slowed on the next road for delivery.

"One-nineteen," Lucy read off.

Miles pulled his truck into the driveway of the next stop and parked. He pushed his door open and turned to Lucy. "You coming?"

She said yes but there was something uncertain in her green eyes.

"The receivers are always happy to see us. We're offering a gift."

Lucy nodded. Then she pushed her door open, too, and met him at the back of the truck. Miles lifted the basket with a huge burgundy bow on its handle into his arms and tipped his head toward the house, gesturing for Lucy to follow him. Once they'd cleared the steps and stood in front of the door, he looked at Lucy. "Mind ringing the bell? My hands are full."

Lucy pressed the button, and they waited.

A moment later, a woman came to the door. Miles knew almost everyone in town. It was his job to know people as much as to protect them. "Hey, Mrs. Pelletier. I have a special delivery for you just in time for Thanksgiving."

The woman opened the screen door with a wide smile and bright eyes. "All that is for me?" she asked with slight astonishment.

"Yes, ma'am. Can I step inside and set it down somewhere for you?"

"Yes, please." The woman looked at Lucy. "Lucy Hannigan? Is that you?"

"Hi, Mrs. Pelletier. Yes, it's me."

"It's been so long but you look exactly the same as you did when you sat in my class, front row." She continued to hold the screen door open for Lucy to enter as well. "Just stick the basket on my kitchen table if you don't mind, Miles."

Miles had been in Mrs. Pelletier's Language Arts class as well. He'd always preferred sitting in the back row. Not because he wanted to goof off, but so that he could monitor who was getting into trouble. He hadn't been a tattletale. He was just a cop in the making.

"The preacher at my church put a box in the reception area for people to drop their names and addresses in if they were struggling for food this time of year," the retired teacher said. "I never do that kind of thing because I figure there's always someone who needs it more than me." Mrs. Pelletier weaved her fingers in front of her midsection. "But I did this year." Her expression looked pained. "Please tell me I'm not taking from someone else who needs it. Because if I am, you take that basket right back and give it to another person."

"It's yours," Miles said. "We have plenty of food."

out the kids is great. I always
big kid yourself."
. "Did you?"
"In a good way. You were always
Nothing seemed to get to you."
ne said.
upset, you never let it show. You
collected at all times. Even when
n." She winked. He guessed the
t she hadn't thought out because
between them coiled. She pulled
l glanced around the room, seem-
istraction. "This is a great space.
it here."
sket from Lucy's arms, balancing
tipped his head toward the third
to leave the baskets in there."
?"
a minute."
t here checking out the facility,"
im. "I might even shoot some

kid in me might want to play too."
ved. "That sounds kind of fun."
notion.
d headed toward the office. He
laced the two unclaimed baskets
ng about the missing cookie inci-
ay. He hoped nothing else would
, he locked the office door before
l Lucy on the small court where
ildren often played.
ball to her chest and eyed the goal.

Mrs. Pelletier looked relieved. She stepped toward them and gave Miles and Lucy tight hugs while thanking them profusely. As Miles and Lucy headed down the porch steps and back to his truck, he looked over at Lucy.

"Well?" he asked.

"That was nice." Her face was lit up. "Can we do it again?"

Miles chuckled. "We sure can. All afternoon."

Chapter Five

The afternoon flew by quickly. Before Miles knew it, he and Lucy had delivered to the last address on the list. There were two spare baskets in Miles's truck, however.

"I need to stop by the Youth Center on the way back to your car, if you don't mind," he told Lucy. "I want to leave these extra baskets there. Jake said he'd try to deliver them tomorrow."

"Sure." Lucy shifted into a more relaxed position in the passenger seat next to him. She didn't seem in a hurry to get home, which made him feel good. Maybe two people who'd once been in love could still be friends after all.

They weren't even really friends these days. They were a bit awkward around each other. Too formal. Too guarded. Today, however, they'd laughed and had fun together. It was a nice shift.

He pulled into the Youth Center's parking lot and cut the engine. "Wanna come in? I'm just going to the office but I think you'd enjoy seeing the place."

"Sure. I've never been inside the Youth Center." Lucy got out and met him around the front of his truck. They walked into the building together, each carrying

"Air ball!" Miles called out at the very moment that she tossed it forward.

Lucy spun to teasingly glare at him. They were having a lot of fun together. It seemed to be the theme of the day. "I'd like to see you do better."

Accepting the challenge, Miles jogged over and swiped the ball off the floor, dribbling farther out so that he could show off his skills. Then he stopped and held the ball to his chest while eying the goal.

As he propelled the ball forward, Lucy called loudly, "Don't miss!"

The ball slipped out of his grasp and shot forward, nowhere near the goal.

Miles turned to point a finger at her. "Hey, that's cheating."

She could barely contain her laughter. "What? You can dole it out but you can't take it yourself?"

"If I remember correctly, you never did like to play fair anyway."

Lucy's lips parted. "What memory are you referring to?"

"Senior year Battle of the Spirit Walls. It was the girls against the guys, and someone tampered with our spirited artwork. The boys should have won."

She giggled quietly. "I think you're just a sore loser."

Miles found himself walking toward her. "Only when I know for a fact that we should have gotten the trophy."

"Such a competitive streak, Deputy Bruno." She folded her arms across her chest. "That was a very long time ago."

"Yes, it was," he agreed.

"It's not good to dwell on the past." She tilted her head to one side. "We should let things go, right?"

He didn't think they were talking about the spirit wall competition anymore.

"I mean it was over a decade ago," she added.

He lowered his voice to a whisper. "In some ways, it feels like it was only yesterday."

Lucy's arms tightened over her chest. "You haven't, um, dated much since high school. Not that I can see, at least."

"Maybe you're not watching closely enough. I dated Gina Manacle last year."

Lucy lifted her brows. "For about a week."

"A month," he corrected, pleased that she'd even noticed. "And why do you care who I'm dating?"

Lucy looked away, her attention appearing to bounce around the room. "I don't. I'm just saying, you're not getting any younger, Miles Bruno."

"Noted. I have a few requirements before I settle down though."

"Oh?" Lucy looked at him with interest. "Like what?"

"Well, I guess there's just one more thing to tick off my list. I already have a job and a stable income with benefits. All I need now is a house." He swallowed. He rarely spoke about his father or those years after his parents had split up. "I don't want to be like my dad and take on more responsibility than I can manage."

Miles wanted to make sure he was better than his father. The next time he committed himself to someone, he was going to be there for the long haul, through thick and thin. "You haven't dated either, by the way."

Lucy's lips parted. "I've been a little busy, caring for

my mom and then grieving for her. I haven't exactly felt romantic, I guess."

They looked at each other.

"I'm sorry about your mom," Miles finally said. "You shouldn't have had to go through that alone."

Pain registered in Lucy's expression. She looked down at her feet for a moment. He heard her soft intake of breath before she looked back up at him. "Tess and Moira were there for me. And Della Rose."

Miles reached out to touch her, hoping she wouldn't pull away. She didn't. "Friends are great for listening and taking your mind off things. But in my experience, they always go home. They aren't there to hold you. Also, speaking from experience, it's when they leave that you usually fall apart."

Lucy lifted her chin stubbornly. "I don't fall apart."

They had both changed since they were eighteen but that was one major change Miles saw in Lucy. She was fiercely independent now. He wondered if she'd even allowed her friends to be there for her while she'd grieved her mom. He also wondered if this change in her was partly due to the fact that she'd leaned on him once and he'd let her down.

"I was just speaking in general." Miles's hand was still on her arm. She looked down at it until Miles dropped it back by his side. He thought that maybe she was going to slap him or yell at him. Or demand for him to take her home. Perhaps he'd crossed an invisible line with his touch. He should have known better.

Instead, surprising him, she sniffled a little, her eyes glossed up, and she buried her face into his chest. Then she began to cry.

∞

This was twice in one week where Lucy felt mortified in front of Miles. He still had his arms around her, and she was suddenly very aware that she was crying on his shoulder—literally.

"I'm sorry." She stepped back and wiped the tears from her eyes. "I'm not sure what just happened."

"Don't apologize. I'm guessing you miss your mom."

Lucy looked up. "Yeah. This time of year is just harder. And something about today peeled back my emotions."

"There's something about bringing people a little bit of joy. It's definitely an emotional experience."

She sniffled and took a shaky breath, her cheeks a ruddy pink. "I'm fine now."

"You sure?"

"Yeah." She laughed quietly, more out of embarrassment than anything. It was so unlike her to cry in front of someone else. "I just feel silly."

Miles's hand was on her shoulder again. "Don't. You know you can break down on me anytime."

Lucy swallowed. "I just try to break down as little as possible. It's not productive."

"I'd argue with you on that one. Holding things in isn't good either."

Lucy's mistake was looking into Miles's dark brown eyes. Once their gazes were locked, she felt like he could see right through her, and she couldn't seem to look away. He was right. She was holding everything in, including a few lingering feelings for him. She wanted to lean into another embrace, but this time, she wanted to tip her head back and kiss him. To be kissed by him.

"You ready for me to take you back to your car?"

The disappointment she felt was as unnerving as allowing herself to cry in front of him. "Yeah. Thank you." They headed back to his vehicle and drove to the Evanses' house where Lucy's car was parked along the curb. "So I guess I'll see you tomorrow," Lucy said. "When you move into my garage apartment."

Miles gave her a serious look. "About that. I would never do anything you didn't want, Luce. If you don't want me renting that space, it's okay. Just tell me, and I'll find somewhere else to go."

"What? Why are you saying that?"

"I realize I'm not your perfect renter," he said. "I'm giving you an out. Just tell me now, and I promise, there'll be no hard feelings."

She wasn't exactly comfortable with him being so close, even if it was only temporary. That was her issue though, and she'd work through it. "I'm not going back on our agreement. You need a place to live, and I need a renter."

"Okay then. I'll move in tomorrow."

"Great." Lucy forced a smile and pushed open the passenger door to step out.

"You won't even know I'm there," Miles assured her.

Lucy seriously doubted that would be the case. "Goodnight, Miles."

"Night."

Lucy walked to her car and got inside. She checked her rearview mirror, where Miles was still parked. No doubt he was waiting to make sure she got off okay, because that was the noble thing. The right thing. The Miles thing.

Miles was a man of honor, a man of his word.

Unless of course he promised to marry her and love her forever. Then he had no problem going back on what he'd said.

"Get over it already, Lucy," she said under her breath. Then she started her engine and drove back to the house on Christmas Lane, where tomorrow Miles would be living next door. She needed rules for this new relationship to work. Her brain worked overtime as she drove, forming boundaries for this new arrangement she'd just agreed to.

Rule #1: She wouldn't go inside the apartment once Miles had moved in.

Rule #2: She wouldn't share a meal with him after dark. Too intimate.

Rule #3: She wouldn't break down on Miles again. Also too intimate.

And Rule #4, which was maybe the most important rule of all: She absolutely would not kiss Miles Bruno like she desperately wanted to—ever.

Chapter Six

Miles was up early Sunday morning and loading boxes into his truck. It was going to take several hauls. His buddy Gil had offered to come help him once he was awake. Gil said he'd text when he was ready.

Since Miles had packed his coffee maker into one of the boxes, he drove over to Sweetie's first to start his day with the necessary jolt of caffeine and sugar.

Darla waved from behind the counter. "I hear you're moving this weekend," she said as Miles approached.

Miles figured Darla's daughter, Moira, must have filled her in. And Moira must have heard it from Lucy. That's how things worked in Somerset Lake. One person told the next, and they told someone else. If it was really juicy information, it ended up as a bullet point on Reva's blog. "I'll be staying in Lucy's garage apartment until I can find a more permanent solution." Like a house of his own. It didn't matter if it was the smallest house in Somerset; it only mattered that it was his. "Can I get a coffee and a bagel please?"

"Of course you can, sweetie. Want to try some pumpkin spice cream cheese on it?" Darla asked.

"That sounds delicious. Thank you."

"You're welcome." Darla turned away from him and started gathering his order. When she turned back, she slid her gaze to someone sitting at a table against the wall of the bakery. Miles's gaze followed. The queen of the gossip chain herself was seated against the wall. "Reva is over there working on the day's blog post."

Miles picked up his coffee and cream cheese bagel, thanked Darla, and stepped over to say hello to the love-to-hate blogger. "Good morning, Mrs. Dawson."

Reva looked up from her laptop, her bright blue eyes lifting over pale blue glasses. "Miles. It's so nice to see you. I thought you'd be moving today."

Miles chuckled. "I am. Just getting a little breakfast first."

"So you're moving into Lucy's place?" she asked, her voice lifting an octave. Reva had hair that was almost a pale pink in this lighting and dark lipstick-stained lips that gave her face a dramatic splash. The woman herself was as colorful as her personality.

Miles sipped his coffee before answering. "The garage is disconnected from Lucy's house, as I'm sure you already know. We'll be living on the same property but not living in the same place," he said pointedly.

"I see." The older woman nodded. "Well, I'm sure she'll be happy to have a man in uniform on her property, especially after that break-in scare the other day."

Which Miles still wasn't sure how Reva had found out about. Did she have a source at the dispatch? Or own a scanner?

"It's an awfully big house for one woman," Reva went on.

Miles was well aware that Reva was fishing for another bullet point for her blog. "Yes, it is."

"I just feel for that Lucy after losing her mother right after the holidays last year. It'll be her first holiday without her mom. I sent her an email inviting her to have Thanksgiving with me, you know. I'm a widow and don't have a whole lot of family. I always invite people in my same situation over."

"Lucy isn't a widow," Miles said.

"No, but she's alone. That's the common thread. And no one should be all by themselves on such an important day."

"So Lucy is going to your house for Thanksgiving?" Miles asked, remembering that Lucy had told him she had plans when he'd invited her over to his mom's before.

"Oh no." Reva shook her head. "She declined. She didn't give a reason but I'm sure she has one."

Miles suspected that Reva was asking if *he* was the reason. And if he was, she'd bullet point him on her blog. Her efforts were almost humorous.

"I hear you two were out delivering food baskets yesterday. What a nice thing for the community."

"The Youth Center raises money and makes the baskets every year." As he was sure she already knew. "The recipients are all confidential," he added, just in case Reva thought she'd put the list of those who'd gotten baskets in her next post.

"Of course they are. No one wants their personal business splashed on a blog for others' entertainment."

"Glad you agree." He needed to say goodbye before he said anything that Reva could use. "Well, enjoy your Sunday, Mrs. Dawson."

"Oh, I will. I'm heading over to the church at the Point in just a bit."

The Point was an outdoor service that happened on the lake. "It's getting colder outside. I thought Pastor Lance would have stopped for the season."

"Oh no. He only stops for rain and snow. He's committed. Tell Lucy I said hello." Reva's eyes narrowed on Miles.

He tried to keep his expression completely neutral because who knew what she'd read from it at the mention of Lucy's name. "I will. If I see her. We're in two separate places," he stressed. "We'll be more neighbors than anything."

"Of course you will be," Reva said, returning her fingers to the keyboard of her laptop. She started typing again, her purple nails tapping in quick succession.

Miles felt a jolt of paranoia streak through him. What was she typing? What had he just said? "Well, I'll see you later, Mrs. Dawson."

"Good luck on your move today, Deputy Bruno," she called as he left the shop.

Miles waved at Darla one more time and stepped outside. Fall was in full effect with the chilly air and orange-red colors making a canopy overhead. Miles got back into his truck with his coffee and bagel. He unwrapped the bagel and set it on his lap before putting his truck in drive and heading to The Village.

Who'd have thought he would ever be moving to the nicest neighborhood in Somerset Lake? He was only renting, it was only temporary, but still. Miles Bruno at The Village. He took a bite of his bagel, which was just as satisfying as the thought of where he'd be living for the undetermined future. Ten minutes later, he pulled onto Christmas Lane, his gaze snagging on a sign that was up at the neighborhood's entrance, announcing The Village's annual Merriest Lawn Contest.

The neighborhood of Victorian houses attracted a lot of attention at Christmastime because they decorated so extravagantly. Folks came from all over to drive through and look at the lighted displays. For the folks who lived here, it was a competition with a hefty dollar prize.

Miles pulled into the driveway of Lucy's two-story Victorian pink house with the unconnected garage, also pink and trimmed in white. Another who'd-have-thought crossed his mind. Who'd have ever thought that he would live in a pink home? The guys at the department were sure to give him grief over this. Latoya, the administrative assistant there, would likely give him even more grief.

Miles finished off his bagel and stepped out. Lucy's car was in the driveway, but knowing her, she'd be going to church at the Point soon, just like Reva. And Reva would undoubtedly needle her for information about this new arrangement.

Miles walked to Lucy's door. He just needed to get the key to the garage apartment. Then he planned to stay out of Lucy's hair for the rest of the day.

He rang the doorbell and waited, hearing Bella's barks grow closer as she headed in his direction. Where was the little dog the other night when Lucy had been terrified that someone was breaking in?

Lucy opened the door and glared at him.

Uh-oh. Judging by his new landlord's stance, she had a bone to pick.

She lifted her chin, jaw muscles clenched tightly, making her high cheekbones even more defined. She crossed her arms and lowered her voice. "What did you do?"

∞

Lucy was about to explode. She hugged her arms around herself as Bella ran past the door's threshold to get Miles's attention. *Traitor.*

"What do you mean?" he asked, a cup of coffee in his hand.

"I just read Reva's blog—yes, I subscribe to it—and she told the entire town about our new living arrangement." Lucy arched a brow high on her forehead.

"Okay." He sipped his drink and looked at her, ever calm, cool, and collected, which was infuriating at the moment. "That's a problem because...?" He trailed off.

Lucy blew out an exasperated breath. "Because she recapped our past for everyone in town who didn't already know it," she explained.

Miles lowered his cup of coffee and shook his head. "Everyone already knows about our history, except maybe the one or two new people here who probably don't subscribe to Reva's blog."

"You don't care that she told everyone we used to date? That we were..." She hesitated. Maybe it wasn't worth recapping. "That we were once engaged." Something ached deep inside her heart.

Miles's gaze locked on hers. "I don't care that the town knows that. There's no changing the past. Or hiding it. It is what it is."

Lucy felt a little silly for caring so much in light of Miles's lackadaisical response. "You have to be careful what you tell Reva."

"I know, and I was. I'm staying in your garage apartment temporarily until I find somewhere else to live. That's all I said."

Maybe she was overreacting. Yeah, that was likely

the case. She was overly sensitive about what people thought of her. Being the pregnant–not pregnant, engaged-and-then-dumped girl will do that to a person. "Good," she finally said, loosening her arms and letting them drop by her sides.

"What was in the post that was so upsetting to you?" Miles asked.

Lucy blew out a breath. "Nothing really. Just the way she painted us. You know how she likes to embellish things. She said we were two star-crossed lovers, a modern-day Romeo and Juliet, because our families didn't want us dating."

Miles took another sip of his coffee. "For the record, my family was fine with us dating. My mom has always adored you."

Lucy avoided his eyes. Her mom had liked Miles well enough. She hadn't been terribly pleased about the pregnancy scare though. Lucy looked away. Maybe talking about this wasn't a good idea. She looked past Miles to his truck full of boxes. "I'll get the key and show you the apartment." She walked inside for a moment, leaving Miles standing on her front porch. Then she returned and walked past him, leading him across the lawn toward her garage.

Miles stepped in behind her.

"Since the staircase is inside the garage, I'll give you a key to both doors. Sorry for the mess," Lucy said, gesturing at the garage. "This was a catch-all for my parents when I was growing up."

Miles looked around. "You have a lot of Christmas decorations in here."

"My parents loved to decorate."

"I remember. Their displays got bigger every year."

"That's because they won the neighborhood's Merriest Lawn Contest every year," Lucy said, even though she knew he was already aware of that fact. "They used the enormous cash prize to buy more decorations. It was their winning strategy." Everyone who entered paid a registration fee, which added up to be the huge cash prize for the winner.

Lucy began to climb the steps up to the apartment. Once she'd reached the landing, she turned and handed him the key. His fingers brushed against hers as he took it and opened the door. Then he stepped inside.

She stayed and watched from beyond the door.

Miles gave her a funny look. "You're not coming in?"

Lucy shook her head. "I have some ground rules for this arrangement."

Miles lifted his cup and took another sip of his coffee as he seemed to wait for her to continue.

Lucy took a breath. "Because we do have a history together, I think we'd be wise to set some boundaries."

"Such as?"

"For starters, I don't think I should come into the apartment while you're living here. It's not very big anyway and, well, it's just too personal. It's where you sleep and eat and shower." She was rambling. "And I don't think we should share meals. It might be tempting to do so since we'll be living on the same property and we'll be alone. But it's too intimate."

"Fair enough. Any other ground rules?" Miles asked.

Lucy nibbled softly at the inside of her lip. She could keep the one about breaking down on him to herself. And the one about kissing too. She shook her head. "Nope. That's it."

"Well, I can handle those two things."

"Great. Me too," she said, still standing on the welcome mat outside his door.

"Well, if you can't come inside this apartment, then I guess you can't help me move in today."

Lucy hadn't thought that she was expected to help. But now she realized not offering would be rude. "Oh."

"Just teasing. I suspect you're going to church this morning."

"I am. Aren't you?"

"Planning on it. I was going to unload these boxes and head over."

Even though the weather was getting cooler, most people drove to the service on golf carts and bicycles, bundled up with knit hats and lightweight jackets.

"I'll help you get the boxes up here," Lucy offered. "And then we can ride together on my mom's golf cart."

Miles grinned at her. "You're already proposing to break your first rule."

"Well, you're not officially moved in yet. The ground rules can start once you are," she said.

"I see. And you're willing to go to church together? That's not crossing some unspoken boundary?"

"We're friends," Lucy said. "And going to church is one of the most platonic things you can do with someone. It's fine," she said. Because being here together and making him drive his truck while she rode separately in a golf cart implied that the history between them was such that they couldn't ride together due to hard feelings or unresolved feelings—neither of which she wanted people to speculate on.

"Okay then." He set his cup of coffee down on the countertop inside and headed past her. "I won't turn down help but you only get to lift the lightweight boxes.

I don't want to be responsible for you being sore at work tomorrow."

Lucy followed him to his truck. "Which ones are lightweight?"

Miles reached into his truck bed and pulled a box toward him. "This one is pretty light." His fingers brushed over her skin as he set it in her arms.

Lucy stiffened.

Miles must've noticed because his eyes narrowed. "Is it too heavy?" he asked, preparing to remove it from her arms.

"No." She shook her head. "I got it." Then she turned and headed back toward the garage and up the steps, pausing at the welcome mat on the landing before stepping into the living area. She hadn't broken Rule #1, she'd just modified it a tiny bit. And she didn't intend to break or modify any more.

∞

Just as Miles had expected, there'd been quite a few eyes and questioning looks at him and Lucy sharing a golf cart to church, including a raised eyebrow from his own mother. Most folks in town read Reva's blog so they'd already gotten the scoop that he was moving into Lucy's garage apartment.

He'd never been one to care about small-town talk. For the most part, he ignored it. But the fact that Lucy cared made him want to mind the chatter more than usual. For that reason, when she'd shivered during the closing prayer of the service, he'd resisted offering her his jacket like he wanted to. She probably wouldn't have taken it anyway.

Now they were pulling back onto Christmas Lane, heading to her pink house at the end. Miles pointed to the sign he'd seen earlier about the neighborhood decorating contest.

"You going to use all those decorations in your garage to try and win the Merriest Lawn Contest?" he asked.

Lucy shook her head. Her reddish-brown hair was blowing behind her as the wind zipped across their faces. "No, I don't think so. That's a lot of effort. My parents used to spend hours upon hours perfecting their display every year. After Dad died, Mom did all the work herself, hiring Mr. Plumly down the road to do the stuff that required a ladder." She got a far-off look in her eyes as she talked, no doubt missing her family.

"Sounds like fun to me," Miles said. "The only outdoor decorating my mom ever did was to put up a wreath." But that had been due to financial limitations more than an indicator of her holiday cheer. Things were better now, and his mom over-accommodated for all that she hadn't been able to do back then.

"Anyway," Lucy said, "I've got clients, and I'm starting a class for new parents at The Village's community center. I don't really have time to pull off something like entering the Merriest Lawn Contest." She pulled the cart into her driveway and slowed. A tap of a button on a remote had one of the garage doors raising so she could park inside.

Miles's gaze lingered on the holiday decorations he'd seen earlier. They took up nearly half the storage space. It had to be thousands of dollars' worth of lights and metal and wooden characters like Rudolph and Frosty. "I can do it. If you want me to."

She turned the golf cart's key into the off position and looked at him. "No, that's okay. You're busy too. You have your job and your volunteer work at the Youth Center." She stepped out. "And today you're all booked up with moving."

He stepped out as well. "Yes, I am. I need to head back to my former home and get another load of stuff. Moving is a pain but I don't own too much. I should be done by this evening." His friend Gil had offered to help today but something had come up and required his attention as the town mayor. He'd texted Miles during the church service earlier.

"Want me to come with you? I can help," she offered.

Miles stared at her across the golf cart. "You sure that won't be breaking one of your rules?" He said it in a teasing manner to lighten the mood. He really wouldn't mind Lucy tagging along with him today but not because he needed help moving boxes. He'd forgotten how much he enjoyed her company. She was fun to be with, and he suspected she would otherwise be spending the day all by herself in that big house that was all too full of the memories of her late family members.

"Those ground rules don't start until you're officially moved in, remember?"

"I see." Miles grinned. "In that case, I'd love a hand."

∞

Many hours later, Miles scooted the last box against the wall of his temporary home and exhaled as he looked around the small five-hundred-square-foot space. It was appropriate for a college student but not a thirty-year-old man. He wanted room to stretch his legs and a nice-size yard for a garden. Lucy's yard was huge, of course, but it wasn't his.

Miles stepped over and looked out the tiny window above the kitchen sink. The sun was on its descent, and the day had disappeared. Lucy had helped him clean his former place before locking the door and saying goodbye to it for good. "I could go for a glass of water right now but I'm not sure which box has my glasses."

"Guess you need to unpack all this stuff," Lucy said from behind him.

He turned to face her, not pointing out that she was now standing in his apartment. That was against her first rule. What was her other rule? Not having dinner together? "I don't think I'll unpack too much. I'll just have to pack up again once I find a house to buy," Miles said. "Speaking of which, I need to contact Della Rose."

"So you're serious? You're going to buy a house?" Lucy looked surprised.

"I've never lived in a house that didn't belong to someone else," Miles explained. "My mom always had a landlord when I was growing up. Owning a house of my own just seems like a milestone. It'll feel as if I've finally made it somehow." He felt a little silly saying that out loud, but it was true. "Plus, I know you don't want me here as a long-term tenant. You'd probably prefer someone who won't cause such a stir on Reva's blog."

Lucy shrugged. "It seems like I can't do anything without making the news on Reva's blog anyway. Apparently, my life is good fodder."

Miles understood what Lucy was talking about.

Lucy had left Somerset Lake for a period, but as soon as she'd returned to care for her sick mother, she'd gone right back to being the subject of gossip. There'd been speculation about how long she would be staying at first. Then on whether she was dating the male hospice nurse who'd tended to her mother. She hadn't been as far as Miles could tell, and admittedly, he'd followed that story closely.

After Lucy's mother had passed, there'd been speculation on whether Lucy would sell the beloved pink house. When she didn't, there'd been a story on the possibility that the pink house was haunted by her parents, and that's why she was staying. Reva hadn't given any meat to that story. She'd just mentioned that some people were talking about the possibility.

Miles didn't know where Reva came up with her "news." He liked to think the information Reva purported was harmless but Lucy had always been extra sensitive about being the target. Some of the gossip that had hurt her was his fault, he guessed. And he'd always feel regretful about that fact.

"Thanks for derailing your Sunday to help me today," Miles said.

"I didn't have much else to do. It's going to be a short week coming up, with the holiday and all. I can't predict if one of my clients will go into labor, but assuming they don't, I'll only be seeing clients on Monday through Wednesday."

"And what will you be doing on Thursday?" Miles asked for the second time in a week. It was starting to feel repetitive, but he was worried about Lucy.

She didn't meet his gaze. "I'm not sure yet, to tell you the truth."

"So you weren't telling the truth when you told me you had plans the other day?" he asked.

"Not exactly. But maybe my plans are to just stay home with Bella and have a quiet day. Is that so wrong?"

Miles propped his body on one of the stools at the small kitchen island. "Not if that's what you want. As long as you don't find yourself missing the people you would normally spend the holiday with too much."

Lucy swallowed as she looked down for a moment. "The last few years, that's just been my mom. My dad has been gone awhile now, and my grandparents too. I'll miss my mother even more than I'm expecting to probably. But that's going to happen regardless of where I am and what I do."

"If you don't want to have a huge meal with someone else's family, maybe it can just be you and me. That way you're not all by yourself."

Lucy shook her head. "No. I'm not going to let you skip Thanksgiving dinner with your family on my account. You need to be there for every holiday you get because you never know if you'll get another one together."

Miles wished he could help Lucy in some way. Grief took time though. "Reva said she invited you. You could go there."

Lucy lifted a shoulder. "Maybe. We'll see." She turned and headed back to the door. Conversation over. At least for now. "Goodnight, Miles."

"Night." He resisted the urge to walk her out. "See you tomorrow." And the day after that. Maybe living here temporarily wouldn't be so bad after all.

Chapter Seven

Where am I?

Miles awoke in the middle of the night. He felt disoriented for a moment. He was used to the moonlight streaming in through the blinds on his right side. Now it streamed from his left.

He rolled to his side to avoid the light as his mind connected the dots. *Right.* Two days ago, he'd moved into Lucy's garage apartment. He'd awoken in a similar fashion last night. He supposed it would take a few nights before he fully adjusted to his new home above Lucy's garage. She was a mere hundred feet away somewhere, lying in her bed sleeping. Or awake like him.

Miles kept his eyes closed as he pondered that thought a bit too long. Thinking of Lucy lying in her bed was probably against one of her rules.

He sighed loudly into the night. This was not a good way to start what was supposed to be a platonic relationship. Unable to return to sleep, he got up and walked out of his room to get a glass of water. He drank it standing at the kitchen sink. This apartment was much smaller than his rental home had been. It took just a few short steps to get to any place in the apartment.

Miles checked his cell phone to gauge the time. He had to work early tomorrow so he'd better sleep if he wanted to be alert on the job. He set his glass down and headed the short distance back to bed, pausing at the loud, creaky floorboard beneath his foot. He shone the light there for a moment, thinking that it looked a bit water damaged. Then he shone his phone's light at the ceiling where there was a dark water spot.

It looked old. Nothing to worry about tonight.

He continued to bed and lay down, forcing his eyes shut and his thoughts to go anywhere except to the pink house next door. His alarm clock woke him a short time later. It felt like he'd only been asleep for minutes instead of hours. He cracked an eye and flinched at the direct sunlight coming through the blinds.

He rubbed his eyes as a yawn stretched his face. Coffee would be nice but he still didn't know which box his machine was in. He'd just have to wake himself with a hot shower. Miles stepped into the tiny bathroom in the apartment. Yesterday he'd discovered that Lucy had placed two folded towels and washcloths inside. That was very much appreciated because he didn't know where he'd packed his own towels either. He stripped off his clothes, turned the nozzle to On, and stepped under the water's spray.

Freezing cold water hit his skin like pointy icicles.

Miles made a series of startled noises as he hopped around on the slick flooring of the tub, nearly falling in the process. Then he maneuvered around the spray to twist the nozzles, turning the knob with the *H* all the way to the right and the knob with the *C* for cold all the way to the left. He waved a hand under the water. Still freezing.

He'd had a hot shower yesterday, but apparently it was a one-and-done kind of deal because only freezing cold water sprayed out right now. This was bad. He was going to have to go coffee-less and take a cold shower after a second night of restless sleep. This didn't bode well for his Tuesday or for his temporary living situation.

An hour later, Miles walked into the sheriff's department wearing his uniform and holding a to-go cup of coffee from Sweetie's Bake Shop.

Latoya Marcus looked up at him from the front desk. "Did you bring one of those coffees for me?"

Miles's smile slipped away. "Uh, I didn't know you wanted one."

"I'm just teasing you. You look like you could use that coffee right about now. Rough night?"

He paused at the front of her desk to talk to her. "My new living situation has a few bumps."

"I read about your move on Reva's blog," Latoya said. "What kind of problems are you having?"

"No hot water for one."

Her face scrunched up tightly as she shook her head. "Oh no. That's a requirement for me. I don't like cold anything. I'd be packing my bags so fast."

Miles lifted his cup of coffee and took several long sips as she talked. "It's probably just a pilot light out or something simple. I hope so, at least. I haven't unpacked yet but I have nowhere else to go short of my mom's couch. I have to find the right place to move first."

"Have you spoken to Della Rose?" Latoya asked. "She's a real estate agent, right?"

"Yeah. I thought I'd check her website first and see what's on the market. I don't need anything too big." Or too expensive. He had a little bit of money saved but not a huge chunk for a big deposit because he hadn't been planning to look for a house just yet.

But it was time, and he was ready. If he found the right house, he could maybe pick up a little overtime at the sheriff's department. Sometimes the other deputies wanted time off to travel and visit family.

"You have big plans for Thanksgiving?" Miles asked Latoya.

She grinned widely. "My boyfriend is taking me to meet his parents."

"That's a big step," Miles said.

"It is. But he's the one. I always thought people were crazy but what they say is true."

"What's that?" Miles asked.

"When you know, you just know." She got a dreamy look in her eyes that made Miles chuckle.

He nodded, even though he was conflicted about that sentiment for himself. Once upon a time, he'd known without a doubt who was the one for him. Then things had gone topsy-turvy. When Lucy's mother had come to see him, Miles had been in the worst kind of way. He'd just found out that Lucy wasn't pregnant, and Mrs. Hannigan seemed over the moon about that fact.

Miles's dad had lost his job and skipped town that summer. To make matters worse, Miles had overheard his mother's crying well into the previous night. She was devastated that they weren't going to have a Thanksgiving meal. No turkey. No stuffing. No made-from-scratch pumpkin pie. They had nothing to speak of.

Miles couldn't have cared less about what they ate for the holiday but the lack was devastating to his mom. And seeing his mother so distraught felt a little traumatizing to him. He was admittedly upset about the pregnancy but also, in some way, relieved that it had only been a scare. He couldn't afford to feed himself, much less a child.

Mrs. Hannigan had sweet-talked him when she came to see him, going on about how she knew he wanted what was best for Lucy.

"You want Lucy to be happy, right?" she'd asked, standing in front of him outside his family's small apartment. The one they were struggling to pay rent on because his dad's paychecks were no longer coming in to help.

"Of course I do, Mrs. Hannigan. That's all I want," Miles had said. Even though there was no baby, he was ready to go through with the marriage. He didn't care that they were young. They had love, which was all that mattered.

"Good. Then we agree, Miles. Love only lasts for so long. You can't eat it or live off it." She gave him a sympathetic look. "You are a good boy, and you've been a great boyfriend for my daughter. But you do understand that there's a difference between a boyfriend and a husband." Mrs. Hannigan held up a hand. "No disrespect to you. It's just, we're from two different worlds."

His world was the one that lived paycheck to paycheck, hand to mouth. Lucy's was the one filled with mansions in The Village. Lucy had never cared about any of that stuff though.

Miles had tried to politely argue but Mrs. Hannigan should have been a lawyer. She knew how to press his buttons.

"Your father tried to do right by your mother. I watched that whole love story unfold. And look how it ended." Mrs. Hannigan held out a comforting hand. "I'm sure she wouldn't trade you or your sister for anything, of course. But your father wasn't the provider your family needed him to be."

"I'm not my dad," Miles objected. He'd been eighteen, raised to never talk back to an elder but he was ready to fight with Mrs. Hannigan that day. To fight for Lucy.

"We're all like our parents, whether we want to be or not. In fact, the harder you try to buck genetics, the more you become the thing you're bucking." Her expression was serious for a long moment, as if she was weighing what she was about to do. Then she held out a crisp one-hundred-dollar bill.

"What's that?" Miles asked. "Are you paying me to break up with Lucy?"

"No." She shook her head, a nervous laugh tumbling off her lips. "Of course not. I do believe you love my daughter. For that reason, I know you'll do right by her."

He understood that right implied ending things.

"This money is for you to buy a nice meal for your family. It's Thanksgiving after all. A time to be together and reflect. There's so much to be grateful for." She forced the money into his hand, closing his fingers around it. "If you want Lucy to be happy, let's not tell her about this visit of ours. I don't think she'd be pleased, and after that whole baby disappointment, well, I'd hate to ruin her holiday."

With that, Mrs. Hannigan walked away, leaving him befuddled, broken, and conflicted.

"Earth to Miles," Latoya said, waving a hand in front of his face. "Where did you just disappear off to?"

Miles blinked his thoughts back to the present, where he was a thirty-year-old responsible man with a good paying job and the town's respect. Nothing like his father. "I haven't had my full dose of caffeine just yet," he explained. "Any calls for me to investigate?"

Latoya slid a list in front of him. "You can take your pick of what you want to go check out."

If there hadn't been a call on his radio, then it wasn't urgent and it made its way to Latoya's list.

"Ready?" she asked.

"Yep."

Latoya tapped the first item on the list. "Do you want to check on a report about Mr. S who was lying in the nude outside the Somerset Rental Cottages again?"

Miles cringed. Mr. S was in his eighties and had once lived in a nudist colony. "First of all, it's freezing outside. Second, I thought he had stopped that behavior this summer."

"Maybe a little relapse," Latoya said with a wink. "Happens to the best of us."

"What else do you have?"

She tapped her finger on the next item. "It appears someone around here is not feeling the Thanksgiving good vibes. The giant inflated turkey on the corner of Hannigan Street and Loblolly was popped overnight."

Miles felt his jaw go slack. "Someone stabbed Mr. Gobbles?"

Mr. Gobbles had been used as a decoration downtown since Miles was a little boy. "Maybe it was an animal."

Latoya grinned. "That terrorizing opossum from Lucy's porch?"

Miles shrugged. "He's on my short list of suspects."

"No. A witness saw a couple kids in hoodies run off just before Mr. Gobbles went down."

Miles frowned. "What a pointless crime. Why would anyone do something like that?"

"Kicks and giggles. Or maybe because whoever did it doesn't have as much to be grateful for as the rest of us. They could be acting out by taking out their frustration on an oversize turkey. May Mr. Gobbles rest in peace," she said in mock solemnity.

Miles frowned. Part of him found the crime humorous. The other part was disappointed that someone in his community would be such a grouch that they'd spoil a little holiday cheer for everyone else.

Lucy's day had been busy so far. She'd completed another house call for her client, Mandy Elks, whose belly seemed to grow impossibly bigger every time she saw her. Mandy was due on Thanksgiving Day but this was her first pregnancy so she'd probably go past her due date.

After checking on Mandy, Lucy stopped in to see a few other clients before returning home. Now it was late afternoon, and Lucy was filing insurance from her client visits and writing daily notes. She also planned to prepare for her first parenting class that was happening tonight. Patient education was one of the things she loved most about being a nurse. She'd invited all her current clients and a few potential clients she'd met with over the last couple weeks.

Bella barked at Lucy as if to tell her to get back to work.

"Thanks for the necessary reminder," Lucy said, bending to pat Bella's head for a moment. Bella panted lightly into her palm and then turned on a dime at the sound of someone at the front door. She took off down the hall, barking all the way.

It was probably just the mail carrier but Lucy stood and followed anyway. Maybe a stretch break would revive her enough to finish up the necessary paperwork on her desk. When she got to the door, she saw the distorted image of Olivia Reynolds, one of her neighbors, through the oval-shaped opaque glass. A visit from a neighbor wasn't unusual. It didn't typically happen during the workday, however.

Lucy opened the door and peered back at the woman. "Hi, Olivia. How are you?" Olivia was in her mid to late forties. She had two adorable children who always seemed to be cutting through Lucy's front yard and irritating Bella as she watched from the window.

Olivia's gaze skittered around, not meeting Lucy's directly. "Great. But I'm afraid I'm going to spoil your afternoon."

A small laugh tumbled off Lucy's lips until she realized that Olivia was serious. "Why? What's wrong?"

"Maybe I should come inside," Olivia said, lowering her voice as if there were other neighbors in earshot. There weren't as far as Lucy could see.

"Okay." Lucy opened the door wider, inviting Olivia in. Olivia stepped past her, bending momentarily to pet Bella's head. Then Lucy closed the door and led her to the living area. Everything was still decorated the way her mom had left it. Lucy hadn't had the time or money to make it her own just yet. Olivia sat on the older couch with a burgundy grid pattern. Lucy took a seat beside her, her insides coiling. She liked Olivia but she didn't like the tone of this visit so far. *What is going on?*

"I'm just going to lay this out there," Olivia said on a breath.

"Okay?"

"You haven't been paying the homeowner's association fees. No one from this address has paid since your mother passed away." She looked horrified as she said it, which is exactly how Lucy felt.

"What? There's a homeowner's association?" Lucy asked.

Olivia's brows furrowed. "After the first few skipped checks, we hesitated to contact you because you were still grieving, and we thought you might be selling this big house anyway. It's just too big for one person. And if you sold, we were just going to let the unpaid dues go. But..." She trailed off.

Lucy was still stuck on the fact that this neighborhood had a homeowner's association. How did she not know that? The Village was one of the nicest neighborhoods in Somerset Lake. *Of course* it would have an association.

"Mrs. Newsome does our accounting. After her appendicitis in the spring, she got a little behind with it. She's all caught up now though." Olivia cringed. "And it looks like we haven't received a payment from this address since last December."

Lucy quickly did the mental math. "That's eleven months."

Olivia looked apologetic. "That's correct. And I really tried to get the board to agree to wipe out those dues if you agreed to start paying from here."

The way Olivia said that led Lucy to know that Olivia's efforts were futile. "I see. Well, how much are the monthly dues?" Lucy asked.

Olivia rolled her lips together for a moment. Then she finally cleared her throat and mumbled a number.

"I'm sorry, what?" Lucy leaned closer.

"It's two hundred dollars a month," she repeated.

Lucy nearly fell off the couch. "What? Why on earth are the dues that expensive?"

"It's a good deal," Olivia said. "It covers all of the road upkeep, your lawn care, and maintenance and use of the community building, which is where you're planning to hold your parenting classes, correct?"

Lucy swallowed as guilt layered inside her belly. She'd thought she had access to the building just based on the fact that she lived in the neighborhood. "How could I be so clueless?"

"You really didn't know there was an HOA?" Olivia asked, her mouth opening in shock.

Lucy shook her head. "No, I really didn't. I had no hand in Mom's finances until after she died. I haven't seen a bill from the HOA."

"Well, most people just write a check and send it in. We only issue bills for those who are delinquent and, of course, with Mrs. Newsome temporarily unavailable..."

"I can't be delinquent on something I didn't even know about," Lucy pointed out.

"How did you think you were having your lawn maintained?" Olivia asked.

Lucy hadn't really thought about it. "Mr. Howey always did the lawn for my mom. She was an older widow. When he continued doing so after Mom died, I kind of thought he was just a nice guy." Lucy let her head fall into her hands. "I guess I wasn't thinking." There'd been too many other things to think about after her mom's passing. Like all the contractors coming out of the woodwork to ask her to pay up on jobs that seemed absolutely unnecessary in Lucy's opinion.

"Well, the good news is that I convinced the board to give you an extension on what you owe. Which is currently twenty-two hundred dollars. Next month will bring it up to twenty-four."

Lucy wanted to cry. "An extension is appreciated. Thank you."

"You're welcome," Olivia said. "I know having an unexpected bill during the holidays is not ideal."

"No, it's not." It wasn't preferable any time of the year. Lucy's budget was already tight. "How long do I have until I make a payment?"

"The board agreed that you can pay in full for the entire year by late December."

"Late December next year?" Lucy asked hopefully.

Olivia's smile wobbled until it flatlined. "No, next month."

Lucy found herself having a hard time taking in a full breath. "That's one month."

"Generous considering you're almost one year behind, don't you think?"

Lucy swallowed but didn't respond.

"The HOA asked me to relay that, if you agree, they'll still allow you to have your parenting classes at the community building as planned."

That was good because the first class was tonight, and Lucy was hoping for a decent turnout.

"And if you don't, they'll be suing you for the money in the new year," Olivia said a little sheepishly. "I'm sorry, Lucy. It's in our bylaws that the HOA will file a lawsuit after a year of unpaid dues."

Lucy would have been making sure to pay them all along if she'd known. Having to pay a whole year in less than a month wouldn't be easy. At this point, after spending every spare dime on her mom's other debts, it felt nearly impossible.

"I see," Lucy said, resisting bringing her hand to her chest to clutch her heart. "Tell the board I'll be sure to pay as soon as I can."

∞

Miles was officially off work for tonight but his mind was still on his sheriff duties as he drove to the Youth Center that evening.

Before he'd left the department for the day, he'd followed up on a few leads about Mr. Gobbles that had amounted to nothing. Other than the witness who had seen a figure running from the scene, Miles had nothing else to go on. He didn't even know if the person was the reason that Mr. Gobbles had deflated. When he had inspected the large inflatable, however, there had been a large puncture near the colorful back feathers. Miles supposed that somebody could patch the large hole up and Mr. Gobbles could be salvaged for Thanksgivings to come.

Miles sighed as he pulled into the parking lot of the Youth Center, got out, and headed into the building. He didn't plan on staying long this afternoon. Lucy was teaching a class at the community building tonight, so he'd offered to take Bella for a walk.

He was kind of looking forward to walking around The Village and looking at the historic homes. The desire for a house of his own was growing stronger the more he thought about it. For a long time, he'd wanted a place that he owned free and clear. A place that he could settle into that no one else could take away. Unlike the homes of his childhood.

"Thought you weren't volunteering tonight," Reese Whitaker said as he approached.

Miles shook his head. "I'm not. Just popping in to say hello to the kids." This was the only night this week that the Youth Center would be open due to the holidays.

"You're checking on Charlie, aren't you?" she asked with a knowing look. What could he say? He was a sucker for a down-on-his-luck kid.

"I wouldn't mind knowing how he's doing," Miles admitted.

"Well, you'll have to go to his house to see. He's not here," she said. "I don't even think he went to school today. Another kid said he hadn't seen Charlie since last Friday."

"Hmm. It's not like him to miss."

"Stop worrying. It's a holiday week," Reese pointed out. "People are going out of town early to see family or they're just taking a break. A lot of the kids aren't here this evening, not just Charlie."

"Good point. And I'm not here either," Miles said, making Reese laugh. "Unless you need me to be."

She shook her head and gave him a playful shove. "Nope. Go find yourself a girlfriend or something," she teased, not for the first time. People in town had a fascination with the singles around here, wanting to fix them up and see to it they got their happy ever after. Miles always ducked when those efforts were directed at him. He didn't need a matchmaker. What he needed was a few days off for Thanksgiving and a new home for Christmas.

Miles chatted with Della Rose's boys, Justin and Jett, before leaving. They were in good spirits tonight despite their parents' messy divorce.

"We're having Thanksgiving lunch with Dad," Justin told Miles. "And Thanksgiving supper with Mom. It's weird."

His twin brother Jett grinned. "But we get double the turkey and pie, so Mom says we should be happy."

Miles offered a serious nod. "Double the good food sounds like a win to me."

"I told Mom that I want double the presents at Christmas," Justin said excitedly.

"Me too. Me too," Jett agreed, making Miles laugh. After wishing a happy holiday to a few more kids, Miles walked back out as a light sprinkle of rain began to fall. He knew there were supposed to be storms tonight so he needed to hurry if he wanted to walk Bella around Lucy's neighborhood.

He checked his phone before starting the engine. His heart skipped at the sight of Lucy's name on his screen.

Lucy: You still okay to walk Bella?

Miles tapped his index finger along the screen's keyboard.

Miles: Heading that direction now. Good luck with your class tonight.
Lucy: Thanks. After the day I've had, I wouldn't be surprised if it's a flop.

Miles texted a reply.

Miles: That bad? What happened?

He watched the dots bounce, anxiously awaiting her reply.

Lucy: I'll tell you about it tonight.

Miles was looking forward to that just to be able to spend time with Lucy. He tapped a reply more quickly than his mind could censor what he typed.

Miles: It's a date.

Chapter Eight

Miles found the key to Lucy's house just where she'd told him it would be. Under the rainwater jar on the back porch.

"This is not where you hide your house key, Lucy," he said to himself as he looked at the nearly empty rainwater jar. It would be full after tonight's storm. This little jar in his hand had stirred up trouble for an opossum and Lucy last week, starting a domino effect that led Miles to Lucy's door. If he was one to believe in fate, he'd say it had a hand in his situation.

Or maybe it all was just a mix of good and bad luck.

He retrieved the key and let himself inside Lucy's back door. Bella greeted him with a bark and wagging tail.

"Hey, beautiful." Miles squatted low to pat her head for a moment. "I'm your designated walker tonight. Where's your leash?"

Bella turned and ran straight to a purple leash draped over a dining room chair.

"You're smart and beautiful. Just like your owner." Miles needed to be careful with sentiments like that. He was walking a fine line being around Lucy, but he couldn't cross it. He had broken Lucy's heart once. He knew he'd hurt her, and he didn't want to risk doing so again.

Miles snapped Bella's leash into place as he headed out the back door for a walk. The air was chilly now. The sky rumbled just slightly, warning of the oncoming storms tonight and competing with Miles's memories of long ago.

Miles never told Lucy about her mother's visit or the money she'd given him. Instead, after determining that Mrs. Hannigan was right all those years ago, he'd gone to see Lucy on a mission.

"We need to talk," he'd said.

"Okay. About what?" She was still wearing his great-grandmother's ring on her left hand.

"I'm not sure how to say this, so I'm just going to put it out there. Lucy, I can't afford to be dragged down with a girlfriend right now. And you can't afford to let me drag you down either." He knew he sounded like one big jerk. And if he hadn't known it, the look on Lucy's face would've told him as much.

She lifted her chin, hiccupping a breath. "Dragged down?" she repeated, taking a step back and hugging herself. "I'm dragging you down?" She audibly swallowed.

"Lucy, you have everything you could ever want," he'd told her, blinking away the sting in his eyes. "You have a huge house and a yard and two parents who give you anything you ask for. You're going to sit down tomorrow and have a Thanksgiving meal fit for the president. It's not like that for everyone."

Lucy's eyes widened as if maybe she'd never fully considered his situation. Or hers. "Well, don't let me drag you down any longer," Lucy whispered, taking one more tiny step away from him. She had pulled the ring off and tossed it at his feet. Then she'd walked—run—away.

The sky rumbled softly as Miles kept walking. He stopped momentarily as Bella squatted on the base of a neighbor's mailbox.

"No, Bella. No." Miles wondered if that was against some rule in this neighborhood. "Don't do that again, girl. I'll find you a nice tree somewhere," he promised, looking ahead. He spotted the community building farther down. There weren't that many cars in the lot, which meant Lucy didn't have too great of a turnout. He inwardly cringed, remembering that she was already having a rough day. He also remembered that she said she'd tell him about it tonight.

A thread of excitement ran through him at the prospect of spending any amount of time with her. As friends. A few folks left the community building and headed to their cars as Miles and Bella walked in that direction. The cars pulled out and headed down the road, passing him as he approached the building. By the time he and Bella were walking up the parking lot, the only car left was Lucy's.

Miles hesitated. He could keep walking Bella and return to Lucy's house. He could let Bella inside the pink house, return the key under the jar, and go up to his garage apartment where he belonged. Better yet, he could go up there and do that online search of the local housing market.

Or he could go inside that community building and check on Lucy. Bella tugged against her leash, clearly voting for the latter option. Miles followed, aware of another rumble of thunder. He opened the front entry door to the building and called out. "Lucy?"

"Back here!" she responded from a room that was off the main entryway.

Miles headed in that direction. He poked his head in the doorway, clutching the leash in his hand more tightly because Bella wanted to run to her owner. "I saw the last car leave so I thought I'd check on you. To see if you need help cleaning up."

Lucy plopped down on a chair and sighed wearily. "I had four students tonight. Four." Her expression told him that wasn't a good thing.

"How many were you expecting?"

"Ten," she said.

"Well, there's a storm coming. That likely kept people at home."

She offered a weak smile. "Maybe."

Miles looked around. "This is a nice building. Anyone can use it?" he asked.

"Anyone who lives in The Village. Or outsiders can rent it out for a fee."

"So you get free access to this if you live here?"

"That's what I thought," she said with a touch of exasperation. "Until this afternoon."

Sensing that Lucy was going to catch him up on her day and that it might take a while, Miles stepped into the room, finally let go of Bella's leash, and took a seat that had been set up for Lucy's students. Bella dragged her leash along the floor as she scurried over to Lucy's arms.

"What happened this afternoon?" he asked.

Lucy blew out a breath, sinking lower into her chair as she hugged Bella to her midsection. "Someone from the homeowner's association knocked on my door to inform me that I haven't been paying the monthly dues."

Miles lifted his brows. "Why haven't you?"

"Because I didn't *know* there were monthly dues. I didn't even know The Village had an HOA. Mom had it automatically deducted from her account, and that account was closed when she died." Lucy sighed. "I've had other things to think about, like, oh, I don't know, roofing and plumbing bills. So now I owe a huge bill by the end of the year. I mean, not huge to some, but I don't have a wad of cash lying around to pay twenty-four hundred dollars."

"Whoa," Miles said. "That's a chunk of money."

"Yes, it is. Maybe I should have sold my mom's house immediately instead of deciding to stay awhile," she said quietly. "I just, I didn't want to lose everything all at once."

Miles stood and walked over to her, squatting down to look her in the eyes. "Hey, it'll be okay. We'll figure this out."

Her gaze fluttered up to meet his. "We?"

"Yeah, why not?"

"Because my problems are not your responsibility."

"No, but you're my friend." He reached for her hand and squeezed it, feeling a rush of something more than friendship for Lucy. "I know you're perfectly capable of doing things all on your own. I'm just offering you someone to bounce ideas off. I would do anything to help you. You know that."

The corners of her mouth curled upward.

"If you don't want to move out of your parents' house, you don't have to. We'll figure out how to pay the HOA bill and how to keep you there as long as you need."

Lucy appeared to swallow. Her eyes were shiny as if she wanted to cry. "Thank you, Miles. I'm just feeling overwhelmed with life these days."

He was still holding her hand. Thunder boomed, and suddenly the sound of the rain's downpour on the roof surrounded them. Miles didn't break eye contact.

"You only feel overwhelmed because you've been doing everything on your own. I suspect you haven't asked for help or leaned on anyone. I get that you're strong and independent but I'm here and I'm not going anywhere. We'll fix this and everything else. Together."

Her shoulders seemed to slump as she exhaled. Then the lights in the room flickered, once, twice, and they were out. Lucy clutched Miles's hand. "I can't see anything."

"Me either," Miles said. "I can get my phone and shine some light." He started to pull his hand from hers but she didn't release it. Instead, she tugged the way Bella had tugged on her leash outside. And he didn't resist. He'd just told her he was here for her, for whatever she needed. And right now, she apparently needed him to kiss her.

Lucy's mouth opened on his, and their lips seemed to melt into one another. His heart was pounding along with the drumming of rain all around them. There was something about the veil of darkness that made this okay. And there was the fact that Lucy was upset and needed him. That she'd initiated this.

But she was vulnerable right now.

Miles broke away from the kiss. "Lucy?" he asked.

She came down off the chair and sat on the floor with him. "Are you sure this is what you want? Kissing me won't fix anything." In fact, it was likely to be just one more thing that overwhelmed her once the moment was over.

"I don't need you to fix anything," she whispered. "All I need is for you to keep kissing me."

ꝏ

The lights flickered and came back on, abruptly ending the moment.

Lucy pulled away from the kiss and looked at Miles, her gaze searching his for answers. Like what did that kiss mean? Did it change things? What happened now?

He exhaled softly and reached for her hand, giving it a slight squeeze. "Ready to get home?"

"Yes," she said, even though there was a part of her that wouldn't mind leaning over and kissing some more. "Yeah. It's been a long day."

They both stood, and Lucy collected her things quietly. They got into Lucy's car and drove back to her house.

"So," Miles began, not moving to get out once they were parked in the driveway, "Thursday is Thanksgiving."

Lucy blew out a breath. "Are we really going to go through this again?"

Miles nodded. "Yeah, we are. I can't in good conscience leave you alone. So if you don't want to go to my mom's house, then I'll stay back with you."

"Miles, that kiss back at the community building—" she started, shaking her head slightly.

He cut her off. "Isn't the reason I want to spend the day with you. The reason is that it's your first Thanksgiving without your mom, and I don't want you to be alone."

"So it's a pity invite?" she asked, knowing that wasn't fair.

He narrowed his eyes. "Or," he said, "I can call in Moira or Della Rose. Or Tess. Trisha. Any one of them will be sure to drag you to their family's home."

"You're not going to let me be alone?" she asked with a touch of irritation.

He shook his head. "That's what you think you want. And I'm not the kind of guy to think he knows better than you. But I've seen a lot of people in my job over the years who think they want to be alone. It's not a good place to be when you're hurting. When you're hurting, the best place to be is with the people who care about you."

Lucy tried not to read too much into that statement. Miles cared about her. Something about that took away her irritation and melted her heart at the same time.

She looked at her hands in her lap for a moment and then glanced over at him. "First we spent the day together delivering food baskets. Then you moved into my garage apartment. Now we're spending a family holiday together?" She shook her head. "What will Reva's blog read on Friday?"

Miles shook his head. "I don't really care right now, to be honest. I only care about you. So, what do you say? Come to my family's home with me? And eat turkey until you put yourself into a food coma?"

Lucy knew that he was right. The last thing she

needed on Thursday was to be lying on her couch and wallowing in her own self-misery. "Okay."

Miles smiled. "Okay. It's a—"

Lucy held up a finger. "Don't say it," she warned. "It's not a d-word."

He laughed quietly. "It's a solid plan." He looked out on the rain. "This is where we say goodnight and run to our respective doors." He looked at her again, his gaze dropping to her mouth just a moment. Her gaze dropped as well. A true date ended with a goodnight kiss.

"Goodnight, Miles," Lucy said before tucking Bella under her arm, pushing her car door open, and racing through the rain toward her front awning. Rule #4 was no kissing Miles. She'd already broken that rule once tonight. She didn't plan on breaking it a second time.

On Thursday morning, Lucy stared into the depths of her closet, trying to decide what to wear to Thanksgiving dinner at the Bruno house. She'd never spent a holiday without her mom or away from the pink house. Her mom had always insisted on dressing nice for the holiday even though they weren't going anywhere. It was a special day. But maybe the Brunos dressed down. Maybe they wore jeans and T-shirts.

Lucy scrutinized her things, finally pulling out a skirt and a cotton top. One could never go wrong with a fun skirt and cotton top. Good for church or a football game. Or Thanksgiving dinner at her ex-fiancé's home.

Lucy showered, changed, and waited for Miles to come get her.

She'd only ever been to Mrs. Bruno's house for a

meal once when she was younger. It was an awkward meal because there was this ubiquitous awareness that it wasn't enough food for the family much less a guest as well. And Mrs. Bruno had served Lucy the biggest portion.

Times were harder for the Bruno family back then. Things had gotten easier from what Lucy could tell. Even so, she'd pulled items out of her cupboards this morning and had put together a side dish of green bean casserole. Attending a nice dinner empty-handed wasn't Lucy's style.

Lucy's cell phone chirped loudly from her kitchen counter. She walked over, expecting it to be Miles telling her he was ready to go. Instead, it was one of her clients.

> ***Mandy Elks:*** My water broke!

Lucy's heart took off in a wild sprint at those three words. She tapped out a quick reply.

> ***Lucy:*** That's exciting news! It's going to be fine. I'll meet you at the birthing center.

Lucy pulled up Miles's contact and tapped a text to him as well.

> ***Lucy:*** I'm sorry but I need to cancel going to your house for Thanksgiving. My client just went into labor.

Lucy raced back to her bedroom, changed quickly into a pair of scrubs, pulled her thick hair into a ponytail, and tugged a pair of medical sneakers on her feet. Then she grabbed her keys, purse, and the green bean casserole as she dashed out the door. Miles was outside waiting for her.

"Did you get my text?" she asked.

"Yeah. I understand. My mom will too."

"I'm sorry." Lucy offered the foil-wrapped casserole dish. "This is proof that I was planning on going. Will you bring this to your family's meal?"

Miles looked disappointed as he took it. "It's Thanksgiving. What better thing to be thankful for than the miracle of life, right?"

Lucy swallowed, grateful that he was so understanding. "Right."

"You better go. Mind if I take Bella? She shouldn't spend the day alone if she doesn't have to."

Lucy melted at the offer. "Your mom won't mind?"

"Mom is a dog lover. She hasn't had one since Ginger died. She'll be happy for the canine company."

"That would be great then. Thank you."

"Bella and I will eat your share today," Miles teased.

Lucy laughed and headed to her car with a flutter of feelings swirling inside her chest. Excitement. Relief. Disappointment. There was also that nameless feeling that came with a growing crush. It was more than attraction, resembling hope, feeling like the anticipation of the night before Christmas. That nameless feeling made her feel constricted in her chest but not because she was stressed. It was more because it was swelling with a million butterflies, all competing for fluttering space.

Lucy got behind the steering wheel and cranked the car. Her gaze lifted briefly to note that Miles was heading to his own vehicle with Bella tucked under one arm like a wiggling football. He carried Lucy's casserole in the other hand.

Lucy's brain hummed with a question that she couldn't for the life of her find the answer to right now.

Why am I not supposed to fall for him again?

Miles walked through his mother's front door with Bella in one arm and a warm casserole in the other. His senses were immediately accosted with the sights, sounds, and delicious aromas of Thanksgiving.

"Where's your dinner guest?" his mother asked. She had an apron tied around her waist and a wooden stirring spoon in one hand.

Miles looked down at Bella. "My guest is right here. Happy Thanksgiving, Mom."

She petted Bella's head and took the casserole from his other hand. "Dogs don't get to sit at the table. I prepared a spot for Lucy," she said, talking over her shoulder as she headed toward the kitchen.

"She got called into work. One of her clients is in labor." Miles followed his mother, his mouth watering as he drew closer to the food. The Thanksgiving meals of his childhood were never this good. "This smells great. Is Ava here yet?"

"Your sister brought two guests," his mother said, lifting a brow at him. "You brought a dog. Looks like you might lose the challenge."

"Hold that thought. I invited Reese from the Youth Center. Maria Bates and her kids, Charlie and Brittney. I also invited Trisha Langly, Jake Fletcher, and Kim and Chris Evans." Miles looked at the time on his cell phone. "They still might show up. You said one p.m. That means I haven't lost yet."

This challenge was sort of a way to celebrate the fact that their family had more than enough finances and food these days. They weren't rich by any means but they could feed as many guests as they wanted on this special day. And they were thankful for that.

"Kim and Chris Evans?" his mom asked, carrying Lucy's dish to the stove.

"They're going through a rough patch," Miles said.

"And she's pregnant. That could count as three guests if she comes," his mom said, making Miles laugh.

"We'll see what happens. I won't be staying long today though," he said, feeling a little trepidation as his mom whirled from the stove.

"Why? You have other plans?"

Miles placed Bella at his feet and faced his mother. "Just in case Lucy returns home earlier than expected, I don't want her to be alone. It's the first holiday since her mom died."

His mother's stance softened. "I see. Yes, you're right. Someone should be there for her. *You* should be there." She gave Miles a knowing look. Miles supposed it wasn't hard for his mom to see what he tried to hide from everyone else. He was still hopelessly devoted to his first love.

He swallowed because he even hid that fact from himself most days. There was something about a mother who saw through the defenses and pretenses. She'd never asked why he'd broken up with Lucy when they were younger. Everyone else had, of course, and his answer had always been the same. *It's personal.*

"I'll make a plate for her. You'll take it to her." His mom turned and started collecting to-go plastic bins. "And you can't stuff yourself too much here because you'll need to eat with Lucy. She shouldn't eat her meal alone."

Miles just watched. There was also something about a mother who wanted to see their child happy and in love. He hated to tell his mom that he and Lucy were over—no going back after he'd broken her heart.

Except that kiss on Tuesday night begged to differ.

"Hey, loser." Miles's sister, Ava, walked into the room.

Their mother turned with a scowl. "It's Thanksgiving Day, Ava. What kind of language is that?"

Ava laughed. "Miles knows I'm just playing with him."

There was a tall man with dark brown skin and a friendly demeanor standing beside Ava. Miles guessed it was her new boyfriend.

"This is Malachi. My guest." Ava folded her arms over her chest. "And where are your guests?" She flashed a victorious look.

"Lucy couldn't make it but I have a few who might." Miles offered his hand to Malachi. "Nice to meet you. Happy Thanksgiving."

"Likewise." Malachi looked at Bella, who was sticking close to Miles's feet. "Is that your dog?"

"It belongs to my friend-slash-landlord. This is Bella." Miles offered Ava a pointed look. "And Mom says that Bella counts as a guest. So we're tied at the moment."

Ava looked at their mother. "What? A dog doesn't count."

"I'm the host, and I say it does," his mom said with a conspiratorial look at Miles.

"Only spots at the dinner table count," Ava objected, whining like the young sister he'd grown up with. "And dogs don't sit at the dinner table."

"We can make an exception for Bella," their mom said.

Ava looked like she might protest some more but then the doorbell rang. They all turned toward the front of the house.

"I'll get it!" Miles said, hoping it was one of his invited guests. He headed through the living room and opened the door to Mrs. Bates and her children. "Hey, Bates family. I'm glad you guys could make it."

"Well, we appreciate the invitation," Mrs. Bates said. "Is it still okay to be here?"

"More than okay," Miles's mother said, walking into the room. "Welcome, welcome. The more the merrier."

Charlie looked down at his feet while everyone talked, looking shy for once. Miles had once been in his shoes. It wasn't always easy depending on the kindness of others. It was awkward. Or it could be.

"Hey, Charlie, do you want to see my old soccer trophies?" Miles knew the boy was a fan of the sport.

Charlie glanced up at Miles. "You never told me you played soccer."

"I played everything. I was what one might call competitive. Still am," he said, flashing a grin at his sister, who lingered in the doorway. Miles returned his attention to Charlie. "Come on. I'll show you." He looked at Brittney. "You can come too," he said.

The teen girl shook her head. "No, thanks. I'll just play with your dog if that's okay."

"Bella loves attention," Miles told her. And something told him that the teen girl could use Bella's attention too.

&

Two hours later, Miles left his mom's home carrying several trays of food with him. All his invited guests had come so he'd won this year's guest challenge. That meant he was also carrying a pie home.

Miles tucked Bella into his passenger seat and drove back to the pink house on Christmas Lane. He noticed a couple neighbors already beginning to decorate outside for The Village's annual Merriest Lawn Contest.

One neighbor was putting out a giant present with a huge velvety red bow on top. Another was stringing lights on one of the trees out front. His competitive streak made him want to join in the fun too. But he didn't live here, not really. It wasn't his contest to win.

He pulled into the driveway, disappointed that Lucy wasn't home yet. He had a ton of food that he didn't want to leave in the truck or haul up the garage steps. Plus, he needed to let Bella in the house. Maybe he'd just use the hidden key under the rainwater jar and go inside. She'd been okay with that earlier in the week. And this food was for her after all, with his mom's strict order that Lucy not be allowed to eat it alone.

Miles looked at Bella. "Ready, girl? Let's set up a surprise for your owner."

Chapter Nine

Lucy was still coming down off the high of helping to deliver a baby. She would never get over how much she loved the whole process. The labor and helping the mother breathe through the pain. The newborn's cry. The look on the parents' faces when they first held their child.

Lucy felt satisfied right now. And exhausted. All she wanted to do was go home, strip off these scrubs, and crawl into a steaming hot bath. Preferably with a glass of wine because it was Thanksgiving and she deserved a little luxury while the rest of the country was snoring off their turkey dinners.

Lucy pulled into her driveway and glanced over at Miles's truck. She wondered if he had Bella or if she needed to walk up and retrieve her dog.

First the bath and wine.

She headed to her front door, poked her key in the lock, and turned the knob. Then she unloaded her purse and keys on the small table beside the door.

Bella came charging toward her with a welcoming bark.

"Hey, sweetie! You're here!" Lucy knelt to pat Bella's head. "Miles must have let you in with the key, huh?"

"I hope that's okay," Miles said, startling Lucy.

She wobbled in her crouched position but caught herself on the wall by bracing a hand. "Oh, you're here too."

He gave a slight smirk. "Not trying to scare you to death. Just trying to surprise you."

She stood and stepped toward him. "I'm surprised." She noticed now that the house smelled of deliciousness. "What were you doing in my kitchen?"

"Warming up the food my mom sent over. She insisted, and I promised I wouldn't let you eat alone. A guy can't very well argue with his mother."

This made Lucy laugh. "No, you always have to listen to your mom," she said, suddenly breathless as her eyes filled up with tears.

"Hey. Are you crying?"

She shook her head, even as tears pricked behind her eyes. "A little bit." She pressed a hand to her chest and tried to steady her breathing. "I'm a mess, aren't I? This is the second time I've cried with you in a week. I'm not even usually much of a crier."

"I know. That's why I know you're going through some things right now."

She felt him stepping toward her, even though her eyes were closed. Part of her wanted to step away. The other part wanted to step closer. Instead, she just stood there and waited. "It's been a year since my mom passed away. I shouldn't still be crying."

Miles's hand was on her shoulder. "There are no shoulds or shouldn'ts when it comes to grief. She was your mom. You miss her."

Lucy's eyes blurred with even more tears. "I do miss her. Every day. When is that going to stop?"

Miles shook his head. "I don't think it ever does. Especially not on a day like today."

"My mother loved Thanksgiving," Lucy said. "She loved waking early and cooking for hours on hours. She also loved to scrutinize faces as all the guests took their first bites. It was a bit creepy to tell the truth." Lucy laughed now. She finally sucked in a huge breath and let it out. She thought that she should feel foolish for getting so upset in front of Miles, but she didn't. "I'm done crying for tonight. I promise."

"You could cry all night if you want. I want to be here for you."

Lucy tilted her head as she looked at him. "Were you always this nice?"

Miles's brown eyes narrowed. "Probably not," he said quietly. "People change, people grow."

Lucy could see that he'd done both of those things. He was such a good person, and he was just as good-looking as he ever was. "So about that dinner?" She was glad he was here. She didn't want to be alone tonight after all. And she was especially thankful that Miles was the one she was spending the evening with.

Miles reached for her hand. "Let me show you your surprise."

Lucy ignored the gooey warmth that radiated through her at the feel of his palm against hers. She followed him into the dining room and then her lips parted. "You went through my mom's china cabinet?"

Miles suddenly looked worried. "I didn't want to serve you on paper plates. Which your mom had a lot of, by the way. Why did she need so many paper products?"

Lucy shrugged. "Why did she need a lot of the

stuff she purchased before she died? I don't have the answers," she said.

"Well, I thought tonight called for your mom's good china. I hope that's okay..." He trailed off.

Lucy looked at the dinner table, set beautifully with her mother's prized willow pattern dishes. Miles had located the good silver in the top drawer of the cabinet as well. It looked exactly like the way her mom would've set it. "There are four spots at the table. Who are the other two spots for?"

"That's part of your surprise." He looked excited about whatever he was about to tell her. "I invited Tess, Moira, and Della Rose for dinner. Trisha and Jake stopped by my mom's earlier but they're eating with Jake's grandma Vi tonight. Della's kids are with their father so she was going to be alone too."

Lucy was slowly processing what Miles was telling her. "You're not staying?"

He shook his head. "You set a ground rule about not having dinner together. I wasn't about to break that. My mom just said not to let you eat alone tonight."

"Sounds like you thought of everything." Lucy tried to temper her disappointment. It was her rule after all.

"I hope so. Everything is on the stove or in the oven warming. Even a full pie because I won my mom's guest challenge."

"Even without me?" Lucy asked.

"Bella tipped me over the edge."

Lucy grinned. "Good thing you brought her then. What time will my guests be arriving?"

"Any minute. You better go change. I'll stay until you're ready to take over."

Lucy hesitated. "You can stay the whole time. It's your mom's food after all. And I just meant we shouldn't have dinner alone."

Miles shook his head. "Truthfully, I'm tired. I'm looking forward to the apartment and maybe doing an online search about the housing market."

"I see. Well, I'll just go freshen up and be right out. Thank you, Miles."

"You're welcome, Luce." He looked at her for a long moment.

She couldn't read his mind but she was remembering the kiss they'd shared the other night. She'd thought about it a lot in the last forty-eight hours but she still hadn't decided if she regretted it or wanted it to happen again. When Miles was this nice to her though, it was the latter.

Miles climbed the steps to his garage apartment, his gaze trailing to the decorations off to the side of the garage as he headed up. Every time he looked in that direction, there was something new to catch his eye. Tonight, he spotted a large, plastic penguin wearing a red knit hat and snowflake sweater.

When he was a kid, his family used to love driving through The Village just to look at all the decorations. It was like a winter wonderland come to life. It was one of Miles's favorite Christmas memories because his parents were together and happy in the front seat while he and Ava wrestled for window space in the back. They turned the holiday music up as they drove, and for a captured moment in his memory, life was beautiful.

There were no struggles. There was just the crooning of Bing Crosby on the radio and all the twinkling lights blurring together as he refused to blink for fear that he'd miss some magical detail.

Miles realized that he had stopped at the top step leading into his garage apartment and he was still staring at the Christmas decorations. He blinked, noting wooden cut-outs of a chorus of carolers before continuing into his temporary dwelling. Where there was still no hot water. And where there was a leak he'd discovered during the storm a couple days ago. The last thing Lucy needed was to hire yet another contractor and rack up more bills. He'd fix it himself when he got a day off.

Miles grabbed his laptop on the way to his bed and propped himself up along the headboard. He opened the computer and pulled up a browser so that he could search the housing market in Somerset Lake.

As he waited for the website to load, his phone buzzed to life beside him. Miles picked it up and read the text from his sister.

> ***Ava:*** Hey loser. I had four more guests arrive after you left.
> ***Ava:*** So that pie you think you rightfully won is actually mine.

Miles didn't want to disappoint his sister but that pie was going to be eaten by Lucy and her friends at any moment.

> ***Miles:*** You mean the pie that I just finished eating?

Ava: You ate loser pie.
Ava: Mom said she'd make me another pie tomorrow.
Ava: Just wanted you to know that...
Ava: I'm the WINNER!

She followed that text up with a GIF of a baby doing a victory dance.

Miles laughed even as his competitive side set in. He'd always loved a friendly challenge. He liked being victorious as much, even more, than the next guy. He tapped his finger along the screen.

Miles: At Christmas, we'll set a time that guests have to show up by.
Miles: Otherwise, they're invalid.
Ava: Fine. But I'm still today's winner.
Ava: And next time, dogs don't count as guests.

Miles grinned to himself. Ava was just as competitive in nature as he was. A board game in their house was never simple.

Ava: Christmas!

Miles returned his attention to his computer screen, pulling up Della Rose's home page to view all the properties she was currently representing. He'd grown up with Della Rose, and she was in the house next door right now keeping Lucy company. That won her all the points in Miles's book.

Miles sorted the properties to show the least expensive first. He was a single man. He didn't need a mansion, nor could he afford one on a deputy sheriff's salary. All he needed was a little house with a porch where he could sit. A decent view of the mountains would be nice, maybe on a creek somewhere. Hot water and a roof that didn't leak when it rained would also be a plus.

Miles stopped scrolling as a tiny yellow house that matched that description popped on screen. The home was familiar. He'd seen it before. It was quaint. He tapped a link that led to more information.

Three bedrooms, two baths, original wood floors throughout. It was exactly the kind of house he had in mind. He scrolled through the pictures, noting the porch that overlooked Mallard Creek, appropriately named because there were wild ducks out there.

Right. Miles knew exactly where this house was. He'd patrolled this area many times, and his eye had caught on the bright yellow color. His pulse quickened with a little thrill of knowing he'd found what he'd been looking for. *Could it be that easy?*

He returned to the home screen because he hadn't looked at the asking price just yet. He blinked the number into focus. It wasn't too high but it was a little more than he'd been planning to spend. Disappointment settled in his stomach, and he decided to continue searching. After another ten minutes of doing so, he returned to the yellow house on Mallard Creek. He guessed it wouldn't hurt to at least take a look. He'd call Della Rose and schedule a viewing tomorrow.

He stayed on his computer another hour before

closing his laptop and laying it on the table beside his bed. It was early yet, but he closed his eyes anyway, his thoughts drifting to Lucy. The longer he stayed here, the more difficult it would be. He'd learned the hard way that she was easy to fall for and nearly impossible to get over.

Somewhere in the minutes with his eyes closed, he fell asleep with his thoughts centered on Lucy. He didn't wake until early the next morning—and he still had Lucy on his mind. He quickly climbed out of bed, pulled on a pair of jeans and a sweatshirt, and headed down to the garage. Lucy might kill him for digging through this stuff but it was far too early to knock on her door and ask permission. He figured she'd have the day after Thanksgiving off and want to sleep in.

He had the day off, too, even though he didn't go Black Friday shopping and he wasn't out of town visiting family. He'd told Sheriff Mills not to hesitate calling him in today because there was no good reason he needed to have the day off. Except now he had an idea and something to occupy his time. He wanted to dig out all these lawn decorations, pull them to Lucy's front lawn, and get started on winning the Merriest Lawn Contest. The cash prize would wipe out Lucy's HOA bill and the rest of her mother's unpaid debt.

In theory, it would make Lucy happy, and suddenly that's all he wanted to do.

∞

Lucy stirred under the covers. She didn't want to get up even though the sun was determined to pry her eyelids open.

Bella huffed loudly from the end of the bed where she slept most nights. She had her own set of steps to get up on the bed because she was a spoiled little dog. Lucy's mother's doing.

Lucy finally sighed and rolled onto her side, opened her eyes, and entertained a few memories from last night when her best friends had come over. They'd cheered her up so much when she otherwise might have cried in a hot bath with a glass of wine. And they'd been there because Miles had invited them. He'd brought food over from his mother's house, set a table worthy of one of her mother's Thanksgivings, and then he'd left so that he didn't break one of her rules.

He was amazing. Why was she resisting him so hard again?

Lucy sat up in bed. She shuffled her socked feet down the hall toward the coffee maker, flipped it on, and leaned against the counter. As far as she knew, Miles hadn't gotten his coffee maker out of his boxes yet. He was determined not to unpack because he was looking for somewhere else to live. Which was for the best. But maybe she could return his favor from yesterday and make him a cup of coffee and bring it over.

Yeah. Good idea.

She grabbed a Thermos from her cabinet while the coffee brewed. Then she went into the bathroom and brushed her hair and teeth, deciding that it was okay to leave her flannel pajamas on. She might stay in them all day since she didn't expect to have to head out for work. Not unless Mandy needed her. She was one day postpartum, after all.

When Lucy returned to the coffee maker, the coffee

was ready. She poured herself a cup and then poured Miles a Thermos.

Bella barked and jogged over to the front door. Lucy was vaguely aware of some noise out there too. Lucy hoped it wasn't another visit from Olivia or someone else from the HOA, nagging her about her negligence in paying. How was she going to pay that bill before the end of the year? Maybe she could dig out some of her mother's old things and have an estate sale. Or pawn some of her appliances.

That sounded like a lot of effort. It also sounded desperate, which she guessed she was. She didn't want to be sued in the coming year. And she wanted to be in good standing with the HOA if she was going to stay in this house.

Was she going to stay in this house?

Bella continued to bark. Lucy walked over to her window with the cup and Thermos of coffee in her hand. She peeked through the blinds and a gasp whooshed out of her lungs.

She headed to the door, opened it, and headed in Miles's direction on the front lawn. "What do you think you're doing?"

Miles looked up and grinned, little dimples digging into his boyish cheeks. "Fixing your problem."

Chapter Ten

"I don't have a problem." Lucy folded her arms over her chest.

"Yes, you do. You said that you owe a bill with your HOA," Miles reminded her.

Lucy looked at the scattered lawn ornaments. "Okay. Yes, that's true. What does that have to do with all this?"

Miles grinned. "When a woman tells a man her problem, he lies awake in bed trying to find a way to solve it for her."

"You're going to fix my HOA issue by tossing Christmas cheer all over my front yard?" she asked in a sarcastic tone.

Miles bent to hug a Frosty the Snowman to his side. "We're going to win the Merriest Lawn Contest."

Lucy nearly dropped her mug and the Thermos she was holding. "What?"

"It's a twenty-five-hundred-dollar prize. It'll cover your overdue fees with the homeowner's association."

Lucy looked around again, processing what he was suggesting. "I don't feel like being merry this year though. I just want to say bah humbug and skip Christmas, like that movie."

"*The Kranks*?" Miles shook his head. "You're not skipping Christmas under my watch. And this is perfect. You have all the lawn ornaments and decorations. You just need to put them out."

"You make that sound so easy. Believe me, it's not. Outdoor decorating is a big job. My dad used to spend days doing this stuff. Weeks even. The people in this neighborhood are serious about this contest. It's not as easy as throwing everything out on the lawn and plugging it in."

"I'll do all the work for you," Miles said.

Lucy stepped toward him and handed him the Thermos of coffee she was holding. Then she sipped from her own cup as she thought. "I can't ask you to do that."

"You didn't ask. I'm offering."

She still shook her head but she had to admit it was a good idea. "I don't know."

"Winning would wipe out the bill. You wouldn't even have to worry about it. Then I'll be out of your hair soon, and you can rent that garage apartment to someone you actually want living next door to you."

Lucy nibbled at her lower lip.

"After I do a few repairs, that is."

She frowned, meeting his gaze. "What repairs?"

"Well, there's no hot water in the garage apartment for one," he said.

Lucy sipped more of her coffee. "I didn't know that. I'll call a plumber right away."

"It's okay. A cold shower isn't the end of the world. I can probably fix the issue myself." Plus, the last thing Lucy needed was one more bill on her house. "So what do you say? Want to win this year's Merriest Lawn Contest?"

Lucy hesitated.

"What if we do it together? It might be fun," he urged.

She tilted her head to one side. "You have a strange idea of fun."

Miles grinned. "Also, I think it's my turn to make a rule."

Lucy lifted her brows. "Okay?"

"Whenever we decorate together, we have to blast Christmas music and drink hot cocoa with extra marshmallows."

She cringed as an image of Olivia walking next door and handing out a neighborhood warning ticket crossed her mind. "I think the HOA probably has a noise ordinance."

"They can't object if we're playing Christmas tunes," he said. "Only a grinch would be upset about that."

Lucy hesitated. "Fair enough. Any other rules?"

"Yeah. I don't want you to feel weird about that kiss we shared the other night," he said. "I know you were just...having a bad day. I know it didn't mean anything."

Lucy cupped her hands around her mug of coffee. "You're saying that as if it was a one-sided kiss."

"No." He shook his head. "It was definitely two-sided."

"But you're blaming it on my bad day."

"No." He shook his head again. "I'm blaming you kissing me on a bad day. Me kissing you back was more...bad judgment."

Lucy's jaw dropped, and her voice rose an octave as she gasped, "What?"

Miles waved his hands in front of him. "Not in the way you're thinking. I just, I know where we stand, and I like the fact that we can still be friends after all we've been through together. I also kind of like having a roof over my head. I don't want to give you any reason to kick me out."

She gave him a faint smile. "I'm not kicking you out. But you're right. That kiss the other night was just a *When Harry Met Sally* moment."

Miles furrowed his brow, obviously clueless to her reference.

"You know. When Sally is crying and upset over her ex-boyfriend getting married. Then Harry tries to comfort her, and she kisses him. And he kisses her back, even though they know they shouldn't," she said, explaining quickly. "Sally just wants to feel better, and he just wants"—Lucy looked around at the scattered lawn decorations that Miles had dragged out—"to fix things for her."

Miles shook his head. "I've never seen the movie. Harry sounds like my kind of guy though."

"I think you'd be friends. If he was a real person. Then again, you're that guy who makes friends with everyone."

"I don't like to keep enemies," he said.

And despite how hard she'd tried to hate him once, she'd never quite been able to. "So we have an agreement?" She reached out a hand to him. "We'll decorate the yard and gazebo, blast holiday tunes, drink hot cocoa, and *not* kiss." Heat flushed her cheeks and body with the last word.

"Sounds like a recipe for a merry holiday to me," Miles agreed, taking her hand in his. The touch zinged through her palm and zipped all the way to her toes.

"Okay," she said a little breathlessly. "Let's create the merriest lawn that The Village has ever seen."

Miles was beginning to realize that Lucy was right. Decorating a lawn for Christmas wasn't easy. He'd strung lights at his mom's house before, and he'd helped put up the tree. But this was ten times as hard. There was an entire two-car garage full of elaborate decorations. They were meant to be set up as scenes. First, he needed to pull the decorations out and organize which ones belonged together. Rudolph didn't belong in the nativity scene any more than the Grinch who stole Christmas got to stand with a group of festive carolers.

The last couple hours had been devoted to figuring out what exactly was in the garage. He'd pulled each item out while Lucy made a running list of what they had. None of the decorations seemed to go together, and in his mind, didn't equal a winning combination. Whatever he and Lucy came up with needed to be more original than everyone else's display.

Miles finally stopped and sat down to rest in the gazebo. Bella wandered over and propped her front paws on his thigh, attempting to lick his cheek. He dodged the slobbery kiss and blew out a breath. "I need to take a break and tend to a few errands," he told Lucy.

She had changed out of her pajamas into a pair of fitted jeans and a light pink sweater that brought out the rosy colors of her cheeks and lips. Her auburn locks were pulled back in a ponytail and reading glasses framed her bright green eyes. He'd never seen her in glasses before. It gave her an adorable librarian look that made him all kinds of attracted to her right now.

He pulled his gaze away because he was pretty sure that Lucy would make a rule against being attracted to each other if she could read his mind. "One of my errands is to contact Della Rose about a house I saw online."

"Oh?" Lucy lifted her brows in his direction. "That sounds interesting."

"I was hoping to see it today but I know it's a holiday weekend."

"Can I tag along if you go?"

"I thought you wanted to stay home all day and do absolutely nothing."

"Well, you ruined that with this whole Merriest Lawn Contest idea." She grinned at him. "And touring a house actually sounds like fun."

This house that Miles was interested in wasn't anywhere near as nice as Lucy's. But it would be his, and it seemed cozy. The creek would be an amazing view to look out on every night while sitting on his back porch. He might even be able to do a little fishing there. "I'll contact her and see what she says. Of course, you're more than welcome to come with me if you want."

Lucy propped her reading glasses on the crown of her head. "Really?"

"Sure. I'd love the company. I'll call Della and see when she's available. Then we'll schedule our day from there." Miles pulled his cell phone from his pocket. He pulled up Della Rose's contact and tapped Dial.

Della answered after two rings. "Della Rose here."

"Hey, Della. It's Miles. I'm calling for business this time."

"Did I do something wrong, Deputy Bruno?" she asked, a playful lilt to her tone of voice. "I might welcome spending a night or two in a jail cell after the boys return home. All on my own with some peace and quiet sounds delightful."

Miles chuckled. "I'm afraid you'd be disappointed. The jail isn't such a quiet place."

"Hmm. Well, what can I do for you, Miles?" she asked.

"I'm actually calling you for your real estate expertise. I'm interested in viewing a house I saw online."

"Oh? Tell me which one, and I'll see if I can arrange a viewing."

"I don't expect you to drop what you're doing for me."

"I'm not doing anything at all," she assured him. "The boys are still with their father until this evening. I'm all yours."

Miles gave her the address he'd found online, and they planned a time to get together. He disconnected the call and looked up at Lucy. "The house is uninhabited. She'll meet us there in half an hour."

Lucy bounced softly on the balls of her feet. "Let me just go freshen up." She looked excited. Maybe it was just because it meant he might be out of her hair sooner rather than later.

"I'll do the same," he said.

They parted ways, and he went upstairs to the apartment, where he took an ice-cold shower. The water pressure was also fickle which meant it trickled down in a small, chilly stream. He soaped and got out as quickly as possible. Afterward, he dressed and headed back downstairs.

"You ready?" he asked as Lucy came walking out her front door at the same time he left the garage.

"Absolutely. I'm excited. This could be *the one*," she said, talking about the house. He thought of her though. She was always the one for him, and some part of him worried that, even after he'd checked off his list of requirements for settling down, there would be no one for him. Maybe his one chance for love was past.

He walked over to his truck and opened the door for her. Then he headed around and got in on the driver's side. As they drove, he listened as Lucy told him about Mandy Elks's baby that she'd helped deliver yesterday.

"I could never do that," he said. "I mean, I did one time, like I already told you, but it was unnerving."

"Well, I could never do what you do. Running toward danger. If you remember that night you came to my house, when I thought I had a break-in, I was cowering in the corner." She laughed at herself. "I'm not as brave as you."

"You're plenty brave." He watched the road as they both grew silent for a moment.

"So if you love this house, is our arrangement off? You won't have time to decorate my lawn with me."

"Buying a house takes a while. I would need to make an offer and secure a loan. It wouldn't happen overnight."

Lucy shifted and angled her body toward his as he drove. "Good, because I'm not ready to get rid of you just yet."

"Thought you wanted me out ASAP."

"You've only been at my place for a few days. And it hasn't been so terrible. For me at least. You're the one taking cold showers."

"Yeah. That's not my favorite. I plan to look into fixing your water heater for the apartment today."

"I shouldn't be charging you rent." Lucy shook her head. "I'm getting the better end of this arrangement."

"It's just a few things that need tending to. Sounds like your mom did quite a lot of work on the house before she died."

"She did. I didn't even know she was having those things done. I mean, why did she need a hot tub? Why did the house need a fresh coat of paint? It was fine the way it was."

Miles shrugged as he held on to the steering wheel. "I'm sure she had her reasons."

"And I may never know them now that she's gone." There was a note of sadness in Lucy's voice.

"Are you regretting keeping the house?" Miles asked.

Lucy shook her head. "No. I love that house. That's where I need to be, especially this year. I just didn't realize that there was so much involved in being a homeowner."

Miles thought on that for a moment. He'd always thought that owning a house would be his proof that he had finally made it in the world. But Lucy had never owned a house before now either. She didn't need to in order to feel successful.

Miles lifted his foot off the gas pedal and slowed to turn onto the quiet street that bordered Mallard Creek. Miles had been down here several times before. Not that there were a lot of crimes or illegal activity. But a couple of times he'd been called down here to an older couple who were homebound and didn't have any family. They'd passed away now, and he hadn't been down this street in months.

"There's Della Rose's SUV." Lucy pointed to the driveway in front of the yellow house that Miles had seen online. There was a FOR SALE sign in the front yard. "This is so exciting. Look how cute it is!"

Miles remained nervously quiet as he pulled into the driveway and looked out on the property. The house was quaint. It was the perfect house from where he was sitting. He just hoped that the inside lived up to his expectations. At the same time, another part of him hoped it didn't.

*

Lucy finished her walk-through of the little yellow house and met Miles and Della Rose back inside the front room. "It's perfect. I mean, I'm not the one buying, but if I were, you'd have a fight on your hands," she teased Miles.

He'd been oddly quiet the entire time they'd been inside the house. Della Rose had been the chatty one.

"Miles, what do you think?" Lucy finally asked.

He looked up, his gaze bouncing between her and Della Rose. "Well, it's a great house. I need to think on it. Is that okay?" he asked Della Rose.

"Of course it is. But don't think too long. This one will probably be snatched up fairly quickly."

Lucy scrutinized Miles's expression. She thought he looked pale. His hands were fidgeting in front of him, which wasn't like the confident man she knew. Buying a house was a big deal. It wasn't a decision to make lightly. Not that she knew firsthand. She'd inherited her house.

"I'll call and check on you tomorrow," Della Rose told him. "Sound good?"

Miles looked relieved. "Yes. Thank you. I just don't want to rush into something unless I'm one hundred percent sure."

"Of course. Buying a house is one of the biggest decisions a person makes. And you're doing it on your own." Della looked at Lucy. "Well, you have a little help, but it's you who'd be buying this house and moving in," she told Miles. "I like for my clients to be completely satisfied when they buy a house from me."

"Thanks."

"You're welcome. If you want to look at any other houses today, I'm available until supper time," Della said. "That's when Jerome is bringing the boys back. Divorce is hard on them, and they need time with their dad. I just wasn't expecting that I'd feel so jealous when that happened."

Lucy laid a hand on Della's shoulder. "If you need company, feel free to come over to my house. Miles and I are going to be decorating for Christmas today."

"While blasting holiday music and drinking hot cocoa," Miles added, smiling for the first time since they'd walked into the little yellow house.

Della looked between them. "I love Christmas as much as the next person but the outdoor decorating was always Jerome's forte. I have no desire to do any of that. No offense, but it sounds like torture." She chuckled softly. "I'm going over to Tess's place. We're reading the book club selection together and bingeing Hallmark movies. Maybe you should come hang with us."

Lucy glanced over at Miles, surprised at her realization that there was no one other than him that she wanted to spend the rest of the day with. "I'm afraid our plans are set in stone. Miles and I have a lot to do if we want to win the Merriest Lawn Contest."

"Wouldn't that be something?" Della Rose asked. "Well, have fun, you two. Miles, I'll call you tomorrow, after you've had time to think about this place."

"Sounds good," he said.

Once Lucy and Miles were back in his truck, she looked over at him and reached across the center console to touch his arm.

His eyes widened.

"Okay, spill it," she said. "What's bothering you?"

Chapter Eleven

Lucy shivered as her palm met Miles's warm skin. It was meant to be a platonic touch but her body didn't seem to understand that.

"What do you mean?" he asked.

"Well, you got quiet as soon as we arrived here. I can tell that something's weighing on your mind. Want to share?"

He blew out a breath and looked forward at the house. "I love it," he finally said. "It's exactly what I envision for myself."

"And that's upsetting to you because...?" She drew out the last syllable.

He shook his head. "I don't know. I thought I wanted a house before I settled down but now I kind of feel like this is something that I'm supposed to do with someone else."

Some part of Lucy wanted to volunteer herself. Which was crazy. They were done and over. But another part of herself was already jealous of whoever he did settle down with.

"Buying a forever home should be something you do with the person you're going to spend your life with," he said. "It shouldn't be my house. It should be our house."

Lucy swallowed. "Our house?"

He looked at her. "Mine and my girlfriend or my future wife's."

Lucy laughed nervously. "Right. Yeah, that's what I thought you meant." She waved a hand. What was wrong with her? Spending too much time with Miles was going to her head. "Whoever you end up with, it will be your house together. They bring all of their stuff and their preferences, and it blends together with whatever you've already established."

"Right." Miles was quiet for a moment. "I'll just sleep on this like Della Rose suggested."

"Things are usually clearer in the morning," Lucy agreed.

Miles turned the key in the ignition and started the truck. "Thanks for giving up the remainder of your afternoon to come check out the house with me."

"I didn't have any real plans. Certainly not Black Friday shopping."

"Yeah, I've been on duty for quite a few of those," Miles said on a laugh as he reversed out of the driveway of the yellow house. "People act foolishly when they get in a crowd, all going after the same good deal."

"I bet." Lucy laughed quietly, looking at the yellow house as they drove past. It really was beautiful. Although small, it was cozy, and the view from the back porch was so serene. She could almost picture herself sitting there after a long day. If Miles purchased the house, however, it wouldn't be her sitting on that porch. She had a house—assuming she could find a way to pay off her mom's debt and keep it.

"I do need to go to one store on the way home," Miles said.

She liked their shared idea of home. "Oh?"

"I need to stop at the hardware store for a couple quick items that should allow me to have hot water again. That's the hope, at least."

"Well, by all means, crowd or not, we should get you those items. I want you to have hot showers," she said. "No reason to be taking cold ones."

He slid his gaze over to meet hers momentarily, humor dancing in his eyes. "Great. We'll grab the supplies and then head back to Christmas Lane for decorating and shower fixing."

Lucy nodded. "Perfect."

∞

Two hours later, after fixing his shower issue, thanks to a couple YouTube how-to videos, Miles stood in the middle of the front yard with three wise men, an angel, and Lucy.

"Where do you want the nativity scene?" Miles asked.

She scanned the yard with a thoughtful look. Then she took a few steps toward the left side of the house and swept her hands over the ground. "Maybe right here in front of the gazebo. I don't want it to be right up on Santa's workshop."

"Good idea." Miles carried one wise man at a time to the spot that she'd indicated.

"I'll get started on the front porch while you do that." She cast him a huge grin. "This is kind of fun. I thought putting out these things that my parents loved so much might make me sadder this year, but it's actually kind of the opposite. I'm having these flashbacks of them laughing together. They used to bicker over where to place things or how tacky some of the things my dad brought home were. But they loved doing it." She gave him a meaningful look. "Thank you for suggesting this, Miles."

"You're welcome."

"If there's ever anything I can do to repay the favor," she said. "I mean, I guess I owe you a few favors right now because you also offered to complete the repairs in that garage apartment."

"That won't take me long, and it's as much for me as for you. I'm not a fan of cold showers."

She grimaced and then burst into more laughter. It seemed to be the theme of the afternoon.

Miles watched her for a moment. Her cheeks were nipped from the chilly air. Her green eyes were sparkling with excitement. She was the most beautiful woman he had ever seen. And he was in so much trouble this holiday. "Seeing you happy is enough for me." He looked away. "I know how you could repay the favor though. If you really wanted to."

"Oh?"

He shrugged. "When I move into my new house, I'll need a few pointers on how to make it less of a man cave."

"I would love to." She looked pleased at the invitation. "Well, I'll leave you to work out here. I'm going in to locate a wreath my mom always hung on the front door. I think there are some porch decorations inside too."

"You mean that stuff in the garage isn't all of it?" Miles couldn't imagine that there was more.

"The garage has most of it but there's a closet in one of the upstairs guest rooms with more. What can I say? My parents loved Christmas."

Miles always loved the holiday, too, but he was enjoying it even more this year. Thanks to Lucy.

Miles worked another three hours, making good progress in that amount of time. He set out the nativity scene, minus one missing wise man, a winter wonderland scene, and a group of child carolers. He still had several displays to put up, including one that would involve climbing a very tall ladder and crawling onto the roof to lay out Santa's sleigh and reindeer. He would leave that for another day, along with stringing the lights and patching the roof above his garage apartment.

Decorating for the Merriest Lawn Contest was a big job, for sure. It would take most of his free time. When he wasn't at the sheriff's department or the Youth Center, he'd be here.

Miles headed toward Lucy, who was still on the porch, untangling a strand of lights. "You've done some work up here."

She beamed back at him. "Not as much as you. But the wreath is up. I have the North Pole mailbox there." She gestured by the front door. "My dad was very proud of that piece. He even got a few letters in there from neighborhood kids who thought the mail really went to Santa."

"A pipeline to the North Pole. What kid wouldn't want that?" Miles leaned against the porch railing, his muscles pulling and aching just enough to remind him he'd worked hard today on Lucy's behalf. Somewhere between hauling decorations from storage and setting them in the yard, he'd also tinkered with and fixed the hot water heater. "I'm done for the afternoon." It was nearing dinnertime, and he wanted a chance to relax.

Lucy shoved her hands in the pockets of the coat

she was wearing. "I have leftovers from your mom's house. It's not the day after Thanksgiving if you don't eat leftovers, right?"

Miles hesitated, remembering her rules. And the fact that he could try not to be attracted to Lucy all he wanted but his efforts were futile.

"There's pie in my fridge that you earned fair and square from your mom's house."

"Actually, my sister informed me that I lost that challenge after all. She's the rightful winner."

Lucy's mouth made a little O. "Well, I can't eat all that food by myself. And it's silly, that rule about us not eating together. I mean, we're two adults, and our relationship was so long ago. And that kiss the other night..." She trailed off.

"Right. Yeah," he said, really unsure of what exactly he was agreeing to.

"So a turkey sandwich and a slice of pie?" She looked up, a hopeful gleam in her eyes.

Miles understood why Lucy had made those rules of hers to begin with. It was to keep them from getting too close. That was already happening though, and Miles couldn't say he minded. "Sure."

∞

"Leftover turkey sandwiches are my new favorite food." Lucy leaned back in the dining room chair beside Miles.

Miles waved his fork at her. "Nope, nope, nope. You're not done eating yet. You were supposed to save room for pie."

Lucy giggled and then groaned as she grabbed her

belly again. "I don't think I can eat another bite," she protested as she watched him cut a generous slice of pumpkin pie and slide it toward her.

He cut another slice for himself. Then he held up his fork in her direction.

She gave him a curious look. "What are you doing?"

"Tapping forks. We'll make a toast."

"Most people toast with wine."

"Or pie forks." He waved his fork in the air again.

On a laugh, Lucy lifted her fork as well and clinked it against his, her gaze locking on Miles's brown eyes.

"To winning," he said.

"But you lost the guest list challenge, remember?"

Miles lowered his fork and carved a bite from his slice of pie. "Yes, but we're going to win this decorating thing."

"Are you always so sure of yourself, Deputy Bruno?"

"Have to be. Confidence goes a long way in winning. I guess it stems from all the sports I played in school," Miles said, lifting a bite of pie toward his mouth. "Baseball, basketball, swim team. I was fortunate that my aunt Ruth paid my way for those things because my family would never have afforded that otherwise."

Lucy knew that Ruth was his father's sister. Over the years, she'd helped Miles and Ava pay for school-related things and sent them nice gifts on special occasions.

"That was very nice of her. And if I remember correctly, you were sports obsessed. It was hard for a girlfriend to get alone time with all those extracurricular activities of yours."

Lucy focused on her pie, silently amending her list of rules. She'd missed a very important one that needed to be added to her list. *Rule #5: Don't bring up the past.*

Miles looked at her. "I always made time for you."

She swallowed and dug her fork into her own slice of pie, even though she was too full to put it into her mouth. She wanted to ask him why he'd ever stopped making time for her but that was futile. The pregnancy scare had made him see clearly that he didn't want to be "dragged down" with her for the rest of his life.

Ouch. Those words still hurt when she remembered them.

"What's wrong?" Miles asked.

She shook her head. "Nothing. I think I just ate too much." She put her fork down. "But I agree about left-overs. Food is always better the next day. Your mom is an amazing cook."

"I'll tell her you said so. She prepares even more food at Christmas. And the guest list challenge is happening again. It'll give me a chance to reclaim the champi-onship for the year."

Lucy tilted her head as she eyed him across the dinner table. "Is that an invitation?"

"It is. I mean, I'm helping you win this Merriest Lawn contest and a pot of winnings. The least you can do is help me win a pecan pie at my mom's house."

Lucy lifted a brow. "How about we make a deal? If we win, I'll go with you to your mom's Christmas dinner."

Miles wore his best victory grin.

Lucy pointed a finger at him. "I said *if*."

"Well, we're definitely going to win so there's no question in my mind." He took another bite of pie and then finished his slice off in three solid forkfuls.

Lucy didn't touch hers. She was too full. "So, I was thinking..." she began as Miles shifted and prepared to stand. He was likely planning to go back across the lawn to the garage apartment. "You said you haven't seen *When Harry Met Sally*."

"That's right, I haven't."

"Well, that's practically a crime, Deputy Bruno."

"Is it?" Miles's voice dropped to a deep baritone. Was it just her or did it sound flirtatious? And what was she even suggesting? She had rules against being alone in her house together, and with good reason. She was already beginning to have feelings for him again. And yet thoughts of the past were never far behind when she was with him.

"We could stream it," she told him. "And it's a Friday night. I think we should watch it."

"I don't know. Does it have action in it?" he asked.

Lucy shook her head. "No, and it's still the best movie ever."

"I need at least one chase scene."

Lucy thought for a moment. "There is one scene when Harry is running down the street. It's at the end. Plus, it's kind of a Christmas movie, so we can call it research for our decorations."

Miles furrowed his brow. "It doesn't sound like a Christmas movie to me."

"Any movie that spans across Christmas is a Christmas movie in my book," she said. "Plus, it's my favorite movie, and you've never seen it. That needs to be corrected."

Miles crossed one leg over his knee, leaning back and appearing like he was preparing to stay a while. "Well, if we're watching Christmas movies, we should add my favorite to the queue."

"Oh? What is it?" she asked.

"*It's a Wonderful Life.*"

"Really? That's your favorite?"

Miles's eyes flashed with amusement. "You look surprised."

"Well, I don't recall any chase scenes in that one."

"Maybe not, but George Bailey is a man fighting for his life. This guy thinks he has nothing to live for. Then he realizes everything he ever wanted was right there in front of him all along." Miles looked at her so intensely that she momentarily forgot to breathe. Maybe she should cancel the whole movie idea before she dug herself in too deep with this attraction she was harboring.

Before she could say anything, Miles stood and headed toward her living room, calling behind him, "Which movie should we play first?"

It seemed like Lucy had only closed her eyes for a moment when suddenly she awoke to a knock on her front door. At first she wondered who would be knocking after midnight. She and Miles were on the last leg of *When Harry Met Sally*. Then she realized that the movie was over and somehow it was morning.

The knock grew louder. Bella scurried in that direction, barking up a storm.

"Shh, Bella," Lucy said in a sleepy haze. "Don't wake Miles."

Lucy's eyes widened as she looked over to the other side of the couch, where Miles was asleep. *Oh no!* He'd slept over, and there was a possible witness standing on Lucy's porch.

Lucy pressed a hand to her rapidly beating heart as

her thoughts raced and the knocking continued. Bella barked again. Lucy looked at Miles a second time. He didn't even stir with all the commotion. And for a moment, her heart slid up into her throat. He looked adorably handsome when he slept. His silky black hair was all messed up, and there were creases from the couch on his cheek.

"Lucy?" someone called from the other side of the front door.

Lucy guessed she couldn't avoid the visitor. Her car was in the driveway and Bella was at the door. She got up and headed in that direction.

"Lucy?" the voice called again.

The voice was familiar. Was it Olivia Reynolds from the HOA again?

Lucy opened the door. *Yep, that's exactly who it is.* "Oh hi, Olivia," she said, unsure if this visitor was the best-case scenario or the worst. She didn't know Olivia very well so she wasn't sure if Olivia was the type to judge her for answering the door while looking like such a mess. "What brings you here so early?"

"Well, it's seven a.m. Early bird gets the worm, right?" Olivia's gaze went to Lucy's hair.

Lucy lifted a hand and tried to smooth it down. "I, um, just woke up. It was a late night."

"I see. Well, I noticed all your lawn decorations on my morning walk," Olivia said.

Lucy looked past her to the yard for a moment. "These were my parents' decorations. I thought why not. 'Tis the season, right?"

"Right." Olivia's smile wobbled. "Well, the reason I'm at your door is to make sure you're not planning to enter the Merriest Lawn Contest."

Lucy furrowed her brow. "Why is that? I live here now. I'll pay the registration fee, of course."

"Yes, but..." Olivia hedged, shifting lightly between her sneakered feet.

"But?"

"Well, there's a little byline in the contest rules that says entrants must be up to date with their HOA dues. Otherwise they're disqualified."

Lucy's heart sank. The whole point of entering the contest was to pay those dues. "I see."

"I'm sorry, Lucy. I hate to be the deliverer of bad news again." Olivia looked sincerely apologetic. It was hard to be upset with her when she was just following the rules that Lucy seemed to keep breaking.

"No, it's okay. I understand." Even though Lucy felt like crying.

"Well, I don't," a deep voice said behind her.

Lucy turned to see Miles in his adorable rolled-out-of-bed look.

"Oh, Deputy Bruno." Olivia's eyes went wide. "I didn't realize you were here. So early." She looked between him and Lucy, eyes widening even more.

Lucy waved her hands in front of her. "No, no, no. It's not how it looks." She noticed that two neighbors who'd been out walking had stopped in the street and were seeing the same thing that Olivia was. Both Lucy and Miles had just-rolled-out-of-bed hair and crumpled clothes. The natural conclusion was that Miles had slept over last night. And that was kind of, sort of true.

Chapter Twelve

Miles waited for Lucy to say something. After saying goodbye to Olivia and closing the front door, Lucy had grown scarily quiet.

"Luce?" he finally said.

Her gaze lifted to his. "That was not good. Do you realize how bad that was?"

"So a couple of your neighbors realized I slept over," he said. "We were both dressed, and it was just an accident."

"That's not the story that will be spun once word gets around," she said, her breaths audibly shallow. "This will make for juicy gossip on Reva's blog."

Miles stepped toward her and placed a hand on her shoulder. Her lips parted. "We fell asleep watching a movie. It was harmless. If anyone tries to say differently, we correct them."

"Easy for you." She shook her head. "You weren't the one who took all the gossip after our breakup. People just couldn't seem to help themselves and were concocting stories about what happened. Someone had seen me leave the doctor's office and, coupled with the ring on my finger, the assumption was that we were having a shotgun wedding."

Miles grimaced softly. "Which was true."

Lucy looked away. "Except the home pregnancy test I'd taken at home was a false positive. The baby we thought we were having before I walked into that doctor's office had turned into nothing by the time I stepped out. By then, folks in town were saying we were pregnant. I didn't just have to break the news to you but to everyone who asked. It was embarrassing. I was horrified."

"No wonder you left town."

Her gaze cut back to his. "I left town to go to college. And because you broke up with me."

Miles realized his hand was still on her shoulder. He lowered it. "The only real gossip we have to worry about now is Reva, and I'm not the least bit concerned. It'll be fine, Luce. I promise."

Her posture softened. "Even so, we should try to make sure this never happens again."

"No more sleepovers. Got it," Miles said with a growing grin.

"And we should maybe split up for the rest of the weekend. So this little event can blow over."

Miles took a step back. "I have plans with Gil and Jake today anyway."

Lucy gave him an amused look. "It's so funny that you and Jake are pals. You two couldn't stand each other in high school. I think it's because of those few dates you had with Jake's girlfriend back then."

"It was," Miles agreed. "Jake and Rachel were broken up though. And I hadn't caught your eye just yet," he said, regretting his slip back into the past.

"Oh, you caught my eye. You just didn't know it yet," she said quietly.

Yeah, time to get out of here before this completely innocent sleepover turned into a kiss.

"I'll just head out the back door and try not to be spotted on my way to the apartment."

"Good idea." She followed him out of the living room and into the kitchen. "Your hot water is still working in your apartment?"

"Perfectly," he said. "Thankfully, it really was just the shower valve cartridge like the YouTube tutorial suggested it might be."

"You're a handy guy to have around, Miles Bruno." She lingered in the doorway as he stepped out onto the back deck. His gaze moved to the Jacuzzi tub that Lucy's mom had purchased. "You should try that out over the weekend. It's too good to go to waste."

Lucy side-eyed the tub. "Not until I pay it off. Until then, I'm resentful of it."

Miles looked at it again. "I don't have any bitterness toward the hot tub—just saying."

She laughed while shaking her head. "You taking a dip in that tub would definitely stir up some chatter around here."

Miles was only teasing though. "You're probably right about that. See you later, Lucy. Last night was fun."

She gave him a small smile, her arms folded in front of her. "Yes, it was. See you later, Miles."

He turned and headed back to where he belonged, at least according to his head. His heart, however, tugged and begged him to stay right where he was.

After a hot shower, he dressed and drove over to meet Gil and Jake at a launch site. Gil owned a huge sailboat that he took out on Somerset Lake a couple times a month. When Miles had the day off, he typically joined his friend on the water for fishing or just nature watching, which was best out on the lake with the Blue Ridge Mountains rolling lazily in the background.

"It's nice to have friends in high places," Miles told Gil as they launched the boat in the water.

Gil gave him an amused look. "Jake's the one with the plane."

Jake had a private sea plane that he took them up in sometimes too.

"I have a deputy cruiser," Miles offered jokingly. "I'll let you guys ride along sometime. I'll even let you put on the siren."

The jovial nature of the visit continued as they traversed the lake. It was a beautiful day on the water, the sun unobscured in a clear sky.

Gil managed the helm, but once the sails caught the wind, he sat back and focused on the guys. "I'd ask one of you to join me out here for next week's Christmas flotilla but I'm guessing you'll both be watching from the sidelines with your other halves."

"That's a fact," Jake said. He and Trisha Langly were connected at the hips these days as they prepared for their New Year's wedding. Trisha had a young son who also went everywhere with them.

Gil looked at Miles.

Miles held up his hands. "I don't have another half."

"The way Trisha tells it," Jake said, "the book club ladies seem to think you and Lucy are heating up."

"We're friends," Miles said, even though that wasn't exactly the whole truth.

"But you would like to be more?" Gil asked.

"Lucy is having a rough season. She's still mourning the loss of her mom. I'm not sure she's ready to date." That was the truth. Miles did think Lucy was vulnerable, and even if he wanted to act on his attraction, it wasn't the right time. "And you guys know how I feel about getting serious with someone. I won't do it until I'm one hundred percent stable." Miles gestured at Jake. "I mean, you have a job and a dozen rental properties. There's no worry about being able to keep a roof over your family's head and food on the table."

"That's your childhood talking," Jake said. He leaned against the hull of the boat as he sat with a soda in his hand and a visor shading his face. "You don't have any reason to worry either. You're at the sheriff's department. You're set."

"Almost," Miles said. Because his father had a stable job too until layoffs happened. His father had been able to pay bills too—until he couldn't.

"So, you mean to tell me that if you find yourself in a romantic situation with Lucy," Gil said, "you won't act on it? Because you're too busy worrying about the future?"

That kiss from the other night flashed in Miles's memory, stirring up all kinds of feelings he didn't want to wade through right now. The timing wasn't good for him or Lucy—period.

"Whoa. Did you see that?" Jake asked Gil.

Gil propped his feet up on the side of the boat. "Yep. Sure did."

Jake tipped his soda can toward Miles. "You're holding out on us. Something has already happened between you and Lucy. It's written all over your face."

Miles wished he had on a visor right now too. "I'm

pleading the Fifth, okay? But I will say that, whatever did or didn't already happen with me and Lucy, it's not going to happen again."

Lucy didn't mind the quiet but her thoughts were obnoxiously loud as she poked around the attic where her mom kept the decorations for the inside of the house.

Lucy could remember her mom taking her time, almost savoring the experience every year. There was an artificial tree in the corner and several boxes of ornaments. Lucy examined the tree distastefully. She'd grown to love a live tree since she'd been an adult. There was a local tree farm nearby, Hannigan Farms—yet another business that had once been owned by her family and was sold off years ago. She'd get a tree there, bring it home, and use the boxed ornaments here to decorate.

Lucy headed over to pick up the first box when another box caught her eye. Her breath caught as she immediately recognized it. She lowered herself to the attic floor and sat in front of the box, remembering how much her mother adored the items inside. She lifted the lid and peered at the ceramic houses that her mom put on the mantel every year, creating a little Christmas village that in some ways resembled the neighborhood Lucy had grown up in. There were tiny houses, streetlights, mailboxes, and miniature people that Lucy used to play with.

"Careful," her mom would warn. "Those are fragile. They're not toys."

Lucy gently picked up the tiny gazebo now, admiring

its fine details. It had a pointed roof decorated with garland and red bows. There were festive wreaths hanging from the railings and a decorated evergreen tree standing in the center. Her mom had loved this Christmas village.

Instead of grabbing the box of ornaments, Lucy placed the gazebo in the box with the other miniature items and picked it up. She carried it out of the attic directly to the mantel in the living room. Like her mother, she took her time, savoring each house as she pulled it out and decided where it should go. There were nearly two dozen houses along with the gazebo. Her mom had added to it each year just like she and Lucy's father had added to the outdoor decorations.

When Lucy was done, she felt a little less lonely somehow. She didn't fancy the idea of going right back up to the attic. Instead, she thought it was a beautiful day to make a trip to the tree farm and get herself the fullest blue fir on the Hannigan Farms lot.

She pulled out her phone and dialed Tess.

"Hey, Lucy. Shouldn't you be spending your day with your new tenant?" Tess asked.

"My new tenant is out with friends. And I'm about to go buy my Christmas tree. Want to come along?"

"Tree shopping? That sounds like fun," Tess said. "I mean, not as much fun as staying curled up on the couch and reading my book."

"Which you can do while enjoying the twinkling lights of your tree all month. Come on. Please."

Tess sighed into the phone receiver. "They'll need to load our trees onto our cars, so I'll meet you there."

They said goodbye, and then Lucy disconnected the

call. She freshened up in the bathroom and grabbed her things. Then she headed over to Hannigan Farms, circling the lot until she located Tess's midsize SUV. She parked and got out.

Tess stepped out of her vehicle and tugged her purse over her shoulder. "I have to admit, this does sound like fun."

"Are you getting a tree for your home or the bookstore?" Lucy asked as they walked.

"The bookstore, I think. I don't decorate my house too much. I don't get enough visitors to make it worthwhile. And I practically live at Lakeside Books anyway."

The two women stopped to admire every tree. They all blurred together for Lucy.

"I guess I just need to pick one. None of them are standing out to me," she said.

Tess stood beside her. "I'm holding out for that special one that's meant for me."

Lucy looked over at her friend. "It always surprises me to hear you sound like such a hopeless romantic."

Tess gave Lucy an eye roll. "Just because I don't date very often doesn't mean I don't believe in fate and soul mates." She pointed at the tree in front of her. "Speaking of soul mates. This tree is perfect. I've found *the one*."

Lucy assessed the tree in front of Tess. "Good choice. I'll have the one right next to yours."

"Good thing you don't pick your men that way," Tess quipped, giving her friend a wink.

They tagged their trees, purchased, and waited by their vehicles for someone to load them.

Lucy looked at Tess. "How are you going to drag

that thing into your store all by yourself? Want me to follow you to Lakeside Books? I can help."

"Then how will you get yours inside your house?" Tess asked.

"Miles can help me when he gets home."

Tess's eyes widened a touch. "Wow. I know he's just a tenant but you sound awfully cozy with him already. And I think that's good, Lucy. I know you're hurting because you're missing your mom. But maybe a little romance is exactly what you need to help you through this Christmas."

Lucy narrowed her eyes. "So you're suggesting that I use Miles for my own emotional needs?"

"Is that so wrong?" Tess asked with a half shrug. "I mean, we all use each other. That's kind of the point of relationships."

"I take it back. You don't sound like a hopeless romantic at all."

Tess glanced at the man who was still tying her tree to the top of her SUV and lowered her voice. "You were using me when you called to invite me here this afternoon. You didn't want to be alone. And I was using you right back because I wanted a tree but didn't want to have to come out and get one on my own. All I'm suggesting is that having Miles close by might be a nice distraction. Let the past go and focus on the now."

"I have. I've forgiven Miles for breaking my heart when I was eighteen. I'm not one to hold grudges."

"Then what's the problem?" Tess asked. "Forgive and forget."

Lucy held up a finger. "That's the problem. It's not as easy to forget. I loved him once. He was my entire world back then," Lucy said.

"First love is like that. Wonderful until it's over. Then it's bone crushing."

"Exactly." Lucy watched her tree being strapped to her vehicle now. "A distraction for Christmas would be nice but I'm not sure Miles is what I need for the long-term."

"You don't think you can trust your heart with him?" Tess asked.

"Exactly." Lucy nodded even though she didn't just think that—she knew it.

*

Miles was always in a good mood after a day of being on the lake with his friends. He drove back to The Village, pulled onto Christmas Lane, and turned into the driveway, parking beside Lucy's car. There was a huge tree strapped to the top. As soon as he stepped out of his truck, she opened her front door and headed in his direction.

"I need a favor."

He chuckled. "I bet I can guess what it is." He glanced at the tree. "Did you pick the biggest one on the lot?"

"Well, I have a big house," she explained.

"That's an understatement. I'll get it for you. Do you have the tree stand already in place?"

"Yep. And the tree skirt. All I need is the tree."

"Well, I'm your man." He opened her passenger door and stepped up on the floorboard, leaning over the roof to start loosening the strap. Lucy did the same on the other side. Once the tree was free, Miles gently pulled it to himself. Lucy picked up the end with the tree's conical-shaped top, and they carried it toward the front porch, up the steps, and into the house.

"Over there." Lucy tipped her head in the direction of the living room.

Miles gave her a teasing look. "You mean that spot where you were hiding from the opossum a couple weeks back?"

She gave him a playful scowl. "Yes, that's the spot. You're never going to let me live that down, are you?"

"Not anytime soon." He dragged the tree to the stand, and together they lifted it up and placed it inside. "There." Miles pulled his pocketknife from his keychain and began to cut the twine wrapping the tree's branches tightly.

Lucy worked on fanning the branches out as they were released.

Miles kept glancing through the limbs at her, finding her more beautiful with each glimpse. Her hair, her eyes, her rosy complexion—a telltale that she'd been out in the chilly air all afternoon too.

"How was the boat?" she asked.

"Great. Gil's going to have it out in the flotilla next weekend. He invited me along but I declined."

"Oh?"

Miles was hoping that he might have other plans with Lucy. That maybe they'd be watching the flotilla from the shore together. But that was crazy. "I like to watch from the lakeside and see all the boats as they go by."

"Me too. It's one of the most exciting celebrations of the season."

"That and The Village's Merriest Lawn Contest," he added. He finished cutting the straps and took a step back to admire the tree. It was big and full. "I couldn't have picked a better one myself."

Lucy looked pleased that he would say so. "Tess came along with me. Hers is just as big. I helped her drag it inside her bookstore before coming home."

"Ah. Do you need anything else while I'm here?" Miles asked, knowing he should leave even though he wanted to stick around.

Lucy gave him a hesitant look, pulling her lower lip between her teeth. "There are several boxes of ornaments in the attic. Would you mind helping me?"

"Not at all. Lead the way." Miles followed Lucy upstairs and down the hall. "I don't think I've ever been up here before. This is nice." He glanced in the bedrooms as he passed. "What did your family do with all these rooms?"

"Well, one was mine growing up. My mom and dad kept separate rooms so one of these was my dad's." Lucy laughed softly as she stopped in front of the attic ladder. She'd left it down earlier. "My mom did a lot of work on the upstairs before she got sick. I'm not really sure why she invested the time or money but it looks amazing up here. Like a picture out of one of those home magazines she loved to look at."

"Maybe she was planning to invite some friends to stay as her guests."

"I wouldn't doubt it. She was a social butterfly." Sadness crept into the green of Lucy's eyes for a moment. Then she blinked, and it was gone.

"I'll get the boxes. Are they labeled?" he asked.

"Yep. And I pulled them right to the opening. All you need to do is reach for them," she said. "Hand them down, and I'll take them."

"You got it." He climbed the steps and peered into the large attic, full of yet more decorations. It was almost comical. He grabbed one box after another and handed them down to Lucy. When he was done, he returned to the second floor.

"Since you're up here," Lucy said, "want me to give you a tour?"

Miles looked past her at the long hall, where there appeared to be several rooms. "Sure."

Lucy led him into the first bedroom and then the second. They were decorated to a T with what appeared to be new linens and spreads, curtains and décor.

"Wow. It is very nice up here," he agreed.

"Mom loved to decorate, and not only for the holidays. I guess, after my dad passed away, she needed a hobby." Lucy looked around the last room. It was decorated in a soft mint green with golden accents. The feel was calm and serene. Fancy drapes were pulled back from the large windows with rope ties and gold tassels, streaming in just the right amount of natural light.

"Too bad she never made it to the garage apartment," Miles teased.

Lucy's lips parted. "I would have offered you one of these rooms, but..."

"No, I get it. What would people say?" he asked.

Lucy offered a teasing eye roll. "If the hot water still wasn't working, I'd invite you to move up here. You're more important than rumors. I'm really sorry I didn't see that until now."

Miles was tempted to lie and tell her the water was still cold. Living up here would be nice. These rooms were five-star hotel quality. "Thanks for the tour. You should have a girls' night with your book club over here."

Lucy's eyes lit up. "You know, that's not a bad idea."

Miles headed out and lifted one of the boxes of ornaments to carry down. "You can talk about books all night."

"You know that's not really what we do, right?" She lifted the second box and carried it behind him.

"Oh? What is it you all do then?" he asked over his shoulder.

"Talk about our lives. Give each other advice. Girl talk."

They reached the first floor, and Miles carried the box to the tree, setting it down in front.

"That's kind of what me and the guys did today on the boat."

Lucy looked at him with interest. "Let me guess. They asked about you and me?"

Miles shook his head. "Pleading the Fifth."

Her grin stretched across her face. "And you told them that there was no you and me?"

"Not exactly," Miles confessed. "I told them that you were too smart to ever give me another chance."

Her eyes widened just a touch. She didn't agree or deny that claim. Her hesitation made him suspect the answer was the former though. Not that he'd asked a question. Not formally.

"Well, a hot shower in the garage apartment is calling my name. Goodnight, Lucy." He forced himself toward the door before he said or did something that might put all of his feelings on display. If she truly never would give him a second chance, why put his heart out there for her to break?

Chapter Thirteen

On Monday morning, Miles walked into the sheriff's department bright and early. He headed straight to the staff lounge where the coffee maker was.

"Long weekend?" Sheriff Mills asked, stepping into the lounge.

Sheriff Mills was only a couple years older than Miles. He'd been a high school senior when Miles was a freshman. The sheriff was well-respected among the folks in town and did a good job. For the most part, everyone loved him, including Miles.

Miles set the pot to brew and turned to face his boss. "You might say so. It was good though."

"So I hear." Sheriff Mills smirked.

That got Miles's attention. He braced himself and asked, "What's that supposed to mean?"

The sheriff chuckled. "I'll deny it if you tell anyone else, but I read Reva's blog. And her post today was quite a doozy."

Miles frowned. "What did she post this time?"

"All I can say is that I understand why you need coffee this morning." He walked out of the lounge, leaving Miles baffled and dreading what he might read on Reva's site. He pulled out his cell phone and opened a browser. With a few quick taps, he was staring at a new entry from Reva, with one bullet point titled REUNITED FOR THE HOLIDAYS?

"No, no, no." Miles wished she'd stay out of his personal life. And if she was going to get into his business, he wished she'd at least get her facts straight.

"So you've got a girlfriend for Christmas, huh?" Latoya asked as she entered the lounge. She pointed at the pot. "I want a cup of that coffee you're brewing."

"Help yourself. And I don't have a girlfriend," Miles protested as he returned to reading Reva's blog.

- REUNITED FOR THE HOLIDAYS? It seems there's a lot to be grateful for in the Christmas Village. Several Somerseters witnessed the good deputy leaving Lucy Hannigan's house at seven a.m. on Saturday morning. Sure, he could have walked over early, but a little bird reported that there were sleep creases still on his face. Maybe, this season, these two star-crossed lovers will be reunited once and for all.

Miles growled under his breath. He looked up at Latoya. "Where does Reva get this stuff?" The only people close-up enough to see creases on his face were Lucy and Olivia, and he doubted Lucy was feeding Reva gossip.

Latoya stepped up beside him and poured herself a cup of coffee. "So it's not true that you slept over at your ex's house this weekend?"

Miles opened his mouth but no words came out. Because technically it was the truth.

"Ah ha." Latoya jabbed a finger in his direction.

"It wasn't like that, okay? We fell asleep watching movies."

She lifted a brow. "What movie?"

"*When Harry Met Sally.*"

"Ah ha," she said again as if that had proved her point. "No man agrees to watch that movie unless he's into the woman who's asking."

Miles couldn't argue that point either. He *was* into Lucy. But he couldn't tell Latoya that.

"Hmm." Latoya narrowed her eyes at him as she sipped from her coffee mug. She should have been a detective because she could read people like a good book. "That is the look of a man with lady troubles. Don't let Reva get a whiff of that."

"Why can't she just blog about gardens or crafts or other stuff that people write about?"

Latoya cackled quietly. "Because no one would read that," she said. "Everyone on the lake reads what Reva writes."

"Great." Miles had a feeling that he'd be explaining himself to everyone he crossed paths with today. He finished preparing his cup of coffee to go and headed out of the lounge, calling to Latoya behind him. "I have work to do. There's no time for gossip, especially when it's aimed at me."

He headed out of the station and got into his cruiser. Then he circled the lake, responding to a few minor issues in the community. He kept waiting for Lucy to call or text once she'd heard what Reva had written but his cell phone remained quiet. So much so that he picked it up to make sure it was charged. Maybe Lucy was the one person in town who wouldn't see the blog post this morning.

An hour later, his cell phone finally rang. Miles reached for it, ready to tell Lucy that everything would settle down soon. It wasn't his new landlord on the other line though. Instead, Della Rose's name appeared on his screen.

He still didn't feel one hundred percent certain about the yellow house, as much as he loved it. Maybe he'd tell Della he needed one more day to roll it around in his mind. He wasn't sure what exactly was giving him pause. The house was everything he wanted. Wasn't it?

"Hey Della," he answered.

"Bad news," she said immediately.

Miles wasn't sure he could take any more disappointment this morning. "Okay?" He held his breath as he continued his patrol.

"The house you were interested in on Mallard Creek has been taken off the market."

Miles released his breath. "What? Why?"

"The owner didn't give me a reason. Sometimes they discover something wrong with the home that they want to fix first. Sometimes they have a change of heart. I'll let you know if I hear anything more."

"Thanks. I appreciate that."

"Were you going to put in a bid?" Della asked.

"I wasn't ready just yet," he said. "I was still weighing the pros and cons."

"Well, no harm, no foul, right?"

Miles felt like something had been taken from him though. And it had. His choice had been taken.

"Wanna meet this week and look at some other places?" Della asked. "I have plenty of time on my calendar. And even if I didn't, you know I'd make it for you."

"Maybe. I'll let you know," he said. "Thanks, Della."

"Anytime."

They hung up, and Miles stared at his phone for a long moment. He considered sending a message to Lucy, but she was working today, and he didn't want to bother her. Maybe, if she hadn't seen Reva's post yet, it was for the best.

&

Every time Lucy thought about Reva's blog today, her blood pressure spiked. Consequently, she had a slight headache that thrummed steadily at the center of her forehead.

So far, Lucy had avoided showing her face anywhere she didn't have to. She'd made a couple house calls today and had gone into the birthing center to check on a client who was admitted with false labor pains. She'd gotten a few questioning looks from acquaintances but she'd dodged any conversation about whether or not she and Miles were reuniting.

They weren't. They'd just flirted a bit and fell asleep together watching Lucy's favorite chick flick.

Lucy nibbled at her lower lip. Yeah, if she was an outsider looking in, that would qualify as dating in her book too. But couldn't two former lovers be friends? Couldn't they hang out together without causing a frenzy of onlookers to think they were getting back together?

Lucy turned into The Village and drove slowly. She could put off a lot of things but she couldn't avoid the next stop on her list. Not if she had any hope of paying off her HOA dues and avoiding getting sued in the new year.

Lucy drove past her house on Christmas Lane and rounded the loop past the community building, where she was set to give another parenting class tomorrow night. Then she turned onto the next street and pulled into Olivia's driveway. As part of the homeowner's association, Olivia was as good a place as any to start.

Lucy parked and got out of her car, nerves tightening her chest as she approached the porch, climbed the steps, and rang the bell. There was a huge wreath made out of real evergreen limbs with sprigs of holly interspersed. While she waited, Lucy touched the holly to see if it was real as well, accidentally knocking a piece off.

"Oops." Lucy bent quickly, grabbing up the sprig. By the time she'd straightened, the front door was open.

"Lucy. What a surprise." Olivia dropped her gaze to the holly in Lucy's hand.

Lucy felt her cheeks flare. "This, um, fell off your wreath." She handed it over. "I was hoping I could talk to you. If you have a moment."

"Of course." Olivia shoved the holly back into the wreath and held the door open wider. "Come on in."

"Thanks." Lucy stepped past the woman into a house with a similar layout to hers. Olivia's furniture was more modern though. Lucy's parents liked antiques and old things—even the upstairs that her mother had renovated and recently decorated was still laden with furniture from the late fifties and sixties. Some was perhaps even older than that.

"We can sit on the couch." Olivia gestured toward a brown leather sofa in the living room.

Lucy took a seat and sucked in a shuddery breath. It went against her nature to ask for help. Being in debt for anything also went against who she was. She didn't like to depend on others. She liked to be self-sufficient. She'd once thought the same about her mother.

Olivia gave Lucy an expectant look. Finally, she asked, "What can I help you with, Lucy?"

Lucy threaded her fingers together to keep them from fidgeting. "I came here because I want the board to approve an exception for me. I want to pay my bill, I do, but that's a lot of money to pull out of nowhere by January."

"Yes, it is," Olivia agreed, something akin to sympathy flashing in her eyes. "It would be much easier if you'd been paying monthly."

"That's the problem. I didn't know there was anything to pay," Lucy argued a second time. "It was an honest mistake. Taking over someone's estate isn't easy. I've spent most of this year settling all of my mom's unfinished business."

"Surely your mother left you a bit of money."

Lucy squeaked out a laugh. The money her mom had left her was small. Lucy had used it to pay off her mom's outstanding bills, which it still hadn't fully covered. In her last days, her once responsible mother had hired a slew of contractors and spent what Lucy could only imagine was a small fortune on new curtains, bedding, and a hot tub.

There was no money. Just bills. "She left me the house," Lucy said in explanation, "a dog, and lots of Christmas decorations."

Olivia offered a sympathetic look. "Your parents always did love the holidays, didn't they?"

"It was their favorite time of year. Mom kept up with the decorations after my dad died. I think it made her feel close to him." And Lucy had felt closer to her parents as she'd decorated over the last week with Miles. "Olivia, I want the board to consider allowing me to enter the Merriest Lawn Contest on the condition that if I win, I'll use the prize money to pay my debt in full."

Olivia's eyebrows drew up high on her forehead. "The rules clearly state..."

Lucy waved a hand to interrupt. "I know. You already told me. But I went online and read the HOA's bylines and laws. They also say that homeowners will be contacted after each missed payment. I was never contacted until I'd missed nearly twelve." Lucy flashed a smile because she'd found a little foothold and she planned to make the most of it. "And truly, what does the HOA have to lose with allowing me to enter? If I win, the bill is paid sooner rather than later."

Olivia seemed to consider this proposal. "You'd pay in full immediately?"

"I promise."

Olivia pressed her lips together as she seemed to ponder her decision. "I'll talk to the board. I think you've made a fair request. It would be a win-win, wouldn't it? But if your yard isn't chosen as the Merriest Lawn, what will you do then? The board doesn't take kindly to residents not paying their dues. If we swept it under the rug for one, then everyone would stop paying."

"Don't worry," Lucy said. "Just talk to the board for me, and we'll make a deal." And then she'd plan on winning the contest no matter what it took. With Miles helping her this Christmas, how hard could creating the merriest lawn in the neighborhood be?

∞

Later that afternoon, Lucy was sitting on her front porch when Miles's truck pulled into the driveway. He stepped out and seemed to drag his feet as he approached, looking exactly the way she felt. "Rough day?" she asked.

He blew out an exaggerated breath. "You could say that."

"Anything to do with Reva's blog post?"

Miles stepped up onto Lucy's front porch, where Bella met him at the top step and propped her paws on his thighs. He patted her head and then stepped closer to Lucy on the swing. "If I sit beside you, will tomorrow's blog read something else crazy about us?"

Lucy scooted a few inches to make room for him. "You think the thought of us reuniting is crazy?"

Miles sat and glanced over. He was closer than she expected. "You always used to do that."

"Do what?"

"Put words in my mouth. I didn't say reuniting was crazy." He gave her a long look and then pulled his gaze forward, where Bella was sniffing something on the porch. "What Reva wrote was just a huge assumption."

"Well"—Lucy nibbled at her lower lip—"you did spend the night with me on Friday."

"On the couch. Nothing happened. Not even a kiss."

Lucy grinned. "You don't need to tell me that. I was there, remember?"

He leaned back and folded one leg over the opposite knee. "The last thing I remember was Harry running down the street on New Year's Eve because he'd just realized he loved Sally. Next thing I recall, I was waking up to Olivia's voice at your front door. I don't even know if Sally told Harry to get lost or if she forgave him."

"How can you sleep without knowing how the movie ends?" Lucy scoffed. "Especially that one. You wait the whole movie for that one moment."

"You could tell me what happened and put my mind at ease," he said in a teasing tone.

"I could," she agreed, folding her hands in her lap, "but you need to watch it for yourself. I don't want to spoil the ending for you."

Miles shook his head on a chuckle. "Maybe we can stream the rest sometime."

"Maybe so."

They swung in silence for a couple of minutes. Then Miles looked over. "Della Rose called me today."

Lucy looked over with interest. "Really?"

Miles didn't look happy about whatever he was going to share. "The yellow house was taken off the market. So I guess that means it wasn't the one for me after all."

"I'm sorry to hear that. Why did it get taken off?"

"Della wasn't sure but it doesn't matter. I'm not making an offer on it anytime soon. Looks like you're stuck with me a little longer. Hope you don't mind."

Lucy's heart skipped a beat at the news. Maybe the day hadn't started out so smoothly but things were swinging in her favor this afternoon. "Actually, that works for me," she told Miles. "Because I need you to stay."

∞

Miles's brain understood that Lucy wasn't talking about anything romantic. His heart still took a leap of faith on the slight chance that Lucy actually meant she wanted him here for romantic reasons. "Oh?"

"Mm-hmm. I went to Olivia's house after work to discuss that silly rule about not being able to enter the decorating contest if you're behind on HOA dues. I mean, it's not silly. It's a good rule because some people might take advantage. But not me. I would never."

"And what did she say?" Miles asked. "Will they bend the rules for us?"

Lucy's eyes narrowed with the word *us*. They weren't an *us* unless you believed everything that Reva blogged. "Well, I told her if we won, I'd use the prize money to pay the dues I'm late on."

Miles ran a hand through his hair. "Did she agree?"

"It took a little bit of convincing but Olivia is going to talk to the board tomorrow. I think they'll agree if I use the winnings to pay the HOA bill. And if we don't win—"

Miles held up a hand. "I'm competitive, remember? We'll win. There's no stopping the Hannigan-Bruno team."

Lucy visibly swallowed.

Miles's throat was suddenly parched too. His gaze unwittingly lowered to her dark pink lips. The memory of that kiss they'd shared the other night flashed across his brain. It hadn't stopped flashing there since the night their lips had collided.

"Miles?" Lucy asked in almost a whisper.

He lifted his gaze back to her eyes. "Hmm?"

"Can I ask you a question?"

"You just did. But go ahead. Ask away."

She suddenly looked nervous. "Why did you break up with me? When we were eighteen."

He wasn't sure what he'd been expecting but it wasn't that question.

"I know it was a long time ago, and it doesn't really matter. Or it shouldn't. But it's haunted me over the years. It kind of felt like the breakup was out of nowhere. We were in love and engaged. We thought we were going to have a baby. I thought we were happy."

Her eyes shimmered, flashing a raw pain that he'd caused. "Then..." She trailed off, visibly swallowing back what he suspected was an onslaught of tears. Lucy Hannigan had never been a crier though. She always kept her emotions bottled up. She was tough before him and even tougher after him.

His heart ached. All he'd ever wanted was to make her happy—when they were together and when he'd realized that they couldn't last. "Lucy, we were young. We weren't ready for marriage and kids."

Lucy's eyes were shiny. "I agree. But why did that mean we had to break up?"

Miles hesitated. "We had love back then. But love isn't always enough, Luce," he said.

Lucy visibly bristled. "I can't agree with that. As long as we had each other, we would have been fine. We'd have married and been happy. We'd have a family by now. Maybe a big one with lots of kids. Instead, I'm alone in this huge house."

"You're blaming that on me?" Miles asked quietly.

"Well, you're the one who chickened out, aren't you? If you were in love, like you say, the only thing stopping you was fear."

His calm mood disappeared. Now he felt the

quickening of his heartbeat. "It wasn't that simple. You know that. I was afraid, yeah, but fear wasn't what stopped me from going through with our wedding plans." He stood from the swing, needing to move. There was a restless energy inside him that had him pacing.

"If not fear, what was it? Are you ever going to tell me the truth? Because I don't think our past will ever feel resolved unless I know what happened between us. One day we were in love. The next, we couldn't even say hello in the grocery store."

Miles stopped walking. He turned to face her. She deserved to know everything. Her mom had been gone a year. Maybe now was the right time to give Lucy all the facts. He pulled in a deep breath and let it out. "Not what. Who," he finally said. "Your mom came to talk to me right after the pregnancy scare."

Lucy's face seemed to blanch. "What?"

"On the evening we found out you weren't..." He trailed off.

"That I wasn't pregnant?" she asked. "Why did my mom come see you?"

Miles's heart was racing. He'd never wanted to tell Lucy this story. Her mom had asked him not to, and he'd agreed. He'd always thought it would hurt Lucy if she knew her mom had played a role in convincing him that he wasn't husband material back then. "She wanted to tell me exactly what she thought about the two of us together."

Lucy let out a small laugh but he understood that she didn't find anything about this situation funny. "She liked you, Miles. She thought you were a great boyfriend. She always said so."

"Maybe," he said with a nod. "But she didn't think I was good enough to marry you. I didn't have the resources to support you. My family was poor. I guess in her mind, we always would be. Your mother came to see me and made me realize that I had nothing to offer you, Lucy. I couldn't even afford a ring. I had to give you my great-grandmother's."

Lucy sat very still on the swing and listened to him. "You know I loved that ring, Miles. It was priceless because of the sentimental value it held."

He gave a small shrug, deciding not to mention the money Mrs. Hannigan had given him. It wasn't necessarily a bribe. She'd said it was to buy his family food for the holidays. He understood that it was also meant to drive a point home. If Lucy married him, she'd be entering into his family and a life of very little. Miles cleared his throat. "Your mom made me realize that I wasn't going to be able to support you or any baby we might have."

Lucy lifted a hand to pat her chest, right above her heart. She blew out a heavy breath. "I don't know what to say."

"Your mom was doing what she thought was in your best interest," Miles said. He believed that with all his heart. He didn't really blame Mrs. Hannigan one bit. If he was in her shoes, he probably wouldn't want his daughter dating him either.

Lucy's eyes were suspiciously shiny. "But she knew how much I loved you," she said, voice cracking. She sniffled and looked down at her hands in her lap.

Miles couldn't help it. He stepped over and sat beside her on the swing, wrapping his arm around her shoulders.

"Why would she ever want to take you away from me when she knew that?" Lucy asked, looking up at him.

Miles swallowed. There was one other detail he wanted her to know. "She was looking out for you. She said she didn't want you to end up like her."

"Like her?" Lucy sniffled again, her eyebrows drawing together in confusion. "What does that mean?"

Miles understood that this might hurt Lucy, but if it were him, he'd want to know. "Your mom married your dad because she had to. She told me she felt stuck when she got pregnant."

Lucy patted her hand to her chest again. "What?"

"When we thought you were pregnant, I guess it sent your mom into a panic. I probably looked like the worst thing that could've happened to you." Miles offered a small smile. "So there you have it. That's what happened," he said, his arm still around her.

She looked up at him, eyes shiny, skin pale. "Thanks for telling me."

"You're welcome. Does it change things? Do you want to push me off this swing and throw me in those sticky holly bushes?" He gestured past the porch railing.

A small smile turned up on the corners of her mouth. "Tempting, but no. You were young. You were eighteen."

She was so forgiving, and he didn't deserve her. He released a relieved breath. "Yeah. I'm older and wiser now."

"Oh?" She lifted her gaze. "So what are you going to do with all that maturity and wisdom?"

"Whatever it takes to stay in your good graces and out of those holly bushes," he teased quietly.

This made her laugh, which made his heart skip around in his chest. He tightened his hug around her shoulders, enjoying the feel of her in his arms. Then he kicked off with his feet on the porch, making the swing sway back and forth. He didn't say it out loud, but now that he was older and wiser, he planned on doing everything just right and maybe getting a second chance with Lucy Hannigan this Christmas.

Chapter Fourteen

Thursday night used to mean Lucy would be home and bingeing Netflix. Since moving back to Somerset Lake, however, it meant she'd be attending book club with her favorite ladies.

Lucy walked through the front entrance of Lakeside Books and beelined straight to the back where there was a sofa and a couple worn leather recliners encircling a round coffee table.

"Glad to see you could pull yourself away from your new romance to be with us," Della Rose said.

Lucy put her purse down in one of the recliners and sat. "That's crazy talk. I would never miss seeing you ladies on account of a guy."

"Miles is not just any guy," Moira said, stepping up to the group. She peeled off her heavy coat and draped it on the back of a chair. "He's your first love."

And Lucy's only love. She'd never fallen in love with anyone else. Sure, she'd dated guys, and she'd had serious relationships. But the feelings she'd harbored had always been flat, like the taste of an old soda that lacked the carbonated sparkles that hit your tongue on that first swallow. She'd gone through the motions and had worked hard to convince herself of how she should feel.

With Miles, it was the opposite. She found herself trying to persuade her mind to stop questioning things like the past and follow her heart, which was flooded with emotions after Monday night.

"Don't discuss any of the romantic details without me," Tess called out to them from behind the register. "I'm almost done over here."

"Don't worry," Della called back. "Lucy is being tight-lipped anyway. But we'll break her down," Della said with a wink in Lucy's direction.

The bell over the front entrance rang again, and Trisha, the newest member of the book club, hurried in.

"It's getting so cold outside," she said with an exaggerated shiver. She was dressed in a heavy coat and a turquoise knit hat with a matching scarf. She shut the door behind her and looked around the group. "Don't tell me I missed the discussion about Lucy's love life."

Lucy held out her arms with exasperation as she looked between her friends. "I thought we were here to discuss this month's book selection." The book club only read a few chapters a week and discussed the pages every Thursday night over sugary treats and beverages.

"Yeah, but this is big. You're dating Miles." Tess walked over and joined the group. She plopped down in one of the recliners and crossed her long, lean legs in front of her, wiggling into the seat and making a spectacle of getting comfy. Then she pointed a finger at Lucy. "And you haven't really dated anyone since you came back to take care of your mom last fall."

"Well, caring for a dying mother kind of zaps the endorphins right out of you." Lucy kicked off her shoes and curled her legs up to her chest in the oversize armchair that she was seated in. She might as well get comfortable too. "Okay, if you guys want the scoop, here it is."

Moira, Trisha, Della Rose, and Tess seemed to lean in, anxiously awaiting her confession.

"Miles and I have been decorating my yard for the Merriest Lawn Contest," she said. "And that's all there really is to tell."

"What? There's more than just that," Moira protested. "Come on. I answer nine-one-one calls for a living. All I get is bad news. I need good news for once. Something yummy and delicious."

Lucy pointed at the coffee table of treats, provided by Jana at Choco-Lovers down the street. "If yummy and delicious is what you want, dig in," she said. "I really don't have anything to tell you guys. We've watched movies together, and we've laughed. There's been a lot of laughing. And he's . . . well, he's amazing. He's smart and funny. He's a gentleman and, I mean, just look at him. He's undeniably good-looking."

"But?" Tess asked, tilting her head.

Lucy sighed. "No buts. Not really. It's just, this week he told me the real reason he broke up with me all those years ago."

The women's mouths dropped.

It was a lot to process. Lucy still wasn't sure how to feel. "Apparently, my mom persuaded him to call off the engagement. Miles thought he was doing me a favor."

"By breaking your heart?" Moira asked, her expression revealing that she obviously wasn't buying that reason. If Tess was the most perceptive, Moira was the most skeptical.

"By saving me from a less-than-perfect life. He didn't

have a job or income. He didn't have an education or any special training. He believed my mother when she told him he'd be holding me back." Lucy felt an ache in the center of her chest. She'd let Miles off the hook fairly quickly. He was young, like she'd said. But what was her mom's excuse?

"So Miles told you the truth and you two are moving past it?" Della Rose asked.

Lucy looked around at her friends. "I think so. I'm sad that we couldn't be together back then but our pasts shouldn't keep us from being together now if we can be. Right?"

"Are you asking our permission to make Miles your boyfriend again?" Tess asked with a knowing smile. She looked at the others. "All in favor of Lucy being with Miles even though he's not perfect and made a bad choice when he was eighteen, say aye."

The first one to say it was Trisha. Della Rose followed and then Moira.

"I want you to be happy," Moira added. "And Miles makes you happy." She shrugged as if it was as simple as that. And maybe it was. "Frankly, I'm jealous."

Lucy rolled her eyes. "If you'd just give Gil a chance..." she said, trailing off and knowing that would quiet Moira. Then she tucked her legs beneath her in the chair. "Anyway, enough about my personal life. We need to discuss the book, right?"

Tess reached for her copy of *One Romantic Christmas* and held it up. "Fine, we'll talk about the fictional love lives of these characters even though Lucy's reality is much more interesting."

They all settled into a conversation about the two characters in the book and whether they would end up together. It was a romance, so it was a good bet that they would. Even so, the fun part was pondering the off chance there wouldn't be a happy ever after. That something would come between the couple and tear them apart.

When the book club was over at precisely eight thirty, because Trisha's and Della's kids had a bedtime to meet, Lucy returned home. Miles had turned on the lights in the yard. She drove slowly as she approached, her heart fluttering around in her chest. The decorating wasn't complete yet, but the place already reminded her of her childhood when her parents would string the lights and set out the yard ornaments like this. It was a magical sight to behold.

She pulled into her driveway and stepped out, following the sidewalk to her front door. As she drew closer, she noticed Miles was sitting there with Bella on his lap. She'd been planning to find him tonight. He'd been honest with her on Monday night. He'd told her the truth about what happened when they'd broken up. It was a lot to process, and she'd taken the past couple days to let the information settle in her mind. But she was glad to finally know everything. Now that she did, she felt differently about her past with Miles. And about the prospect of a future.

∞

Miles found it hard to pull in a full breath whenever Lucy was around. His heart was off to the races, leaving him in its wake. He felt short of breath, short of words, and completely helpless due to how much he liked Lucy Hannigan.

After he'd told her the truth, she'd said they were fine, but then she'd ended the night early saying she was tired. When he'd woken up the next morning, her car was already gone, leaving him to wonder what she was thinking. She'd been "busy" for the past couple days with her parenting class at the community center and book club, making him worry that she'd decided he was wrong to listen to her mom all those years ago. Not only that, what if knowing that her mom didn't approve of him somehow made Lucy think less of him?

At this point, there were so many possibilities circulating in Miles's brain. He just wanted to see her and know that everything between them was okay.

She parked her car and headed toward the porch where he was sitting on her swing. She climbed the porch steps and looked at him. "Are you waiting for me?"

The answer to that question was complicated. He'd been waiting for her all his life, whether he'd known it or not. "I thought we should talk about what I told you on Monday night," he said.

"Okay." She gave a nod. "I'll go first."

Miles swallowed as an *uh-oh* bubbled up in his chest. She wasn't smiling but she didn't look upset either. "Okay," he agreed, bracing himself for the worst-case scenario.

"You broke my heart once, and I swore I'd never forgive you for that, Miles Bruno," she said, lifting her chin a notch.

Miles swallowed past a tight throat. "I broke your heart once," he agreed, "and *I'll* never forgive myself either." Pain seared his chest. Was he about to lose

Lucy all over again? He hadn't even gotten her back. Not yet, not really.

Lucy's posture softened, and she stepped closer. Her gentle perfume floated on the air between them, something sweet smelling and enticing. "Well, what if I forgive you enough for both of us?"

"You just said you'd never forgive me," he told her, completely confused.

"No." She shook her head as a small smile played at the corners of her lips. "I said I swore I never would, but we're not eighteen anymore. And right now, I don't want to be mad at you. I even understand why you did what you did."

He exhaled a pent-up breath. "That's good news."

"Our history is in the past. What I care about is the now. And what I really want right now is to kiss you."

Miles blinked. "A kiss would be nice." His thoughts were muddled about anything other than locking lips with Lucy. He stood and reached out to touch her cheek, trailing his fingers behind her ear and down her neck. He wasn't sure if he crossed the rest of the distance or if she did. All he knew was their lips met and their hands clung needily to each other.

Maybe it was as simple as focusing on the now and forgetting about the past. Maybe Reva knew what they were both late to figure out. That in addition to the sparks and unresolved feelings, maybe there was even love, despite the time and distance that had separated them.

Lucy pulled back and sighed, her breath crystalizing in the air between them. "Fine, I'll tell you. At the end of the movie, Harry runs into the party as everyone is counting down to midnight. Then he finds Sally, and she seems like she's not going to forgive him. But he says everything perfectly. And you can see her melting. Then they kiss, and you know they're going to last forever."

Miles looked at her and fell a little deeper for the woman who had always been the one for him. "That's a good ending."

"Yeah. It's the best kiss-and-make-up scene ever," Lucy said wistfully. She jabbed a finger into his chest. "You still have to watch it. I just wanted to make sure you didn't lose sleep wondering what happened."

"Thanks."

They stared at each other for another moment.

"I feel like I should say something but I don't know what to say," she finally said.

"I feel the same." Miles reached for her hand, trailing the pad of his thumb along the smooth silk of her skin.

"So maybe we should just kiss again. If my neighbors see us, we'll just blame it on the mistletoe."

ꝏ

Somerset Lake didn't have a lot of crime, and when they did, it was minor. Case in point, the property damage Miles had responded to first thing this morning was from Mrs. Jennings egging Mr. Jennings's golf cart. Apparently, they'd had a little disagreement about how much time he liked to spend on teeing.

After that, Miles addressed a noise complaint about a barking dog. There was no noise or nuisance ordinance for that neighborhood, so there wasn't much he could do about the situation.

Now he was on his way to a case of vandalism on Mallard Creek Lane. That had him driving right past the yellow house that he'd toured last week. He slowed as he passed by, searching the front of the home as if the answer to why it'd suddenly gone off the market would be there. But no one was moving back in. There was no obvious condition where the house was no longer salable.

It was too bad that it'd been unlisted. Now that it was gone, he wanted it more. It was the right size. The right color. It also had a great view of the creek out back.

His heart dropped a bit as he drove by and headed to the scene of the vandalism at the end of the dead-end road. There at the end was a white, uninhabited one-story home. Once upon a time, it was probably a very nice house. But it'd been abandoned and neglected, and now it was vulnerable to punks with malicious intent and time on their hands.

Miles pulled into the driveway and parked. Then he stepped out of his cruiser and looked out on the spray-painted front where bright blue paint spelled out the words BAH HUMBUG in all caps. It appeared that the perp was not a fan of the holidays. Miles wondered if the same person who'd popped Mr. Gobbles last week was responsible for this handiwork.

He headed up the steps, noting a quarter of a footprint in the blue paint that had dripped onto the wooden porch. He took a few pictures with his cell phone. Then he jotted down the size and location of the print. He also wrote down where the spray-painting was in relation to the house. There were no discarded cans of paint to lift prints from. That would have been an easy way to identify the vandal. Because this house was at the end of the street and bordered by woods on one side, there might not be any witnesses. Even so, Miles walked next door and knocked.

An older woman with tight white curls and glasses answered the door. "Oh, Deputy Bruno, I was hoping they'd send you."

"Hello, Ms. May," Miles said. He hadn't realized the older woman lived at this address. "I was just wondering if you saw any suspicious activity last night that might help me pinpoint who did the artwork on your neighbor's house?"

She glanced past him to the white house and clucked her tongue. "What a shame. So pointless." She shook her head as her lips pursed. "I wish I could help you but I'm afraid I didn't see anything last night. I tucked myself into bed around nine and fell asleep watching the news." Her eyes widened behind her wire-rimmed glasses as she seemed to remember something. She lifted a shaky finger. "I have seen some teenagers walking down the street lately though. Bet they were scoping out a place for that kind of destruction."

"Do you by chance know who the teens were?" Miles hoped it wasn't anyone from the Youth Center.

Ms. May thought for a moment. "I'm afraid not. There was one kid with a purple ball cap and a yo-yo."

"Those are pretty specific details," Miles said, jotting down the notes in his pad of paper.

"And one had a backpack on her shoulder. I bet that's where she kept the cans of paint hidden."

"A she?" Miles jotted down that fact as well.

"I believe so, yes. You know my eyesight isn't what it used to be, but the second one was smaller. That's why

I'm assuming it was a female. I suppose it could have just been someone younger than the others."

"Anything else you can tell me?" The truth was that the vandals would likely never be caught without a witness or prints at the scene of the crime.

"No. I don't have anything else. I'm sorry," Ms. May said.

"Don't be. This is helpful information. Can you tell me who the house belongs to?" Miles asked. "It seems to be abandoned."

"Yes, it is. Mr. Romaine used to live there. But you know he passed away about a year or so ago. It's been empty ever since. Mr. Romaine didn't have family as far as I could tell. Just a cat that I still see roaming sometimes. I set food out for her to make sure she doesn't go hungry. I'd take her in but I'm allergic," the old woman added.

"Thank you for your time," he told Ms. May.

"You're so welcome, Deputy Bruno. Would you like to come in for some tea and cookies?"

"No, ma'am. I'm on the job," he said, feeling a little bad about turning her down. He wasn't sure the woman got a lot of visitors. "Maybe another time."

"Of course. Good luck catching the little grinch," she said.

"Thanks." Miles headed down the steps and walked back to his car in the neighboring driveway. He looked out at the house one more time. *Grinch* was a perfect word for the criminal. If they were the same one that lifted the Christmas cookies from the Thanksgiving baskets and deflated Mr. Gobbles, they were a grinch indeed. For some reason, Miles wondered if the doors of the white house were unlocked. On a whim, he headed back up the steps, reached for the doorknob, and turned it. The door swung open.

"Hello?" Miles called before stepping over the threshold. "Anyone inside?"

No one answered. The house was still furnished with the late Mr. Romaine's things. Nothing seemed to be disturbed. No one had come in and trashed the place. There was a large TV still hanging on the wall. If someone had trespassed, they might have stolen the item.

Miles walked from room to room. The house had almost an identical layout as the yellow house down the street. And despite the exterior of the home, it had held up well on the inside. It was fully furnished as if waiting for Mr. Romaine to return someday.

Meow.

Miles whirled to see a tabby cat sitting on the recliner watching him. "Well, hello to you too. Do you live here?" he asked, stepping closer.

The cat's wide yellow eyes stared back at him. It was wearing a collar. Miles approached the cat hesitantly, not wanting to scare it away. The cat didn't budge though. It seemed unconcerned with his presence. Miles lifted the collar up and saw that it held a heart-shaped metal piece with the cat's name and address engraved on it.

"Purrball." Miles lifted his gaze to meet the cat's unblinking one. "Wow, Mr. Romaine named you Purrball, huh? That's unfortunate."

The cat meowed in response.

Miles looked around the house, wondering how Purrball was able to come and go. If Ms. May next door was feeding the cat, it obviously had an exit point. He noticed that the window above the kitchen sink was pushed up. "I can't leave that open," he told the cat regretfully. "It invites people who shouldn't be here inside." Like the vandals.

Purrball looked at him.

Miles wasn't sure what he was going to do with the cat but he couldn't leave it locked inside an uninhabited house. He reached out to grab the cat, but this time, it leaped off the chair, across the room, into the kitchen, up on the sink, and out the window. Gone in a flash.

Miles followed it to the sink and stared out the window as it disappeared into the woods. He couldn't close the window now and lock Purrball outside in the cold. He'd just have to come back tomorrow and see if he could catch the cat next time. He could take it to the no-kill shelter outside of town. Maybe Purrball could find a new family and a home for Christmas.

At the end of his shift, Miles returned to his temporary home. Lucy's house was lit up with all the decorations that they'd put up last weekend. This weekend, they'd finish putting out the rest. The thought stirred an anxious kind of excitement inside him. He was having fun with the project, which surprised him. He'd offered to help for Lucy's sake, not realizing that he'd actually enjoy the activity. It was almost like a sport, and it definitely gave him that little jolt of competitiveness that he'd thrived on in his youth.

Lucy's car wasn't parked in the driveway yet so he let himself inside the back door of the big pink house so that he could take Bella for a walk. Bella rushed toward him, tail wagging and tongue lolling out of her mouth. He had a weakness for the little dog—and its owner. "Hey, girl. You miss me?"

Bella panted with the attention, her backside swinging with her little tail. Then Miles attached her leash, and they headed outside. They walked past the other houses on the street while Miles scrutinized whether the Hannigan house was in the lead. If not in the lead, it was tied with two others, one of which was the house directly across the street.

The Newsome house was a deep forest green color. Miles had seen Mrs. Newsome's teenaged grandson helping to string the lights. The house was lit up from one corner to the next. Instead of rainbow lights like those on Lucy's house, all yellow lights decorated the Newsomes' house. It was classy and gorgeous.

"Ours is better," Miles told Bella at his feet. The word *ours* tripped him up. He kept thinking words like that. *Us. Ours.* It hadn't taken long for him to sink right back into having romantic feelings toward Lucy. He'd known it was inevitable if he stayed on her property any length of time. He just hadn't realized that it would happen so quickly.

Miles circled back toward the pink house, noticing that Lucy's car was there now. He walked faster, his heartbeat picking up speed. She leaned against her car, bundled up in a heavy coat and knit hat. When she spotted him heading in her direction, she waved.

"I knocked on your door. When you didn't answer and I realized that my dog was missing, I put two and two together."

"You're a good detective," he teased. "Maybe Sheriff Mills should hire you."

Lucy shook her head on a wide grin. "I have a job that suits me just fine, thank you very much."

Miles continued walking until he was standing close

enough to lean in and kiss her. He didn't hesitate to do just that. He bent low and brushed his mouth to hers, giving her a long, lingering hello kiss.

"It's the weekend," she said once they'd pulled away, her green eyes lit with mischief. "Want to go out on the town and make a headline on Reva's blog this weekend?"

∞

The residents of Somerset Lake loved Christmas as much as, if not more than, the next small town. There were lots of festivities on the weekends during the month of December.

Tonight, Lucy and Miles were attending the holiday flotilla, which was one of Lucy's favorite occasions during the season. Lucy had packed two canvas sports chairs and one heavy fleece blanket to share with Miles. They gathered on the downtown strip of the lake where most folks went to watch the flotilla from the shore.

"One of these days, I'm going to get a sailboat like Gil's," Miles said, his gaze on the water where brightly colored boats could be seen on the horizon.

Lucy looked over with interest. "Maybe you're looking for houses in the wrong place. Maybe you should get a houseboat. Then you'd have two wish list items for the price of one."

Miles was holding her hand under the blanket, his shoulder pressed against hers. "There's an idea," he said. "I'm not sure it would satisfy my need to own a house though. I think the only thing that will is something on a plot of land with a fence and a mailbox at the end of the driveway. A place that's completely mine. We always had a roof over our head when I was growing up but my family never owned wherever we stayed."

Lucy squeezed his hand beneath the blanket. "Is that why owning a home is so important to you?"

Miles lifted a shoulder. "I guess so. It was something my mom always wanted and my dad was stuck on before he left. He wanted to buy a house for her, and he almost did. Then he lost everything, and I guess he used that as his justification for packing his bags and taking off."

Lucy leaned into him, urging him to continue. "Have you heard from him since he left?"

"No." Miles shook his head. "And I don't think I will. He left, and there's no turning back. Sometimes the past just needs to stay in the past." He held up a finger. "Stop right there. I'm talking about my dad, not us. Sometimes it's good to revisit the past." He leaned over and brushed his lips over hers.

Even though it was cold outside, Lucy melted into the kiss. She was excited about seeing the flotilla but some part of her wouldn't mind some alone time with Miles. The more they kissed, the more she wanted to stay lip-locked in his arms indefinitely.

"Hey, you two," Della Rose said, interrupting the moment and reminding Lucy that they currently had half the town as a potential audience.

Lucy reluctantly pulled away from the kiss and turned to her friend. "I didn't know you were coming tonight."

Della Rose plopped her chair down next to them with her two boys in tow. "I'd rather be inside where it's warm but I couldn't disappoint these two boys of mine. Do you mind if we join you?"

"Of course not." Lucy waved at Jett and Justin.

The twin boys waved back, all smiles and giggles despite this being the first Christmas that their parents weren't together.

"Tess and Moira are meeting me here too," Della said. "So if you wanted privacy tonight, tell me now or forever hold your peace."

"If we wanted privacy, we wouldn't have come downtown at all," Miles interjected. "We would have stayed on Christmas Lane."

"True enough." Della Rose settled into her seat and looked out at the water with a heavy sigh that turned white in the chilly air. "Jerome's going to be out there tonight. He divorced me and bought a boat. My mother says he's having a midlife crisis."

Jerome was older than the rest of them by about ten years. In addition to the divorce, Jerome's new wife was one of Lucy's midwife clients. That was some midlife crisis he was having. At least from what Lucy could tell, he and his new wife, Sofia, seemed happy. When she was in her role as midwife, Lucy just had to do her best to forget that the parents-to-be had hurt one of her very best friends.

The crowd continued to thicken downtown as the time approached for the flotilla to begin. Everyone was here tonight, and everyone with eyes could see that Lucy was with Miles. They were shoulder to shoulder, gloved hand in gloved hand. And every time Lucy looked over at him, he brushed a kiss to her mouth, which only made her look at him more often. It was as if they were making up for all their lost time.

"You want to go out tomorrow to look at those houses you were interested in?" Della asked Miles. "I have time. The market is slow right now. Folks are too busy present shopping to go looking for new houses. That'll all change in the new year though."

Miles shook his head. "I'll pass. I'm not feeling any of the places I'm seeing online at the moment. I do have a question for you. There's a white house on Mallard Creek Lane. It got vandalized this week."

"Mr. Romaine's old place?" Della asked.

"That's the one. Who owns the house now?" Miles asked. "It seems to be untouched since he passed. Except for the newly painted *Bah Humbug* across the front."

Della grimaced. "That's unfortunate."

"It is," he agreed.

"I don't know who owns it," she said after a moment's thought. "But I can find out for you."

"Thanks. I'd like to contact the owner in case they don't know about the spray paint job. And about Mr. Romaine's cat that seems to still be living there. It's almost as if it's waiting for Mr. Romaine to return."

"Aw, how sad," Lucy said, her face contorting into a frown.

Miles squeezed her hand.

She was inwardly glad that he was putting off viewing any of the houses he was interested in. She wasn't ready for him to move away from Christmas Lane just yet. Having him so close was nice. They were eating meals together, going on nightly walks, and kissing on her front porch. It was perfectly convenient for two people who were falling back in love.

The flotilla began, and everyone grew quiet as they all watched the beautiful display of lights dancing across the water. From the corner of her eye, Lucy saw

Della's boys excitedly pointing, especially when their father's boat skimmed by.

Lucy glanced over at Miles for a moment, her emotions swirling in her chest. It would be so easy to fall for him all over again. Her next thought... Who was she kidding? She was already falling for him.

Miles caught her watching him, leaned in, and brushed his lips to hers. "What are you thinking about?"

"Just how good I feel tonight. How I wish this night," *and this relationship*, "would never end."

"You'll change your tune once you can't feel your toes anymore," he warned. "The temperature is dropping fast."

"Just keep those kisses coming, and I'll stay warm."

Miles obliged with another lingering kiss, only stopping when Della Rose's boys started snickering loudly. Their *eww*s floated in the air. Miles leaned forward and gave them a playful grin. "Don't go back to the Youth Center on Monday and tell all the kids that you caught me kissing a pretty lady."

Jett and Justin giggled.

"We will, Deputy Bruno," Jett said. "I'm going to tell them all."

Miles covered a hand over his face in mock embarrassment. "I thought we were friends, guys."

Justin, the more straight-shooting of the twins, argued against what his brother said. "We won't tell anyone, Deputy Bruno. We *are* friends." He elbowed his brother.

Miles chuckled. "I appreciate it, boys."

Once the flotilla was over, Miles walked Lucy back to his truck. He opened the door for her and waited for her to get seated before closing her in and heading around to the driver's side.

"Mind if I go check on Purrball?" he asked once he was seated behind the steering wheel.

Lucy furrowed her brow. "Purrball?"

"Mr. Romaine's cat that still lives at his house. It's been living all alone on that property since last year. If I can lure it to me, I can at least take it home." He gave Lucy a concerned look. "I mean, if it's okay with you. I was thinking I could set the cat up in the garage overnight and take it to a no-kill shelter somewhere tomorrow."

"No-kill shelters are few and far between," she said. "But we'll figure something out. I don't want Purrball to be out in this weather. It's freezing. Of course we can bring it back to Christmas Lane."

Miles looked grateful. He started the truck and drove to Mallard Creek. They passed the yellow house and continued all the way to the end of the street. As they pulled into the driveway of the white house, Lucy noticed dark shadows cutting across the lawn and rounding the back side of the home.

She jolted in her seat and pointed. "Did you see that?"

"I did. Wait here." Miles pushed open the truck door and hit the ground running, leaving Lucy behind, cowering like she'd done the night Miles had come to investigate the opossum. She held her breath and willed herself to see through the pitch darkness, not that it mattered. Miles was long gone, running after danger. All she could do was slink into the passenger seat and pray he didn't find it.

Chapter Fifteen

Lucy's breathing was shallow as she waited long seconds that stretched across the night. She wasn't sure how much time had passed but Miles should have been back by now.

She pushed the truck door open. Maybe stepping out of the safe confines of the vehicle was risky, but what if Miles needed her? What if he was out there calling for help and she couldn't hear him inside the truck?

"Miles?" she called quietly. "Miles, where are you?"

Meow.

Lucy turned toward the noise and saw two yellow cat eyes shining on the porch. "You must be Purrball." She approached the cat with an outstretched hand, surprised that it didn't run away. Instead, it sniffed her hand tentatively. "Have you seen Miles?" she asked quietly, her heart thumping forcefully against her ribs.

"Over here!"

Lucy looked up to see Miles limping around the back of the house. She stood and darted blindly in his direction. There was no streetlight to illuminate her steps, just the light from the sliver of moon above. "What happened?"

"I tripped while I was chasing some kids." His speech stopped and started as if he was in a bit of pain. "I banged up my knee pretty good but I don't think it's serious."

"Thank goodness for that. Are you sure?" she asked, a little breathlessly.

"Yeah. I think so."

Lucy looked around to make sure there weren't any imminent threats. "You said kids. Did you see who they were?"

Miles shook his head. "No. They ran off."

Lucy bent to pick up Purrball who had followed her over and was now sitting by her feet. The cat purred so loudly that Lucy could hear it over the noisy flow of the creek behind the house. "Well, the good news is that this little guy didn't run. Guess what, Purrball? We're taking you home with us tonight."

The cat's purr seemed to grow louder.

"I'm not sure Bella will be pleased to have you on the premises but I could be wrong," Lucy said. This cat and Bella had a lot in common. They'd both lost their owners in the last year. Maybe they'd instinctually bond over that fact. "Do you need help getting back to the truck?" Lucy asked Miles.

He gave her a questioning grin. "Like you could carry me."

"No, but I could support you. If you needed me to."

"I think I'll be fine. But thank you. And thanks for running out here to check on me. That was pretty brave of you. You must think a lot of me," he said, baiting her.

"Maybe so," she said, swiping her gaze over to meet his. They were still in this in-between stage of flirting and full-on dating. "Or I was just afraid of being stuck out here by myself. You have the keys after all."

"Ah. The truth comes out." They reached the truck, and Miles opened the passenger door for her.

"Nope." She held out her hand and gave him a gimme gesture. "You've proven yourself a gentleman but you're riding shotgun and I'm driving us back to the house. You need to rest that knee. Nurse's orders."

Miles's grin stretched wider as he climbed into the passenger seat. "Okay, Nurse Hannigan. I can agree to that. Drive us home."

∞

Miles had intended to leave Purrball downstairs in the garage but instead the tabby feline was curled into his side as he lay in his bed. The ache in his knee wasn't what was keeping him awake. It was the fact that he'd seen one of the vandals' faces as they'd run from him.

At least he was pretty sure he'd seen one face. He'd thought he'd gotten through to Charlie Bates. He'd told Charlie that he'd help him and his family with whatever they needed. Charlie had been helping out at the Youth Center regularly, and Miles hadn't heard anything more about shoplifting or other trouble.

Miles ran a hand through Purrball's silky coat. Maybe it hadn't been Charlie. It'd definitely been a trio of teens, which by nature, tended to look the same, right? Everyone wanted to fit in, wearing the same hairstyle and similar clothing.

"You're the only real witness," Miles told Purrball. Too bad the cat couldn't talk and confirm or deny

Miles's suspicions. But on Monday evening, when Miles was back at the Youth Center, he'd do a little harmless interrogation to see where Charlie was tonight and who he was hanging out with.

Miles closed his eyes for sleep. The next thing he knew, he awoke on Sunday morning with two cat paws kneading his cheek. His eyes popped open at the same time that his hands pushed Purrball away from him.

Meow.

Once Miles had collected himself, he chuckled quietly and looked at the clock. He didn't have to work today so that meant he'd be finishing up Lucy's yard decorations after church. The judging was two weeks away and consisted of the town being invited to drive through and cast their votes at the community building while being served complimentary apple cider and cookies. Cars were already beginning to drive through to look at the displays. Folks were already forming opinions of which displays were their favorites, even if they weren't allowed to cast a ballot yet.

Miles pulled on a pair of jeans and a T-shirt and then headed down the garage steps. His knee ached, reminding him of last night's little chase scene on Mallard Creek Lane. As he approached the ground level, he heard a rustling noise.

"Hey, sleepyhead." Lucy straightened from where she'd been crouched over another box of decorations. "You're up late."

"And you're up early," he said.

Lucy grinned and continued rustling through a box. "I was awoken by a frantic phone call from one of my clients. She was having acid reflux and wanted to make sure it wasn't something more serious. I assured her that antacids would do the trick and that she should go back to sleep."

"But you didn't return to sleep?" Miles asked.

"No. By then Bella needed to go out and the sun was coming up behind the mountains. I decided to go ahead and have a cup of coffee before getting started on our decorations." She glanced down at his legs. "How's the knee?"

"Sore."

"That means I can't ask you to get on my roof today, huh?" she teased.

"No, it doesn't mean that. I'll do what I need to in order to win this contest."

Lucy straightened and folded her arms over her chest. "You are so competitive."

"Well, it's important to win this time. It's about more than a trophy or a title. You have a bill hanging over your head." He walked over to where she was standing and wrapped his arms around her, unable to resist. "And you're important to me, so I can handle a sore knee to get this job done."

"Thank you. For everything."

"Honestly, it's not a bad gig for me, hanging out with the most beautiful, sweetest, smartest woman in Somerset Lake. I actually think I'm getting the better half of this deal."

She tilted her head. "That's quite the compliment. You must want something."

"Just more time with you. That's all I want for Christmas this year."

Both of their cell phones went off at the same time. Miles reached into his pocket and pulled out his. He answered and had a quiet chat with Sheriff Mills before hanging up.

"Looks like the department is understaffed today. I'm being called in."

Lucy sighed as she shoved her cell phone into the pocket of her jeans. "Looks like my client with acid reflux might be going into early labor after all. I'm being called away too. So much for more time together."

"We'll catch up tonight," Miles promised. "Then we'll keep chipping away on the decorations. It'll be okay."

Lucy went up on her tiptoes to kiss him. "No chasing vandals on that knee today, okay? You need to rest it as much as possible."

"I'll do my best. I better make the trek back up those steps to put my uniform on though. That's unavoidable."

"And I need to go get my scrubs on," Lucy said. She headed toward the garage door. "Talk to you tonight."

"Sounds good." Miles returned to his apartment, changed clothes, and stared at Purrball for a moment. He didn't really want to leave her here by herself, but she had food, water, and a litter box that he'd purchased on the way home last night. Cats were supposedly self-sufficient. He pointed a finger at Purrball for good measure. "Don't stir up any trouble. I'll be back later."

The cat gave him a bored look as Miles headed out.

An hour later, he was patrolling the town, just as bored as Purrball had seemed to be when he'd left his apartment. He'd gotten a few texts from Lucy filling him in on her much more exciting morning. Turns out

JD was the deputy who'd called out because his wife was currently in labor with Lucy as their midwife. How was that for coincidence?

Miles found himself driving toward Mallard Creek Lane, past the yellow house, all the way to the end of the dead-end street. He parked and headed toward the front door. Then he walked around the home, looking for evidence from last night. He guessed, because there was no more evidence of vandalism, that he and Lucy had arrived right before the kids had gotten a chance to cause any more destruction.

Miles glanced around the ground as he walked, coming up on a couple cigarette butts. He sighed, hoping once more that one of the culprits wasn't Charlie. As he looked for clues, he found himself standing on the edge of Mallard Creek. He turned back to look at the back side of the home. Mr. Romaine had been lucky to live here. This was a great little spot, tucked away from the world with the exception of a few rebellious teens.

Miles didn't usually conduct business of any sort on a Sunday if he could help it. But Della had told him to contact her anytime, day or night. She'd made a point of telling him that weekends weren't off limits for her.

He pulled out his cell phone and tapped in a message.

> ***Miles:*** Any word on this house at the end of Mallard Creek Lane?

It took a moment for Della to respond.

> ***Della:*** Not yet, but I doubt whoever owns the place is interested in hearing about its new paint job.

Miles got back inside his cruiser and tapped back a reply.

> ***Miles:*** Maybe not. But I wonder if they're interested in selling.
> ***Della:*** To who?

Miles looked at the vandalized house. He could see himself coming here at the end of a long day. Spending an evening on that creek would be his idea of paradise. He returned his gaze to his phone and texted back.

> ***Miles:*** Maybe to me.

∞

Lucy was sweating bullets, and she wasn't even the one giving birth right now. Loralei Jacobs was having a marathon delivery. Her birth plan detailed an at-home delivery, which was fine since it was a low-risk pregnancy. It was Loralei's first baby though, and she'd wanted the labor process to be natural. At least that's what she'd said before the contractions started.

"Isn't there something you can do for her?" Loralei's husband, JD, pleaded.

"I'm doing everything I can." Lucy tried to exude enough calm for both parents. A drug-free delivery was hard but women had been having them since the beginning of time. Lucy looked at Loralei. "Just breathe and find your happy place. Remember how we discussed that in the parenting classes?"

"I don't want to hear about a happy...place," Loralei said through gritted teeth. Her eyes were squeezed shut, and tears slipped off her flushed cheeks. "You told me you didn't have children. You have no idea how this feels!"

Lucy knew that her client wasn't trying to be mean but the words still hurt a tiny bit. Lucy wanted kids one day. She wanted to ideally be married first and have them within a supportive family. The older she got, the more she wanted those things.

Lucy didn't need a family of her own to be able to guide Loralei through her birthing experience though. "You're right. I've never experienced what you are right now but I've helped dozens of women who have. Trust me. This will pass, and you'll be holding your beautiful baby very soon. Just breathe through it, okay? You can do this, Loralei."

Loralei blew out a breath as JD squeezed her hand.

Loralei jerked her arm away angrily. "Maybe I want to go to the hospital after all," she said.

"It's too late for an epidural," Lucy said calmly. "The baby's head is crowning. Just hang in there a little longer."

Loralei was in what was called the "ring of fire" stage, and she couldn't be consoled right now. The only thing that would make her feel better was the baby out in the world and lying on her chest.

"Just breathe." Lucy sucked in a deep breath as an example and let it out. Loralei did the same, breathing with her. In and out. This was hard work, even for Lucy who wasn't pushing a baby out of her body. She loved her job though. Watching the miracle of life was such an honor.

"This hurts!" Loralei cried.

"I know." Lucy laid a cool compress on Loralei's

forehead. “Breathe. Happy place.” Lucy braced herself to be yelled at again but then the baby’s first cry filled the room.

Tears pricked Lucy’s eyes as she cradled the baby girl’s flailing body in her arms and brought her to Loralei’s chest.

“Aww.” Loralei was crying too. So was her husband. They all had tears streaming down their cheeks. Lucy got to work cleaning up as Loralei and JD got to know the newest member of their family.

By the time Lucy left the happy family’s home, all of her energy was zapped. She told Loralei and JD to call with any questions, needs, or concerns and then drove back to her house for a much-needed shower. Miles was still on his shift at the sheriff’s department. That meant that Lucy could stay home all by herself, but that sounded particularly lonely tonight. She loved helping families grow, but at the same time, she was also painfully aware sometimes that she no longer had a family. Not one single person.

Since she didn’t want to be alone right now, she called Tess and waited. No answer. Lucy was about to come up with a plan B when Tess called right back.

“Hey. Sorry I missed your call. I was trying to put up a Christmas tree. It’s not going well.”

“Oh,” Lucy said. “I guess you’re not up for going out with me then.”

“And you would be wrong,” Tess said. “I would have thought you’d be with your boyfriend this afternoon.”

“He’s working.”

“Ah. Well, let’s go have some fun. Meet you downtown in thirty minutes?” Tess asked.

"I'll be there." Lucy hoped that a visit with a friend would ease her loneliness a touch. Or at least take her mind off the things she was missing, like her mom. There was a lot to be merry about this holiday season, like friends and Miles. They would have to be her family now.

Chapter Sixteen

"Okay, tell me what's bothering you," Tess said to Lucy after a gingerbread-flavored coffee and a walk down Hannigan Street.

Lucy took a moment to think on her answer. "Nothing is wrong. Everything is perfect."

"Well, you don't have to rub it in," Tess teased.

Lucy offered a soft laugh, even though she wasn't exactly feeling humorous. They were both carrying small bags from a couple stores that they'd gone inside. Lucy had bought a couple of trinkets for friends and gifts for her clients. "I guess I'm just missing my mom."

"Perfectly understandable. It's your first Christmas without her."

Lucy looked down for a moment. Even the mention of her mom made her feel emotional these days. "Some part of me feels like I didn't know her as well as I thought I did. I'm discovering sides of her I don't even recognize."

Lucy headed over to a nearby bench and sat down. They couldn't just stand in the middle of the sidewalk and discuss her life. Tess sat beside her and waited patiently for Lucy to say whatever was on her mind.

Lucy sighed, her breath releasing in a white puff of

frosty air. "She played a role in my breakup. She never even wanted to marry my dad. She was in a mountain of debt for things that don't even make sense." Lucy glanced over. "The mom I knew wasn't perfect but she was pretty close."

Tess reached over and rubbed Lucy's back for a moment. "We all have hidden sides to ourselves."

Lucy pulled her shopping bag up on her lap, hugging it to her midsection, partly for the added layer of warmth and partly for something to hold in her restless hands. "Okay, I have a secret stash of chocolate in my cabinet and I cheat on the Hallmark Channel with Lifetime sometimes, but that's about it."

Tess laughed softly. "I'm sorry. I know it's hard."

Lucy felt a little better. "This is just what I needed to hear. Thank you."

"Anytime. You know that. You can call me, text me, visit me. I'm always here for you. Blood-related or not, we are family. Don't think for a moment that we're not."

∞

Miles pulled up to the white house on Mallard Creek Lane, parked, and stepped out of his car. "Sorry to make you work on a Sunday."

Della Rose waved a dismissive hand in his direction. "I'm the one who called you. And the kids are with my ex again so..." She redirected her attention to the white house with blue spray paint across the front. "I spoke to the owner of this place. They said we could look around. It's not for sale yet. She said she was really just ignoring this house because it was too much trouble for her to do something about it."

"Does she live in the area?" Miles asked.

"Chicago," Della explained. "She's some high-powered businesswoman. It's cheaper for her to let this place sit and crumble than for her to lose time sorting out what to do with it. She said she'd talk to a real estate agent about fair market value and what to ask for it." Della pointed a finger. "I have to warn you, you've set yourself up to look like an overeager buyer."

"I'm not a sure thing. I'm just interested," Miles said, walking toward the front porch. "I like the location and the creek out back." He also liked the feeling of serenity here. The house wasn't too big or too small. It was just right for him and perhaps a small family one day.

Della held up a key. "The owner gave me permission to call a locksmith and get this door opened."

Della let him in, and he walked through the home once more, loving it even more than he had last time. He looked at it through fresh eyes this time.

"To be honest, I thought you'd stay at Lucy's garage apartment a little longer," Della said. "You two are getting along well. Maybe you won't need to buy a place of your own after all."

Miles turned to look at Della. "Having a place of my own is important to me." And besides, he could never live in that pink house with Lucy. It was her mom's house, and her mom had made it clear that Miles wasn't good enough for her daughter. Living there would never feel right. "Is there such a thing as real estate agent confidentiality?"

Della lifted her brows. "I guess so."

"Mind not mentioning to Lucy that we were here?" He put his hands on his hips. "She knows I'm looking for a place to live but this house isn't even on the market yet." He didn't care about looking overeager to the seller's agent but he didn't want to appear that way to Lucy.

Della narrowed her eyes at him. "It's your business. I won't tell anyone if you don't want me to, as long as I'm not hiding anything from Lucy that might hurt her."

"I would never intentionally hurt Lucy," he said, meaning it. That was the main reason he wanted to withhold this bit of information from her right now.

∞

Four days later, Miles was summoned to Latoya's desk at the sheriff's department.

"The Christmas Crankster has hit again," she said.

"Huh?" Miles furrowed his brow. "The Christmas Crankster?"

"That's what I've decided to call him or her. Cute, right?" She looked proud of herself. "Cranky prankster equals crankster." She waggled her brows for effect. "Anyway, another place has been vandalized with *Bah Humbug* in large blue paint."

Miles shook his head. "You've got to be kidding. Where?"

Latoya gave him the address.

"That's one of the Somerset Rental Cottages." Jake owned all those properties these days.

"Yep. Trisha called it in. She was pretty upset too. It's Bear Cottage," Latoya told him.

Miles knew the one. It was the last cottage before a thickening of woods that led to Lost Love Cemetery, a local place where folks buried trinkets from relationships gone bad. Miles turned toward the door. "I'll check it out. I wish I could figure out who was committing these petty crimes."

"All you have to do is ask yourself who in this town doesn't like Christmas," Latoya said behind him. "That's gotta be one short list of suspects."

She had a point. The folks in Somerset Lake were crazy about the holiday season. The whole month of December was one big celebration. Before stepping outside, Miles turned back and looked at the department's administrative assistant. "You're on that short list. You never attend any of the festivities."

Latoya cackled. "Doesn't mean I don't like Christmas. I just don't like crowds. Good luck," she called.

"Thanks." Miles continued outside and walked to his cruiser. He checked his phone for messages. There were several, but none from Lucy. A bit forlorn, he drove to the Somerset Rental Cottages, where Jake met Miles at his car.

"Hey, Jake." Miles stepped out of his cruiser.

"Hey, buddy. I wish this visit was under better circumstances."

Miles gestured forward, toward the south side of the lake. "Me too. Lead the way to the scene of the crime."

They walked along the lake toward Bear Cottage. As they did, Miles admired the other cottages. He'd joined the teens at the Youth Center in painting the cottages' exteriors over the summer. Now the homes were a variety of bright colors along the lake shore.

"It's such a shame," Jake said. "And it's not even a vacant cottage. Mr. and Mrs. S live there. Who would spray-paint an old couple's home?"

Miles could already see the large message in bright blue paint as they approached. BAH HUMBUG. "Someone with a lot of nerve, I'm guessing." He glanced over. "I'm suspecting it's a group of teens. I ran into them the other day in the dark outside another house they hit. I didn't see any faces but the way they moved made me guess they were teenagers."

"I haven't seen any teenagers hanging around," Jake said. "Although Lost Love Cemetery sometimes invites them in. The teenage years are big for broken hearts. Please tell me you're not going to bury this thing between you and Lucy in there."

Miles glanced over. "Not this time. Not if I can help it." He pulled out his notebook to take notes on the vandalism. "We're doing really good these days. I've been thinking that I want to show her how I feel. We haven't really said the L-word yet, and I think it's too soon. I don't want to scare her off."

"Well, might I recommend that you bring her a present," Jake said.

Miles found this suggestion to be interesting. "What kind of present?"

Jake dug his hands in his jean pockets. "Well, when Trisha and I were dating, I brought her a photography book."

"Doesn't exactly sound romantic."

Jake chuckled. "Trust me, it worked. Bring her something from the heart."

They headed up the steps for Bear Cottage and knocked on the door. Mrs. S appeared a moment later, looking fretful. She wrung her hands together nervously as she welcomed Miles and Jake inside.

"I heard noise last night but I didn't think anything

of it. You know my husband likes to go outside and lie on the shore."

Everyone in town knew that Mr. S was a nudist who still liked to lie outside naked in the wee hours of the night. The sheriff's department had responded to many a call about the behavior. "Did Mr. S see anything?" Miles asked.

She shook her head. "He must have already been lying outside on the lake. It was just me inside the house. I rolled over and went back to sleep while those vandals put a damper on Christmas."

"We'll paint over it," Jake assured her. "I'll do it this weekend, if that doesn't interfere with the investigation," he told Miles.

"No, that's fine. I'll have everything I need by the time I leave here today."

Mrs. S nodded. "That's good. Thank you." She shook her head. "Who in this town doesn't like Christmas?"

That was the million-dollar question. Miles finished talking to the old woman and then he walked around the cottage one more time, looking for evidence he might have missed. Once he was done, he shook Jake's hand. Instead of heading back down the lake shore where his deputy cruiser was parked, he headed into the woods, following a path to Lost Love Cemetery.

He came to a sign nailed to the tree about a hundred feet from the spot. FOR ROMANTICS ONLY. CYNICS TURN BACK. He'd always been a romantic at heart so he kept walking until he reached the gate. He opened it and carefully stepped down the narrow space between rows of markers, indicating where some little memento of a love that had gone bad was buried.

It took Miles a moment to find his old marker from

over a decade ago. He had been one of the first to bury something here so it was on the outer edge near the gate. He squatted low when he saw the lid of the metal trinket box shining up from the ground. Miles used his fingers to dig away the dirt and loosen it from the ground.

The box was rusted now. Miles sat back against the gate and held it in his hands for a moment, remembering how his heart had hurt when he'd buried this here all those years ago. Remembering what was inside the little box and how he'd hoped he'd never see it again.

He pinched the clasp in the front, preparing to lift it. Instead of moving smoothly, the clasp just fell off into his lap. Holding his breath, Miles lifted the lid and peered inside the box. Time might have worn away the outside of the box in his hand but it hadn't touched the memento on the inside. The copper penny was just as shiny as it'd been a decade earlier. Maybe it was just as lucky too.

Chapter Seventeen

Festive music was playing in the background at Lakeside Books. Lucy was wearing a smile on her face but some part of her was wishing she was with Miles instead. When did she become that person who picked a boyfriend over her best friends?

Moira handed her a glass of eggnog and sat on the couch beside her.

"I don't like eggnog," Lucy said, frowning at the milky liquid in her glass.

"Too bad. It's tradition, and if you don't keep tradition at Christmas, when do you keep it?" She took a sip of her own glass, her face scrunching in distaste. "So what's going on between you and Miles?" Moira finally asked once she'd swallowed the liquid.

Della, Tess, and Trisha stopped talking and almost comically leaned in to hear.

Lucy lifted her glass of eggnog to her lips but didn't sip. Instead, she took a whiff and decided that this tradition could fall to the wayside. "I have nothing new to tell you since the last time you all invaded my privacy. We're still dating. We started kissing." She gave them all pointed looks. "Just kissing."

Moira looked disappointed.

"Any utterances of the L-word?" Tess asked, lifting her eyes over her red Solo cup.

Lucy shook her head. She'd almost said the word the other day as they'd gone their separate ways though. It'd been an accident. They'd kissed, and she'd said, "I..." before stopping herself short. No way was she saying it first. "Nope. Just dating. Nothing wrong with that. We can take things slow."

Moira rolled her eyes. "Oh, come on. You're my best friend, and I know you better than that. You just started dating again, but in your mind, you're probably adding in all the time you were together the first go round." She pointed a lazy finger in Lucy's direction. "I'm betting you're disappointed that he hasn't proposed marriage already."

Lucy's jaw dropped. "Am not."

"Are too," Moira said on a giggle. She was just teasing, and Lucy knew it, but there was some element of truth to what Moira was accusing her of. She did want Miles to profess his feelings sooner rather than later. "It's just..." She trailed off, wondering if she was really going to confess her true thoughts to the ladies of the book club. "I have very strong feelings for Miles."

"I think we all can see that," Tess said, crossing her legs and swiping them off to the side.

Lucy looked at her friend. "And, well..." Lucy hesitated. "I just don't want to get too far into this relationship without knowing where Miles stands."

Tess folded her hands in her lap. "You're afraid Miles doesn't feel the same way. He implied that he was marrying you out of obligation before, which makes you think he never really loved you at all. You have a fear of unrequited love."

"Wow," Moira said. "You're good. You missed your calling."

"You'd be surprised how much counseling goes on at this bookstore," Tess told them.

"Is that true?" Trisha asked Lucy. "You're in love with Miles again? And you're worried that he might not feel the same way?"

Lucy sucked in a breath that didn't seem to reach the place inside her that needed air the most. "I never really fell out of love with him, I guess." She looked at Tess. "Yeah, I think that's what's going on. I don't want to be the only one falling because that'll mean I'm the only one getting hurt in the long run."

"Like last time," Della said, a sympathetic look in her eyes.

Lucy looked around at her friends. "So what do I do?"

"You have to tell him how you feel," Tess supplied. "He might be falling for you as well."

"But what if he's not?" Lucy asked, afraid of the answer.

"If he's just having a casual thing with you, then you need to know. You might want to step things back."

Lucy knew that was true. And if Miles's feelings for her weren't as strong, she also knew that it was too late to avoid getting hurt.

ꕥ

The book club eventually moved to the book they were reading. Lucy barely listened though. If she was falling in love with Miles, she needed to know if he felt the same way. Tess was right, per usual.

"Lucy, did you read the chapters?" Tess asked, leading the discussion.

"I did."

"And what did you think?"

Tess, Della, Moira, and Trisha were all looking at her.

Lucy swallowed. "I think...I think..." To tell the truth, she couldn't even remember the title of the book they were reading right now; her thoughts were so convoluted. "I think I'm going home and talking to Miles. I don't want to be the first to say *I love you.* But I also don't want to be the last to know if he doesn't feel the same."

Miles looked out on Lucy's lighted yard as he waited for her car to pull into the driveway. He knew she was at the book club tonight but he wasn't really sure how long it would last. It didn't matter. He'd sit right here with Bella. And Scrooge, Santa and his reindeer, the three wise men, a choir of carolers, and Frosty.

All these yard ornaments could be considered tacky. At a *National Lampoon's Christmas Vacation* level. Somehow though, he and Lucy had spaced out the decorations just right and weaved them with a variety of beautiful multicolored lights that wrapped around the fence and trees and gazebo. Even Bella gazed out quietly, seemingly in a festive daze over the magical wonderland.

Headlights streamed down the road, blurring with those in the yard.

Miles felt his breaths grow shallow for a moment. He couldn't wait to kiss Lucy and tell her about his day.

He wanted to tell her about the little white house on Mallard Creek. He wanted to discuss the town's Christmas Crankster, as Latoya had dubbed them, striking again, this time on one of the Somerset Cottages.

He wanted to tell Lucy so much more but words seemed to fail him sometimes. That's why he'd taken Jake's advice about getting Lucy a gift.

Her car pulled into the driveway and parked. After a moment, she stepped out. Bella's bark seemed to clue her in that Miles was there. She turned and faced him as he sat in the gazebo and gave him a hesitant wave. "Hi," she said as she headed in his direction.

"Hey."

She broke eye contact and looked at the yard for a moment. "Admiring the lights?"

"Yeah. I think we're a surefire winner."

"I'm usually one to say winning doesn't matter," Lucy said, "but in this case..." She trailed off, and they stared at each other for a silent moment.

"How was book club?" he asked.

She shifted on her feet, looking cold or nervous—he wasn't sure. "Good. More talk about our personal lives than about the chapters we read, as usual."

"Did you talk about your personal life?" Miles asked, wondering if she'd spoken about him.

She tilted her head to one side, her auburn-toned hair swinging over her cheek. "Were your ears burning?"

He took that as a yes. Sensing that she wasn't going to sit on the steps beside him, he stood in front of her. "Lucy, I've been sitting here for the last hour waiting for you."

"Oh? Why is that?"

Miles stepped closer, wishing he could pull her into

his arms. He wanted to shout his love for her from the rooftops. Instead, he reached into his pocket and pulled out the small, rusted trinket box he'd been carrying around all day.

Lucy's gaze lowered. "What's that?"

"I went to Lost Love Cemetery this afternoon. This is something I buried there after we broke up."

Lucy furrowed her brow. "That place is only for those who've loved and lost."

"I know," Miles said.

"But you broke up with me." Lucy's eyes filled with tears as she said the words. "You ended things with me like it was nothing."

"It wasn't nothing." As if to prove his point, Miles lifted the lid of the box, hoping it wouldn't break. It was so rusted that the hinge was thin and brittle.

Lucy blinked as she looked at the contents through her tears. "Oh." She pulled a hand to her chest. "Is that what I think it is?"

"Our lucky penny." He reached inside the box and pulled it out, pinching it softly between his fingers. "Heads, I kiss you. Tails, you kiss me."

Lucy swiped at the tears streaming down her cheeks. The Lucy of old wasn't a crier but the Lucy he knew these days didn't seem to mind shedding a tear in front of him. "That was definitely a lucky coin, wasn't it?"

They'd come up with this game when they'd first started dating. Miles had found the penny on the ground as they'd walked along Somerset Lake in the downtown area. After that, he'd carried that penny with him everywhere he went.

"I loved you back then more than I'd ever loved

anything. More than baseball," he said, hoping Lucy would smile.

She did.

She pressed her lips together, her gaze fluttering up to meet his. "And what about now?" she asked.

Miles felt like he was on the cusp of winning a game. "I still love you more than baseball," he whispered, his eyes locked on hers, refusing to blink in case the moment passed him by too quickly.

Lucy stared up at him, the lights from the decorations reflecting in her eyes. "I really needed to know I wasn't the only one who was feeling this way..." She trailed off.

"You're not the only one, Luce. You and I have never been just casual."

"No, we haven't," she whispered back.

"You can trust me with your heart. If anyone does the heart-breaking this time, it's going to be you."

She blinked, and a tear slipped down her cheek. "That's good to know."

Miles held the penny in his palm. "Okay. So, heads, I kiss you. Tails, I still kiss you." He waited to see her reaction before flipping the penny. A soft grin curled at the corners of her lips. That was a good sign that the penny hadn't lost its charm. He flipped the copper coin in the air and caught it on the back of his opposite hand.

Then they both leaned in to look.

"Heads," Miles said.

"I guess you better kiss me then."

She didn't have to ask him twice. Miles slid the penny into his pocket and stepped a little closer. Then he reached out to run his hands along her shoulders as he looked into her eyes, leaned in, and kissed her.

He was vaguely aware of the festively colored lights twinkling beyond his closed eyelids. Lucy's warm body melted against his as they nestled in the middle of this winter wonderland they'd created.

Clapping cut through the silent night. Then another person joined in.

Miles pulled away and turned to see that he and Lucy had become part of the display. Folks were driving through The Village to see the lights and decorations, and a few had also gotten to see one very magical Christmas kiss.

∞

The following day, Miles's gut was telling him he needed to pay Charlie a visit. Miles remembered being a teen during the holidays. It was hard enough as it was, but add in financial and family struggles, and it felt like the end of the world to a kid.

Miles finished up his shift at the sheriff's department, and instead of driving to the Youth Center, he drove over to the Bateses' home. Charlie hadn't been to the center much lately. Like his big sister, maybe he was getting too old to hang out there.

Miles pulled into the Bateses' driveway, got out, and walked up to the modest blue house with dark black shutters and a large wreath on the door. From the outside looking in, no one would know the family was having troubles this year. That's the way it often went. People continued to say they were fine when, behind closed doors, they sometimes weren't. Miles had learned that lesson while growing up, and he'd seen it repeated many times in his work as a deputy.

Miles rang the doorbell and waited, eager to check in on Charlie.

A moment later, Mrs. Bates answered the door with a friendly smile that quickly fell as she looked to both sides of Miles. She glanced past him to Miles's vehicle in the driveway.

"Where's Charlie?" Her brows lifted high on her forehead.

Miles felt a little hiccup in his thoughts. He shook his head. "What do you mean? I came here to visit him." Miles saw the growing panic in Mrs. Bates's eyes. "Is he home?"

"No." She shook her head. "He's with you, Deputy Bruno. Isn't he?"

Miles wished he had a better answer for the worried mother. "No. Did he tell you that's where he'd be?"

"Of course. He's been helping you at the Youth Center every afternoon this week."

Miles hadn't volunteered at the Youth Center at all this week. Every night, he'd been working in Lucy's yard, prepping it for the contest. He'd called the center before heading over here, and they'd told him that Charlie hadn't been coming. That's why Miles was standing on the Bateses' doorstep right now.

Charlie's mother's eyes grew wider as her skin blanched. "He hasn't been helping you?"

"I'm afraid not."

Her lips parted. "Why? Why would Charlie lie to me?"

The easy answer was because Charlie was a teenager, and by nature, teens pushed their limits. They rebelled and looked for a sense of freedom, which sometimes meant lying to the ones they felt restricted them. "I don't know. But I'll head right back out and find him. Don't worry, Mrs. Bates."

He could see in her eyes that telling her not to worry wouldn't make it so. He'd just have to try to find Charlie as quickly as possible so his mother didn't panic for too long. "I'll call you as soon as I locate him, okay? And you call me if he shows up here."

Mrs. Bates leaned against the doorframe as if her concern might knock her over. "I will. Thank you."

Miles took quick strides back to his deputy's car and got in. He was technically off shift but there was no way he was going home now. Why would Charlie say he was with Miles all week? What was that kid up to?

Miles phoned Sheriff Mills as he pulled out of the driveway and headed toward the stop sign at the end of the road. "Hey, Sheriff. I'm patrolling the area looking for Charlie Bates. I don't think he's in any kind of trouble but his mom can't locate him. Can you radio the other deputies and have them keep an eye out?"

"Will do," Sheriff Mills said. "Charlie has already gotten into a little mischief this year, hasn't he?"

Miles had told the sheriff about the shoplifting incident at Hannigan's Market. "Yeah, but I thought we had resolved that issue." Miles had been making sure Charlie's family had groceries coming in from the local food bank. He'd also contacted a community outreach program that kept the water running and electricity on for families who were struggling. Miles didn't think the Bateses would need help for too long. Mrs. Bates was actively looking for a job, and maybe Mr. Bates would return, despite Charlie's belief that he'd left their family for good. Miles knew from experience that only time would tell.

"You think Charlie's our Christmas Crankster?" Sheriff Mills asked.

Miles thought it was funny that even Sheriff Mills had adopted the nickname for the criminal. "Why would you ask that?" Miles had briefly considered Charlie as a suspect but Charlie was a great kid with a big heart. Charlie was just worried about his family, and rightfully so. Whatever the boy was up to, Miles suspected it was more about helping the ones he loved.

"Well, I ask because our cranky criminal just struck again. Three wreaths have been taken on Wesley Street," Sheriff Mills said with a note of wariness.

"Wreaths, huh? Seems harmless enough," Miles said with a chuckle.

"They were replaced with signs that read *Christmas is Cancelled.*"

Miles burst out laughing. "Well, at least our perp has a sense of humor. Bah humbug indeed." He pulled up to the stop sign, waited for a car to cross the intersection, and continued forward, looking around for Charlie. "I don't think Charlie's our vandal. Shoplifting was just his attempt to feed his family. The crankster's intent is to rob people of their holiday spirit. Those are two very different motives."

"Maybe so. Well, I'll pass on the word to look out for Charlie. Let me know when you locate him and what he's up to?" Sheriff Mills said.

"Will do." Miles disconnected the call and patrolled every place he could think of. Charlie wasn't driving age so, wherever he went, he'd have to walk. There were only so many places within reasonable walking distance. Granted, all the vandalized places were in that radius.

Miles had thought the three shadows back at the little white house on Mallard Creek moved and looked like teens with their hoodies and baggie jeans.

Was that shadowed figure Charlie?

Miles slowed his car as he drove down Hannigan Street where all the downtown shops were. They were busier than usual with the upcoming holiday. The streetlamps all showcased red velvet bows and greenery. All the windows were painted festively for the big day. There were lights and trees, ornaments, Santa hats, mistletoe, and nativity scenes.

And there on the corner in a hoodie and baggie jeans was Charlie.

Miles pulled up to the curb, stopped, and rolled down his passenger side window. "Get in."

Charlie didn't budge for a moment. His expression went from defensive to shock to maybe a bit of fear too. Finally, he opened the passenger door. He slid his lanky body in and plopped the book bag he'd been carrying onto the floorboard at his feet.

"What's in the bag?" Miles asked, flicking his gaze down.

Charlie closed the door behind him and glanced over. Instead of answering the question, he asked one of his own. "Am I in trouble?"

"Should you be?" Miles asked.

Charlie offered a weak scowl. "You went to my house?"

"Yep."

The teen visibly swallowed. "I didn't do anything wrong, okay?"

"So why have you been lying to your mom, saying you were with me this week after school? I haven't been at the Youth Center, and neither have you. I called and checked."

"I didn't want her to worry. She's got enough on her plate," Charlie muttered, his shoulders rounding as he slumped in the seat.

"You want to tell me where you really were?"

Charlie shook his head. "Not really."

Miles couldn't make the kid talk, and Miles had no concrete reason to believe Charlie had done anything that warranted searching his bag. Miles glanced in the rearview mirror and pulled back onto the road. "Best get you home so your mom can relax. Like you said, she has enough to be concerned about without also having to wonder where you are."

Charlie didn't respond. Instead, he angled his body to look out the passenger window as Miles drove.

After several long and silent minutes, Miles asked, "How do you feel about Christmas? Love it or want to skip it this year?" He still didn't believe Charlie was the town's Christmas Crankster but he had to ask.

Charlie glanced over. "It's a holiday for people who have money to spend. I can't afford to buy my mom or my sister anything. So I guess I'd rather skip it."

Chapter Eighteen

Lucy was enjoying the Moonlight and Mistletoe Bonanza. She pulled her scarf more tightly around her neck and stepped under a large branch of mistletoe and eyed Miles. Tonight was a time when the town came together for last-minute gift shopping in the final week before Christmas.

Miles dipped in and kissed Lucy's cheek. Then he held up a shopping bag on his arm. "Okay, I got something for Ava and her fiancé, Malachi. And something for my aunt Ruth and aunt Debra. I still need something for my mom." He lowered the bag and looked at her. "Who's left on your list?"

Lucy swallowed. "Well, I got something for Trisha and Moira. I still need something for Della Rose and Tess." Lucy was acutely aware that Miles had listed family while she only had friends to buy for. "And it's not easy getting a booklover something without going to the only bookstore in town, which she happens to own."

"What about Choco-Lovers?" Miles asked. "Books and chocolate go together, right?"

Lucy's eyes lit up. "Great idea. I can get some of Jana's famous chocolate truffles for Tess. And for Della and her boys." She nibbled her lower lip as she and Miles stepped under yet another twig of mistletoe. She stopped and turned to face him. "And a cup of hot chocolate would be amazing tonight."

"We could share," Miles suggested as he leaned in to kiss her yet again.

Lucy held up a finger. "I don't share my chocolate. Ever. Not even with you."

He kissed her before responding. Then they continued down the festive sidewalk, weaving around other folks who were kissing one another on the cheeks and wishing passersby a merry Somerset Christmas. "You don't share chocolate? That could be a deal breaker for some. Not for me."

Lucy held his hand as they walked to Choco-Lovers just up ahead. They stepped up to the entrance, and Miles held the door for her.

Lucy breathed in the cocoa-tinged air as she stepped over the threshold.

"Lucy!" Jana Martin, the store's owner, called from behind the counter.

Lucy waved at her longtime friend and got in the back of the long line for yummy treats. Lucy looked at the chalkboard of choices on the wall written in brightly colored chalk. "My mom used to love Choco-Lovers. When she was alive, I got her something from here every holiday."

Miles squeezed Lucy's hand. "Bet she enjoyed that."

"She did." Lucy felt her eyes burn but blinked the sting away. "She loved to receive the Christmas snow balls. I think I'll get Della's boys some of those."

"Justin and Jett will be thrilled," Miles said, obviously fond of them.

Lucy loved that he helped out at the Youth Center. He served his community and enjoyed being with kids. How much more perfect could a man be? She reached for his hand, warming at the feel of his palm against hers. "I can make the gift from both of us. As a couple."

"In that case," Miles said, "let's add some chocolate peanut butter balls to their treat box."

"Della Rose will kill us for loading them up on sugar." Lucy laughed. "We'll get her some too to stay in her good graces."

A minute later, they stepped to the head of the line. Jana was about the same age as Lucy. She'd gone to the same high school but they'd run in different circles.

"Hey, you two," Jana said. "It's so nice to see you out and about together. What'll you have?"

Lucy ordered chocolate snow balls and chocolate peanut butter balls and added some chocolate truffles for Della and Tess.

"You got it," Jana said. "Anything else?" Jana asked Miles.

Miles rubbed his hand along his jawline where his five o'clock shadow was filling in. Lucy had to resist lifting her hand to caress the soft growth of new hair too. "I'll have some pomegranate fudge."

"A gift?" Jana asked Miles.

"For Latoya, the administrative assistant at the sheriff's department," he confirmed.

"Aww." Jana pointed at him. "You'll get points for that."

"We'd also like two cups of hot chocolate," Miles told the shop owner. "Apparently, my date here doesn't like to share."

Jana laughed. "I don't blame her. Go ahead and grab a seat. Linus will bring your mugs to you when they're ready." Jana turned and started prepping their orders.

There was only one table left in the crowded room. Lucy headed toward it and sat across from Miles.

"You okay?" Miles asked when she didn't immediately start talking.

"Just missing my mom. I guess it's hitting me that I'll never buy her chocolate snow balls for Christmas again."

Miles reached a hand across the table, taking her hand in his. "Anything I can do?"

"I don't think so. At least I have my mom's house that she loved. And you." There was an unspoken statement between them. Her mom hadn't been so fond of him. Not in the husbandly sense at least.

Miles lowered his gaze and then looked around, appearing to focus on the crowd.

A moment later, Linus approached the table and placed a hot chocolate in front of each of them. "And this gift bag is for you," he told Lucy. "And this one is for you," he told Miles.

"Thank you," they both said in unison.

Linus grinned. "Of course. Enjoy your chocolates." He waved and walked away.

Once he was gone, Lucy looked at Miles again. "After we drink our cocoa, we need to go find the perfect gift for your mom."

"We don't have to. If it's making you feel sad. I wasn't thinking. I can grab my mom a gift after work sometime."

"Don't be ridiculous. Yes, I miss my mom, but I

want to help you find the perfect gift for yours. It's fine. You could probably use a woman's touch in picking out things for her anyway. And lucky for you, I know exactly what a woman likes because I happen to be one."

Miles grinned. "Okay. Well, fill me in. What exactly does a woman like? Because I have one more woman on my list to buy for this year."

"If you're talking about me, all I want for Christmas this year is you." She cupped her hands around her mug of hot cocoa and grimaced sheepishly. "Okay, and admittedly, I also really want to win the Merriest Lawn Contest."

∞

The rest of the night was magical, from the next dozen mistletoe kisses to the reading of the Christmas story down by the large Christmas tree in the middle of the town square. Mayor Gil Ryan always did the reading. The kids adored him almost as much as the adults—all but Moira, who avoided him like the plague. Lucy was willing to bet her friend hadn't even come out tonight in order to avoid the possibility of being caught under the mistletoe by her longtime admirer.

Temperatures dropped as Miles and Lucy finally headed back to his truck at almost midnight, arms full of shopping bags.

"Your mom is going to love that sweater," Lucy said. She'd had a great time shopping with Miles, even though she had no family to buy for. Helping Miles buy for his relatives had somehow soothed a little bit of her loneliness. "Trust me."

Miles nudged her softly. "You should be there to see her face when she opens her gift. Since you helped me pick it out."

"Are you inviting me to your house for Christmas?" Lucy asked. She'd already agreed to go if they won the Merriest Lawn Contest, but that was mostly in jest and she wasn't agreeing to go as Miles's date.

"Well, you didn't make it to Thanksgiving. Bella got me a point but I still lost the guest list challenge."

"Okay," Lucy said without a moment's hesitation. "I'd love to go to your family's home for Christmas. Thank you."

"Not even arguing with me this time. That's progress." Miles opened the door for her.

Lucy stepped inside and turned to him. "I've decided I don't want to be home alone. My mom wouldn't want that for me either. She'd want me to be happy. And I really do want to see your mom's face when she gets that cashmere sweater. She's going to love it."

Miles closed the door behind her and headed around the truck.

Lucy watched him.

"Home?" he asked as he got back behind the wheel.

"How about we take a drive and look at the lights first? Just to make sure we're still in the lead. The judging is a week from today. We can't have any of our neighbors outdoing us with the lights."

Miles laughed as he cranked the engine. "A woman after my heart."

Chapter Nineteen

The following Thursday, Lucy stopped at Sweetie's Bake Shop for a cream cheese bagel and grabbed an extra one for her first client of the day. Ashley Herring was still high-maintenance but she'd come to the last couple Tuesday night classes. She seemed to be relaxing just a little bit now that she had an idea of what to expect.

Lucy knocked on Ashley's door with the paper bag breakfast in hand and waited patiently. It took several minutes for Ashley to finally answer the door.

"Oh." Lucy took in Ashley's exhausted appearance. "Are you okay?"

"Yeah. I just haven't been sleeping well." Ashley stepped back and allowed Lucy to walk inside.

Lucy headed over to the kitchen table where she and Ashley usually met. "I brought you breakfast. Have you eaten?"

"Not yet. Thank you." Ashley maneuvered slowly to sit down. Lucy was sure that Ashley's husband, Allen, was pampering her. He was as doting as Ashley was demanding. "My back aches. My legs are swollen. It's getting harder and harder to find a comfortable position at night." She reached for the paper bag and pulled out the second bagel. "This is so nice of you. Thank you," she said.

"Of course. I like to treat my clients when I can." Lucy waited for a moment while Ashley took her first bite and settled down. "How's Allen?"

Now Ashley's eyes grew shiny. "He's... well, I think he's a little overwhelmed. Maybe I've been too much to handle. He keeps talking about date nights and wanting to spend time together before the baby comes. And I keep ruining it with all my complaining." Tears slipped down Ashley's cheek. "I don't mean to. I just, I didn't realize that pregnancy would be so hard. And he's been wonderful, and he deserves to have time with his wife. But I'm swollen and tired, and I don't feel attractive even though he keeps telling me I am."

Lucy spotted a box of Kleenex on the counter and went to retrieve it. She carried it back over and slid it in front of Ashley. "This is all very normal. Your body is changing and so is your relationship with your husband. It's not a bad thing though. It's good. Having a baby will bring you so much closer together."

"I'm so thankful to have you helping me." Ashley hadn't even finished her bagel yet.

"You know what? You should go on a date with Allen. It'll be fun. You can dress up, go to dinner, hold hands, kiss under the mistletoe."

"Dress up?" Ashley asked. "But nothing fits me."

"That's not true. You have plenty of maternity clothing."

"But they all have elastic waists. They're not date material."

Lucy suppressed her need to expel a sigh. She'd never been pregnant so she didn't fully understand how Ashley felt. "What matters is that you and Allen are together, enjoying quality time before the baby gets here in the next couple weeks."

Ashley sniffled. "Maybe."

"Or what about going on a babymoon?" Lucy had always loved that idea, although most of her clients weren't wealthy enough to go off to some extravagant place for several days before their bundle of joy arrived. And most doctors advised against flying when a mother-to-be was in the final month.

"A babymoon? What's that?" Ashley asked.

"It's kind of like a honeymoon, except two parents-to-be go off on a mini-vacation before the baby is due. It's just a chance to get away and relax." And Ashley definitely seemed to need to relax. "Just going somewhere that isn't your own home, where you don't have to clean or cook or think too much."

Ashley seemed to take a breath. She picked a piece of her bagel off and popped it into her mouth. "I like that idea. I don't want to go far though. You're here and what if I go into labor? I need you by my side. But just leaving this house. Maybe we could go to a bed and breakfast or something. Does that count as a babymoon?"

"Yes," Lucy said, feeling excited. "I think that's a great idea. A babymoon bed and breakfast. I can look up places for you. Let me look into that for you, okay?"

The smallest smile crept up on Ashley's face. "Okay. Thank you, Lucy. I don't know what I'd do without you."

"You're welcome. I'll be in touch."

Lucy couldn't wait to complete an online search for Ashley's babymoon later today. She wished every expectant mother and father could go on a pre-baby vacation. Before the research, she wanted to stop in and check on Kimberly Evans whose due date was also quickly approaching.

Lucy headed over to see the next mother-to-be. Kimberly seemed to be in good spirits even though Chris still hadn't found a job.

"No one seems to be hiring for anything," Kim said. "He's applied everywhere. I don't want to have to move. This is where we want to raise our child, but..." She trailed off. "Anyway, that's what I'm hoping for this Christmas. A job for my husband would be the best gift ever."

Lucy reached out and squeezed Kim's hand. She asked a few probing questions to make sure her friend was okay. "And you've seen your primary care doctor recently?"

"Yes, everything's fine."

"Good." Lucy noted the dark circles under Kim's eyes. She hadn't been sleeping well lately either, no doubt worrying over Chris's unemployment and all the things that came with preparing for a new baby. A babymoon would be amazing for them as well. Just a chance to get away and let someone pamper them with gourmet meals, nice rooms, and a change of scenery. Lucy doubted Kim and Chris had any chance of affording that. But maybe she'd ask around.

After a full day of seeing clients, Lucy drove home, hoping to get a little time at her computer before she inevitably spent the rest of the evening after book club with Miles. Bella greeted Lucy at the door, eager to go outside. If Lucy wasn't mistaken, her dog also looked a little disappointed that it wasn't Miles who'd come to her rescue.

"Just me, girl. But don't worry. Miles will be home soon." Her heart skipped a beat. She hadn't exactly liked the idea of him moving onto her property but now Miles and home felt synonymous.

ꟹ

Miles spotted Gil sitting at a table in the back of the tavern as soon as he walked in. Miles walked over and pulled out a chair, draping his coat over the back before sitting down.

"Hey, man. Glad you could pull yourself away."

Miles always got together with Gil for dinner this time of year. Sometimes they invited another friend or two to join them. This year, they'd invited Jake Fletcher.

"Jake's not here yet?"

"He is. He spotted someone he wanted to say hello to. River Harrison. Do you know him?" Gil asked.

Miles nodded. "Yeah. Of course."

Gil reached for his glass of tea. "Jake went to see if he could get River to join us since he seemed to be sitting alone."

"That's nice of him," Miles said, glancing around and looking for the men in question.

A waitress came and asked Miles what he wanted to drink.

"I'll have a tea as well," he told her politely. Then he noticed Jake leading River toward their table. River was ex-military and had grown up in a neighboring town.

"Looks like Jake convinced you," Gil said to River on a laugh.

"Well, I am a lawyer," Jake pointed out, pulling out his own chair and taking a seat. He tipped his head at Miles to say a hello.

Miles tipped his head right back.

River stood in front of a chair and looked between the guys. "You sure you all don't mind? I was just here for the special on fried shrimp." He looked around uncomfortably.

"You can have the special while hanging out with us," Miles said. "Join us. Please." Miles watched River take a seat. River had a scar that ran just below his left eye. Miles suspected he'd gotten the injury during his time overseas. River was a quiet man who mostly kept to himself as far as Miles knew. He didn't get on law enforcement's radar at least. Or Reva Dawson's.

The waitress returned and they all ordered.

"I think I'll have what River is having," Miles told the young woman. "Fried shrimp sounds delicious."

Jake handed his menu up. "Same for me."

"And me," Gil said, handing his menu up as well.

"You got it." The waitress gave River a wink. "Looks like Lonesome Dove has found a flock of friends." She looked at the others to explain. "He is my regular Thursday night customer. He sits alone in the corner, gets the special, and reads. I call him Lonesome Dove for that reason."

"Except I'm not lonely," River said, lifting his gaze. "Some folks just like their privacy."

"Oh, I know. That's why I'm surprised these handsome fellas lured you to their center table." She pointed at the guys. "For that, I'm going to bring an extra tray of hush puppies and corn stix on the house."

Gil punched a fist in the air, looking like a teenaged boy instead of a distinguished town mayor for a moment. "I love those corn stix," he said.

After the waitress had left, the men shared awkward conversation that stopped and started like a shallow creek bed over rocky hills. Even so, it was nice and they didn't do this often enough.

"Where is your old-new girlfriend tonight?" Jake asked Miles.

Miles popped a fried shrimp into his mouth and chewed, swallowing before answering. "She's at book club, of course."

"That's right. Every Thursday night like clockwork," Gil said with a nod.

Miles chuckled in his direction. "You know this because you have eyes for Moira, who is there every Thursday night."

Gil reached for one of those corn stix. Miles suspected he was on his third or fourth. "I would deny it but I gave up lying a long time ago. So I plead the Fifth."

"Just ask her out, man," Jake said. He was leaned back casually in his chair with one arm draped on the back.

Gil frowned in his direction. "You know good and well that I have."

"Not since we were nineteen though, right?" Miles asked.

Gil looked deflated for a moment. "Well, let's just say that Moira knows where we stand. If she wanted to go out with me, she knows where to find me." He looked at River. "What about you?"

River had said very little since he'd joined them. Miles suspected he was a little uncomfortable and perhaps wishing he were by himself in the corner as usual. But Jake could be convincing when he wanted to be. "What about me?" he asked.

"Are you seeing anyone?"

"No," River said.

"You're working as a private investigator still?" Miles asked.

"Yes," River said.

The conversation, like the shallow waters of the creek bed, ebbed.

River seemed to understand that they wanted more from him. "I'm looking for a place to stay right now. My dad has moved into the assisted living home and we sold his house a while back. It was too big to keep for just me and we needed the money to pay for his room and board at the facility." He took a long, steady breath. "Della is helping me look for a quiet place that suits me."

Miles found this interesting. "Della is helping me too," he told him, popping another shrimp into his mouth. He told River about the few places he'd looked at, and River, in turn, told him where he'd looked. Then the conversation moved to Jake and Trisha's wedding plans over New Year's and what everyone was doing for Christmas. By the time their plates were clean, they all sat back with huge grins on their faces.

"Maybe we should create our own Thursday night routine like the ladies. They have book club and we can have Thursday night shrimp special at the tavern," Gil suggested.

"Your treat, right?" Miles teased.

"We can say it's an official town meeting." Gil seemed to think about this for a moment. "Miles is our sheriff rep. Jake, you're legal. River, you can be a concerned citizen."

Jake shook his head. "Nope. This is a bad idea. How about we just do this every now and again because we want to and we're friends. We already know Lonesome Dove over here comes every Thursday." He tipped his head over at River who laughed quietly. "And since I'm dating Trisha and Miles is with Lucy, we're free on Thursdays because they have book club on those nights. So..." He trailed off.

"So..." Gil agreed.

Miles reached for his glass of sweet tea and lifted it without saying a word. They all followed suit until their glasses clinked. "Merry Christmas, guys."

"Merry Christmas," Gil agreed.

"Bah humbug," Jake joked.

Miles whipped his gaze to his. "Are you my Christmas Crankster?"

Jake laughed and shook his head, holding one palm out. "Not me. I promise."

"Christmas Crankster?" River asked with a curious expression.

Miles recapped what was going on with his case. "So someone is out to steal Christmas cheer and I have one week to catch them. Otherwise, the holiday passes us by and the perps get away scot-free."

"Sounds about right for a small-town crime spree," Jake teased across the table, making them all laugh, including Miles. It was pretty funny if he thought about it. But he still really wanted to catch his Christmas Crankster, and he wanted to find out what he or she had against the holidays.

ꝏ

It was the last Thursday before Christmas, therefore book club wasn't technically happening tonight. Instead, Lucy was sitting in Lakeside Books to exchange presents with these women who meant so much to her. She'd needed these women this year. They'd helped her get through a difficult time.

Lucy uncrossed her legs as she sat on the sofa. Then she leaned forward and picked up a small gift wrapped in golden paper. It had a bright red velvet ribbon encircling it and tied at the top. "This is for you," she told Tess.

Tess's brown eyes lit up as she took the gift and started to shake it.

Lucy stopped her. "That's bad gift-opening etiquette. What if it's breakable?"

"Ohh, a breakable gift." This seemed to delight Tess even more. "Those are the best kind."

Lucy gestured at the package, eager to see Tess's expression when she opened it. "Well, go ahead."

Tess meticulously removed the ribbon first before unsealing the tape with a nail file so that she didn't tear the paper. She peeled it off carefully until the small cardboard box that Lucy had placed the gift inside was visible. Before lifting the lid, she hesitated and looked up. "I like to savor each gift. The older I get, the fewer presents come my way, so I take my time and try to enjoy each one even more."

"That could change if you'd start dating someone," Moira teased.

"You're one to talk." Lucy side-eyed her friend.

"Dating is such a letdown. The guys around here

are not the heroes in these books we read," Tess said. "That's why I love reading romance. It'll always deliver a happy ever after. Whereas dating delivers the one breakable thing I don't fancy."

"A broken heart," Moira agreed.

"Such pessimists," Della Rose said with a shake of her head. "I'm the one going through a divorce, and even I believe there's a happy ending out there for all of us. Look at Lucy." Della lifted a hand in Lucy's direction. "We never thought she'd find it."

"Hey!" Lucy said. "You guys doubted I'd find love?"

"Only because we knew you already had it with Miles, and that no one else would ever be good enough in comparison," Moira said. "We didn't know you two would get back together."

Lucy felt her cheeks warm. There was also a feeling of weightlessness in her chest. This was supposed to be a difficult holiday because it was her first without her mom. Instead, she felt surrounded by loved ones. "I never thought Miles and I would reunite either." She gestured at Tess. "Okay, okay. Open the gift already."

Tess laughed and lifted the lid off one of the boxes. Her lips parted, and she sucked in an audible breath. "Oh, wow. They're beautiful!"

"Show us," Della demanded.

Tess lifted the box and showed everyone the earrings that Lucy had picked out for her. They were tiny golden hearts, simple and beautiful just like Tess.

"I thought they were perfect for someone who loves to read so many romantic stories."

"I'll wear these earrings every day next year," Tess said. Then she opened the gift containing the truffles that Lucy had gotten her at Jana's store. Tess's eyes lit up. "Gold and chocolate, a girl's two best friends." She winked before grabbing a present for Lucy and passed it over.

It took the good part of two hours for them to exchange all their gifts and to sample one of each of the Christmas cookies the others had brought. By the time Lucy left the book club, her arms were full of presents and her heart was overrunning with cheer. She drove home, excited about the coming week when she'd spend more time with Miles, the annual Merriest Lawn Contest would be judged, and she'd go to Christmas dinner at Miles's family's home.

This promised to be the best Christmas ever—even without her mother physically by her side. Her mother was in her heart, and she could almost feel her presence. A large part of that was thanks to Miles, who'd been the one to insist on decorating. Making a merry home had been one of Lucy's mom's favorite holiday pastimes.

Lucy hummed softly to "I'll Be Home for Christmas" as it played on the radio. She turned into The Village and drove down Christmas Lane toward her house, slowing to admire all the neighbors' lights and decorations. Then Lucy looked ahead to her yard and gasped. "What happened?"

Chapter Twenty

Lucy sat in her parked car and stared out at her home for a moment. Everything was ruined. The lights were out. Half the decorations were torn down. Santa appeared to be MIA.

All the hard work she and Miles had done was ruined in a matter of hours. Tears flooded her eyes. It was as if a tornado had come through and tossed the decorations around haphazardly in its path. Lucy knew that wasn't the case. Her house was fine. It was just the lawn ornaments and lights that were strewn about.

With a shaky hand, she finally pushed her door open and stepped out of her car. She felt like the wind had been knocked out of her. As she stood there at a loss for what to do next, headlights streamed in behind her. She turned to squint at Miles's truck.

He cut the lights and the engine. Then he stepped out quickly, slammed the door behind him, and walked over. "What happened?"

"I wish I knew. I just got home from book club." Her voice was shaky. Her legs too.

Miles wrapped an arm around her as he surveyed the lawn. "I think this is probably the work of an overly competitive and jealous neighbor. Or the vandal that's been spreading his or her anti-cheer around town."

Lucy lifted a hand to gently pinch the bridge of her nose, hoping maybe that would keep the headache at bay. "The judging is two days away. There's no time to fix this. We've lost." She gestured down the street. "And no one else's yard seems to have been touched. Just mine."

Miles held her more tightly against him. "Hey. No talk of losing. I like to win, remember?"

"Well, that's a lost cause now." A tear slipped off her cheek. She was doing her best not to cry. Her emotions felt whiplashed though. She'd just had an amazing time with friends. She'd been full of hope and joy. The vandal hadn't just wrecked her lawn; they'd also stolen her Christmas spirit.

Miles dipped his head to kiss her lips before stepping away. "Let me take a closer look. I need to assess how much damage was done."

"Okay." She continued to stand there in disbelief as Miles left her side to investigate the scene.

Who would do this to me?

The next question rolled in and sat heavily on her shoulders. How would she pay the HOA bill now? Short of a Christmas miracle, she couldn't.

ꕥ

Miles had already called in to report the crime. He'd interviewed neighbors, taken pictures, and jotted down notes as he'd walked around Lucy's house, just as he would for any other investigation. Like the other vandalism scenes, there weren't many clues to go on.

He headed back toward the porch where Lucy was sitting with her head down.

"The strings of lights were all cut," Miles said as he climbed the steps to the top one where she sat. "They'll all have to come down, and new strings will have to be put up. And you're missing five lawn ornaments. I'm guessing that's all that could fit in the perp's vehicle. He or she must have had help to lift that many without being noticed."

Lucy looked up at him. The sadness in her eyes clutched his heart and squeezed it painfully. He didn't like seeing her so upset. He'd do anything to make things right.

"We don't have time to restring lights or replace the characters that were stolen." She gestured beyond him. "Half the ones that weren't taken were still spray-painted blue. All of my parents' lawn ornaments look like merry Smurfs." Her voice cracked with emotion.

Miles understood that it wasn't just about the contest. The things that had been destructed held sentimental value to Lucy. Most of them had been used as decorations since she was a kid. Her parents had worked hard to win the contest year after year, using the earnings to add more.

She lowered her face in her palms and groaned. "It's hopeless."

Miles sat down beside her and put his hand on her lower back. "Hey. The judging isn't until Saturday night. We have forty-eight hours to fix this."

She lifted her head and looked at him. "I have to work tomorrow. I don't have money to buy new things. It would cost a small fortune. Besides, most places in town are sold out of lights and decorations because of this contest." She sighed wearily. "I'm sorry, Miles. I know you put a lot of effort into helping me with this."

"Don't apologize. I enjoyed every minute."

She offered a small smile that didn't reach her eyes. "It was pretty fun."

"Yeah," he said. She was right. There wasn't the time or the resources needed to fix this situation. They wouldn't win the Merriest Lawn Contest now. Whoever the Christmas Crankster was, he or she had stolen Lucy's chance at bringing home the cash prize and paying off the last of her mother's bills. "I'm sorry, Lucy."

"It's not your fault," she said. "I'm tired. I just want to go to bed and pretend like this is just a bad dream."

"Do you want company?" he asked.

Her eyes subtly widened at the question.

Miles shook his head. "I'm not suggesting anything. Just offering to stay with you until you fall asleep."

"Oh no, that's okay. I'm fine. Thank you though." She looked out at the destruction one more time, her green eyes shimmering under the moonlight. She took a shaky breath and returned her gaze to him. "My mom spent all that money on updating this house. It's too bad she didn't put in a security system too."

Miles wished that Mrs. Hannigan had. Somerset Lake was as safe as a town could be but having a recording of this one night would change everything.

Lucy stood. "Goodnight, Miles. I'll see you in the morning."

"Goodnight, Lucy." He watched her step inside with Bella at her heels. Then he turned to look at the lawn again. It was indeed a losing battle with such short notice. If there was a way to fix this, he would, but right now he didn't see one.

The next morning, Miles awoke early and headed into the sheriff's department. Lucy's house wasn't the only one that had been vandalized in the night. The crankster had also robbed decorations from other neighborhoods in the area.

Latoya handed Miles a list with two addresses. "Have fun."

"This is getting ridiculous. There are so many missing Santas that the perp will eventually run out of places to put the stolen lawn ornaments."

Latoya folded her arms across her chest and leaned back in her chair. "Maybe he'll be a Robin Hood of sorts. You know, steal Santas from the rich and give 'em to the poor."

Miles chuckled at the idea. "It would still be a crime."

"But it would be an endearing one, at least."

Not in Miles's book. After the hurt he'd seen on Lucy's face last night, there was no scenario that would reduce the vandal's damage.

"If it's some teen, they'll just get community service," Latoya pointed out. "That's not much of a deterrent."

Miles knew she was right. "Well, here's hoping I find something to lead me to the Christmas Crankster before the holidays are over. He stole more than cheer from Lucy. Now she really has no chance of winning the Merriest Lawn Contest."

Latoya's frown deepened. "I know she's disappointed."

"She is," Miles confirmed.

"You are too. I can see it on your face. You worked hard to help her win that contest."

"We would have too," he said.

Latoya shook her head. "Well, listen. If you need decorations, come to my place and take them all. I purchase a new penguin decoration every December. It's kind of my thing. I can spare them this year for a good cause. My neighborhood doesn't put on a fancy contest, so it doesn't matter much to me."

"That's nice of you but that's your Christmas cheer," he told her.

"Christmas cheer comes in the giving," she said.

"Thanks for the offer, Latoya." Although Miles didn't think he'd be taking her up on the offer. Miles turned to leave. "See you later," he called behind him. "Hopefully with the Christmas Crankster in handcuffs."

"Good luck!" she answered back.

Miles was going to need all the luck he could get. Without a strong lead, the case would grow cold. He got into his car and drove to the first address on his list to interview Mrs. Mayberry, who was more than a little distraught over her missing life-size nutcracker.

"I've had him for decades. My kids and I first put him out when they were little. My grandkids love to come visit him now. He was a special decoration for my family. You must find it for me, Deputy Bruno."

Maybe it was a bit comical that Miles was investigating a missing nutcracker, but like Lucy's decorations, the lawn ornament had sentimental value. He felt sorry for the older woman. "I'll do my best. You didn't see anything suspicious?"

"No." She shook her head. "I was fast asleep by nine. No one has ever taken anything from me before. I trust my neighbors. Who would do this?"

Miles wasn't sure. As he climbed into his car to

head to the second address, however, his heart dropped into his gut as he slowed toward the location. Charlie Bates was on the porch doing something. Painting the door?

No. Charlie had insisted that he hadn't been involved with anything troublesome. Miles pulled into the driveway. As he did, Charlie spun to face him. They met gazes. No running now. Maybe Miles would be taking the crankster back to the department in handcuffs after all.

He parked and got out of his vehicle. "Hey, Charlie."

Charlie put his paint roller down in the tray at his feet. "Hi," he said a bit sheepishly. The door behind him was covered in blue graffiti. The paint roller, however, was coated in white paint.

"What's going on?" Miles asked, looking between the pan and the boy.

Charlie held out his open palms. "Let me explain."

"Please do." Miles didn't want to leap to conclusions but the current scene in front of him was more than a little suspicious.

"I didn't do this," Charlie prefaced. "But I'll take full responsibility for my sister's actions."

"Brittney did this?" Miles asked.

"She's having a rough Christmas. I told her this was hurting people but her friends are idiots. They're the ones making her do this stuff."

"Brittney and her friends have been the ones spray-painting and stealing lawn decorations?" Miles had a hard time imagining the sweet fifteen-year-old girl he knew acting so rebelliously.

"I'll paint over it," Charlie promised, a note of desperation in his voice. "It cost me what I was saving to buy my mom a present but my mom will be so upset if she finds out what Brittney has been doing. I don't want her to cry anymore."

Miles understood. Growing up, he'd heard his mom cry a lot when she thought no one was listening. "You're a good son and brother. But," he said, making Charlie visibly tense, "Brittney needs to be helping you clean up this whole mess. Then she needs to go back to Lucy's place and help fix that too. Preferably with her friends."

Charlie was pale as he held his elbows tightly against his sides. "You won't tell my mom?"

Miles didn't like keeping secrets but some could only do harm by telling. "I should. But no, I won't. As long as Brittney helps make this right." Righting the wrong inflicted on Lucy was all Miles wanted. Hopefully, it wasn't too late.

∞

Lucy was just going through the motions today when all she really wanted to do was go home, crawl under the covers, and stay there through the weekend. Tomorrow, folks in town would be driving through The Village to help judge the contest. And they'd all see what a disappointment Lucy's lawn was.

Ashley Herring waved a hand in front of Lucy's face. "Hello? Are you okay today?" she asked kindly.

Lucy blinked her client into focus. "Yeah, just tired," she said, breaking into a yawn. "I'm sorry."

"No problem. I can make you a cup of coffee if you'd like," Ashley offered. "I know I can't drink any but I still love to smell it."

A cup of coffee might be just the jolt Lucy needed. "You don't mind?"

"Of course not. You have helped me and Allen so much with this pregnancy. When we first found out about the baby, I was a nervous wreck. But I'm feeling so much better these days, thanks to you. The classes you've been teaching at the community building have been so informative too. We just can't thank you enough." Ashley stood slowly and awkwardly before moving to the kitchen counter. After flipping the coffee maker on, she returned to the table and placed a small, wrapped package in front of Lucy.

Lucy looked at the cube-shaped present wrapped in festive paper. "What's this?"

"It's a gift. For you." Ashley lowered herself back into the chair. "Allen and I found it the other night when we were shopping at the Moonlight and Mistletoe Bonanza. As soon as we saw it, we knew it would be perfect for you. Finding the right gift for someone is one of the best feelings." She tipped her head at the gift. "Go on, open it."

Lucy's heart felt full for the moment. This whole season had been an emotional rollercoaster, with highs and lows that left her feeling a bit disoriented. "You didn't have to buy me anything."

"You've been a lifesaver. And this isn't anything huge." Ashley leaned back and placed her hands on her stomach.

Lucy carefully peeled off the shimmery paper until there was a plain cardboard box in front of her. Like Tess had done, she took her time and savored the whole process. Her mom had always showered Lucy with a dozen gifts. Lucy didn't have that to look forward to this year, so she was extra thankful for each one that she got. Lifting the lid, Lucy peered inside. "Oh, wow," she said on a quick intake of breath. "That's gorgeous."

Ashley grinned when Lucy looked up. "Hannigan Gifts sells pieces for a Christmas village collection. People collect all kinds of houses and little trinkets to make a tiny village on their mantels."

"I know. My mother collected these. I just set out her pieces last week. She doesn't have a pink house though. This is perfect."

"It kind of looks like your place, doesn't it? Allen and I thought you should have it."

Lucy lifted the tiny pink house out of the box. She turned it from side to side, admiring the little windows, flower baskets, and intricate carvings. "It's so detailed." Lucy set the house on the table in front of her. Then she leaned over and hugged Ashley tightly. "Thank you so much. I love it."

"You're welcome." Ashley pulled away and returned to standing. "Now I'll get you that cup of coffee."

Lucy didn't really even need it anymore. The gift had given her enough of a boost. Even so, Ashley poured Lucy a mug and placed it in front of her. As she did, Lucy told Ashley what she'd found online about babymoons, which was basically nothing.

"I really thought there'd be some place close by that did this but I guess not," Lucy said.

"Well, that's okay. It would have been nice but Allen and I can enjoy a night out on the town together. And he seems to think your classes at the community center are like a date." Ashley rolled her eyes even though she was laughing. "It's kind of sweet. In his mind, just being with me is a date."

"That's very romantic. And when the baby comes, you can always leave her with me for a couple hours. While you two go out and spend some time together."

"I might just take you up on that," Ashley said. "Allen and I plan to drive through The Village tomorrow night and vote on the Merriest Lawn. We might be biased but I'm pretty sure you'll get our vote."

Lucy blew out a breath. "Well, you might be the only vote I get. Someone destroyed my lawn yesterday. It's all ruined."

Ashley's mouth dropped. "Are you serious? Who would do that?"

Lucy sipped her coffee. "We don't know. Someone who isn't exactly feeling cheerful this year, I'd guess."

Ashley huffed and rubbed her belly. "You deserve a good holiday. I'm so sorry they picked your home to unload their anti-cheer on."

"Thanks. Me too," Lucy said. "Well, the baby will be here soon. I have my phone on me. Call anytime, day or night. I'll meet you here and help you welcome that sweet baby girl into the world. Have you decided on a name yet?"

Ashley hesitated for a moment. "We're keeping it under wraps but I'll tell you as long as you promise to keep it to yourself."

"My lips are sealed."

Ashley was practically beaming. "We're thinking..." she said, drawing out her vowels, "Merry would be a great name, since she's due on Christmas Day. Merry as in M-E-R-R-Y. Even if she doesn't arrive on December twenty-fifth, it's close enough."

"Oh, that's beautiful."

"You think?" Ashley asked, rubbing her belly.

"I do."

After leaving Ashley's kitchen, Lucy drove to Kimberly Evans's house next. When she left there, she went to meet a potential client in Magnolia Falls. The potential client had just found out she was pregnant and wanted an at-home birth or one in the birthing center there. She hadn't decided that detail but she did know she wanted Lucy as her midwife.

"You have a reputation for being the new-mom whisperer," the expectant mother said.

"New-mom whisperer?" Lucy asked. "I've never heard that one before."

"Well, it's a compliment. Do you have kids?" the woman asked.

"Not yet." And Lucy was becoming more and more aware of that fact. She was unmarried with no kids. And she had no living parents. There was no family to speak of. Just Bella.

Despite the gift from Ashley and being dubbed the "new-mom whisperer," Lucy felt blue as she drove home that Friday afternoon. She hoped Miles was there, although she might not be the greatest company.

She turned into The Village and glumly admired her neighbors' homes and decorations. Then she sucked in a little breath as she approached her house. Miles was out in the front yard stringing new lights. A teen boy—Charlie Bates?—was working on the spray-painted Mrs. Claus. A couple other teens were also working in her yard.

There were over a dozen large penguins of various sizes and designs set up throughout the yard, connecting the previously unrelated scenes together in a penguin's winter wonderland. On her roof, instead of

Santa driving the sleigh, there was a penguin with a Santa hat and a white beard. In one corner of the yard, there was a snowy scene with a penguin snowman posing alongside Frosty. On the other side of the yard was Lucy's original nativity scene with a small penguin standing alongside the three wise men.

Lights were strung all over the trees and house once again, and if Lucy wasn't mistaken, they were bright pink, complementing the color of the house perfectly.

Lucy parked in her driveway and got out. "What's all this?" she asked as Miles headed in her direction.

Miles glanced over his shoulder. "The grinches' hearts have grown two sizes. Granted they needed help from yours truly."

Miles and the others must have been working all day. Lucy wasn't sure what to say right now. It seemed like Miles had saved the day for her a lot this past month. She prided herself on her independence but she had to admit that she wouldn't have been able to pull off what he had done while she was gone. She'd pretty much given up on the Merriest Lawn Contest. "How?" she asked.

"Well, Latoya let you borrow her penguins for the holiday. All the red and green and white lights were sold out so I bought pink. And I gathered up a couple willing and eager kids from the Youth Center. Offered them pizza in exchange for their time." There was a gleam in his brown eyes as he grinned proudly. "I told you I like to win."

Lucy felt like crying happy tears. "I can't believe you did all this. For me."

"I admit, my motive was partly selfish. I like to see you smile. It probably has something to do with how I feel about you," he said in a quiet voice that only she could hear. "I love you," he said without hesitation. He'd implied it before, but this time he said those three little words, leaving no question about his feelings for her.

Lucy stepped into his arms and tipped her face up to smile at him. "What a coincidence. Because I happen to love you back."

Chapter Twenty-One

Lucy was still on a high from Miles telling her that he loved her the next morning as she loaded the dishwasher. It was the Saturday before Christmas, and if all went well, they'd win the neighborhood contest tonight, and she'd pay off her mom's debt. Things were falling into place splendidly.

She closed the dishwasher door and pressed the Start button. The engine groaned in response. She opened it and made sure all the dishes were secured in place and closed the door once more before pressing the button. This time the motor started with a loud moan that definitely wasn't right. Her breath caught, and Bella hurried over to bark at her appliance.

"I know, I know," she told her dog as she turned the dishwasher off. "It's broken." She shouldn't feel as disheartened as she did—it was just a dishwasher—but it was also one more thing to tend to. Would the list of things to fix at this house ever stop?

She tromped over to the counter and swiped a pen and notepad to make a note to contact a repairman for the dishwasher. Then she lifted her head at the sound of her doorbell. Bella lifted her head as well. On the second ring, Bella hobbled toward the front of the house. Lucy followed, still in a grouchy mood about the dishwasher. Part of her was taking it as a bad omen. Just when she thought she was almost in the clear—she could see the end in sight!—something else broke.

She opened the door and stared back at a woman she didn't recognize. "Good morning," Lucy said, even if it wasn't turning out to be so far.

"Yes, indeed." The woman hesitated. "I'm the manager of the company your mom hired to clear the trees in your backyard last year. When she got sick, we stopped payment for her." The woman looked suddenly uncomfortable. "I'm sorry about your mother," she said.

"Thank you." Lucy appreciated the sentiment but she wished her mother hadn't cleared the trees in the backyard. Why would she do that? They'd been beautiful pines and oaks.

The woman continued to stand wordlessly on Lucy's porch until Lucy understood what she was there for.

"My mother owes your company money?" she asked as dread hung like a heavy stone in the pit of her stomach.

"Yes. I'm afraid so. Our customers usually pay upfront, but your mother was a friend of ours, and we were happy to help her. Then when she got sick, she asked us to give her an extension on the payment..." She trailed off. "After she died, out of respect, we wanted to give you time to grieve."

"Thank you for that," Lucy said, meaning it. She was still grieving in her own way, and maybe she always would be. "How much is still owed to your company?" She braced herself. Otherwise, she might fall apart. There was another bill, and maybe it wasn't the last. Perhaps that was the nature of this house. It naturally needed upkeep and maintenance, repairs and new appliances.

"Fifty-five hundred," the woman said matter-of-factly. "And that was with the friends-and-family discount and no interest on being late," she added a bit sheepishly.

"I see." Lucy blinked back tears. "I can't pay that today. I hope you understand."

"Of course. I assume you didn't know about the bill."

"I didn't." Lucy hadn't known about a lot of her mother's doings and goings-on before she'd come to stay in her mother's final weeks. Her mother obviously had a vision for this house that matched nothing that Lucy could even begin to imagine.

The woman handed Lucy a business card and an envelope which Lucy assumed held an itemized statement. Lucy wished she could just ask for the trees in the backyard to be returned. Then the woman looked out at the decorated front lawn. "Your parents always outdid themselves with the decorations this time of year. I'd say you have followed into their footsteps. This is amazing."

Lucy forced a smile but it felt flat and emotionless. Even if they won tonight, Lucy would still have unsettled debt to pay. She felt overwhelmed and frustrated by her circumstances. And as much as she didn't want to be, she felt angry at her mother for leaving her here with all these bills and unanswered questions.

After the woman left, Lucy closed the door behind her and leaned against it, tears filling her eyes and an unbearable weight pressing down on her from all sides. Another day. Another bill. Another broken appliance.

Maybe this was the wake-up call she'd needed to finally end this dream of staying in this pink house.

She couldn't stay here. She was one person, and it was too much to care for. Her mom must have felt the same way, and yet, instead of selling, her mother had racked up a stack of unnecessary, random bills. How irresponsible. How could she leave Lucy to pay for all this alone? How could she leave Lucy?

Lucy felt like her knees were going to buckle. She allowed herself to slide to the floor before they did. Bella approached and licked away the tears on her cheek but more kept falling. This morning was her breaking point. Everyone had one. Even if she won tonight's yard-decorating contest, she'd still go into the new year paying off bills and struggling to keep this house maintained. It was futile, and she was finally done fighting what felt like a lost cause.

∞

Miles was looking forward to tonight. Yeah, he was competitive and loved a good contest as much as the next person, but his enthusiasm was more about being with Lucy.

He walked into the lounge at the sheriff's station and leaned against the counter with a cup of coffee.

Sheriff Mills poured himself a cup as well and side-eyed him. "Explain this to me."

"Okay. I'll try." Miles prepared himself to discuss the Christmas vandal. He didn't really know how to explain the Christmas Crankster's motives at the moment.

"You're aiming to buy a house but you're falling for

Lucy who lives in that huge pink house on Christmas Lane."

Miles sipped his coffee. "That's not work-related."

Sheriff Mills chuckled. "No, it's not. It's friend-related."

Miles nodded. "Lucy and I just started dating again. I can't live in that small garage apartment indefinitely."

"You could move into that big house of hers though. It's just her living there, right?" the sheriff asked.

Miles nodded. "That's right." He took another bitter sip of his coffee. The lounge coffee was an acquired taste. "She hasn't invited me into the house, and I don't know that I want to cross that boundary before we're ready. I kind of thought I wanted to have all my ducks in a row before I got into a serious relationship."

The sheriff frowned. "What's that mean?"

"You know. The job. The mortgage. I don't want to go into a relationship, counting on what she brings to the table."

"That's a bit old-fashioned," Sheriff Mills said. "Plus, her house is bigger than the one I imagine you'll pick out."

That was true enough. Miles shrugged and stared down into his coffee. "Then I'll sell my place or rent it out. Owning my own house is just something I need. I'm sure it's because my dad failed in that arena and I have something to prove."

The sheriff gave him a steady look. "Now *that* I understand. Whether he respects his father or not, a man always has something to prove in relation to his dad. That's why I wear this badge."

Miles gave him a questioning look. "Yeah? I didn't know that."

"My dad was in law enforcement for a time. He discouraged me from following in his path but you know how that is. Tell a kid not to do something and they decide to do it with even more determination."

Miles grinned. "You stubborn? No way."

The sheriff laughed at that and took another sip of coffee. "So if you need a house to feel settled and ready to enter into a relationship, then you should buy one. It's that abandoned place on the creek, right? That's the one you're looking at?"

Miles leaned off the counter and tossed his empty cup in the trash. He hadn't even told Lucy that he was seriously looking at the house yet. He really didn't want word getting back to her before he had a chance. "That's right. I'm just thinking about it though. I haven't signed any paperwork."

"Well, good for you. And if you end up with a house and with Lucy, maybe you two could live in both. One in the winter, one in the summer."

Miles gave him a strange look. "That's a bad idea, boss."

The sheriff shrugged. "Or maybe Lucy will want to downsize from that big mansion she's always lived in for something smaller. Just saying, do what feels right, follow your heart, and everything will work itself out. It always does."

Miles nodded. "That's good advice. Thanks."

The sheriff placed his coffee mug in the sink and headed out of the lounge, leaving Miles standing there for a moment longer. He'd wanted to be in a house before he got serious with someone, but he'd gotten those two things out of order. Now it felt complicated. He was serious about Lucy, which somehow made him feel guilty about wanting to get his own place. But owning his own house was something he needed deep down in his core. He had something to prove, and he and Lucy still had time in their budding romance for him to prove it to himself. Like the sheriff said, things would work out the way they were supposed to. They always did.

Chapter Twenty-Two

The community building at The Village was a bustle of activity later that night. There was a steady line of cars threading through the streets of the cozy neighborhood. Afterward, most were coming here to cast their vote for the Merriest Lawn.

Miles reached for Lucy's arm to gain her attention. "Want me to get you some cider?"

"Mm. Yes, please. And a cookie, too, if you don't mind."

"I won't forget the Christmas cookies." Miles headed over to the refreshment area for tonight's guests. He grabbed two festively printed napkins off the large stack at the end of the table and then grabbed a couple cookies for him and Lucy.

"Hey, Miles," a voice said, walking up beside him.

"Mayor Gilbert," Miles said quietly.

Gil rolled his eyes at his formal name. "Some things never change."

"That's the beauty of small-town life."

"I think you and Lucy might have a chance at the winner's title," Gil said. "You have the whole *March of the Penguins* theme going for you. And the bright pink twinkling lights are perfect with the pink house."

"Thanks, man. Pink lights were the only color we could find on such short notice but it does help us stand out, doesn't it?"

Gil nodded his agreement. "In the history of this contest, I've never seen anything quite as original or as fun as penguins and bright pink lights."

"Some might call that combo tacky," Miles said.

"Nah. There's a fine line between tacky and genius. I call what you guys did at Lucy's house a stroke of genius."

"Thanks." Miles glanced around at the shoulder-to-shoulder crowd. "I hope so. The prize would be nice for Lucy but I also think it'd help her with how much she's missing her mom."

"We miss our lost loved ones more this time of year, don't we?" Gil asked.

"I guess we do," Miles agreed, thinking about his father for just a brief moment.

Gil turned and offered his hand to Miles. "Good luck tonight, man."

"Thanks." Miles glanced over at Lucy who was also talking to community members.

"Also, it's poor etiquette to vote for yourself," Gil teased.

Miles shook his head. "I'm not voting. Just enjoying the atmosphere and good company."

After pouring two cups of cider, Miles headed back to where Lucy was standing. She was alone again but Miles doubted that would last long. Almost all the folks in Somerset Lake would be here tonight at some point.

"Want to take these with us as we walk back?" Miles asked.

"Great idea."

Even the sidewalk was crowded. Folks who didn't want to drive into the congestion had parked along the roads outside of the neighborhood and walked in.

"I think the temperature has dropped twenty degrees since an hour ago," Lucy observed with a shiver as she sipped her hot cider.

"Maybe it'll snow tonight." Miles sipped his beverage too. "Snow makes my job a lot harder but I still love a white Christmas." He looked over. "I'm glad the snow has held off until this judging. A layer of snow over all the decorations would ruin things. Has that ever happened?"

Lucy got a far-off look as she thought. "I think I remember one time. My parents scraped layers of snow off the lawn ornaments so they could be seen better. They really loved this contest." Lucy bit into one of her cookies and chewed for a quiet moment. "I don't remember my parents ever really bonding over anything, not even me. Except for this contest. It always pulled them closer together this time of year."

Miles noticed the wistful look in her eyes. "It kind of brought us together too."

"So regardless of what happens tonight, we're both winners, right?"

"So, once we win the Merriest Lawn title," Miles amended, "we're double winners. I'm competitive, remember?"

"More than I realized." Lucy's laugh came out in a white puff of air.

"Getting your heart back is the biggest win though." In fact, it was the score of Miles's life. He was in love with Lucy. He wanted to spend the rest of his time on earth making her happy. The future was theirs.

∞

After walking home from the community building, Lucy sat on her porch swing with Miles by her side.

Miles laid a hand over Lucy's. "Stop fidgeting."

"Can't help it. I can't believe how excited this all makes me. I understand now why you love a good competition. This is so much fun."

Miles wrapped his arm around Lucy's shoulders, hugging her close. "Well, you're invested in this for several reasons."

"If I don't pay that HOA bill, they'll come after me in the new year. That's not the way I want to begin the next twelve months. I've spent the last twelve paying off Mom's debt." Lucy snuggled into the crook of his arm, her thoughts trailing to her latest troubles which she'd decided not to bother Miles with tonight. They could wait until tomorrow. "I have been determined to leave all that stuff behind me after this year. The only way that's going to happen now is if we win this silly contest." And even then, it wouldn't happen. The only thing that would save her from her mother's bills was selling her childhood home.

The thought hollowed her out and made her want to dissolve into tears.

"It's not silly," Miles said, oblivious to her inner turmoil. Either she was an amazing actress or he had a one-track mind about the contest. "I've always loved driving through The Village this time of year. Especially slowing to give this pink house a closer look, looking for you."

Lucy tipped her head back to gaze up at him. One-track mind or not, he was adorable when he was excited. "Yeah? That was before we dated or after?"

"Both. You were like the princess in your castle."

"And now you live on the castle premises with me," she teased. "Who'd have thought?" Something ached deep inside her chest. She wouldn't be that princess in the pink castle any longer. Someone else would be living in this beloved house this time next year.

"Actually, I may have found a place to buy," he said.

Lucy pulled slightly back to get a better look at him. "Oh? I haven't heard you talk about a house. Did you look at it yet?"

"You did too. Remember the white house on Mallard Creek? Where we found Purrball?"

Lucy nodded slowly. "Yes, but it wasn't for sale, from what I recall."

"No, but I returned to investigate the vandalism and I found myself standing in the backyard admiring the view. It's amazing out there. The house is the perfect size for one man. Or a small family one day down the road," he said quietly. "No one is living there so Della did a little digging for me and discovered that the owner doesn't want the place. She's a businesswoman with more money than she has time. She's been dragging her feet on cleaning the house out and selling."

Lucy wondered why Della hadn't told her about this. It seemed like something that would have come up in their last conversation. "But you changed the owner's mind about selling?" Lucy asked.

"I guess my inquiry motivated her. She's given Della a price, and she's willing to make a direct sell to me. As is. She doesn't want any of the stuff inside unless I find something valuable or sentimental."

"Wow. So you're serious?" Lucy asked, slightly

stunned by the news and the fact that he'd gotten this far in his search without telling her.

An excited grin crept up at the corners of his mouth. "I guess I am. I've been wanting a place of my own for a while now. It's something I need. And this place strikes a chord. I want a home that's not perfect. I want to be able to fix it up, do the work, and make it my own. The house has character, and I think I'd enjoy living on the creek."

Lucy felt a tinge of sadness even though she knew that was completely selfish. He was buying a house, and she was losing hers. "Have you made the offer yet?"

"No. I wanted to sleep on it first. And talk to you. I want to talk to my mom too." He pulled his arm from around her and clasped his hands in his lap. "It's a big decision so I guess I'm not jumping in without being absolutely certain."

"Well, I think you should do it. Being a homeowner is important to you, and you've found a house that you love." She swallowed as unexpected emotion whooshed to the surface. "Maybe it has a garage apartment for me to rent," she said, voice shaking.

He looked over at her, brows gathering above his dark eyes. "What?"

Lucy felt her smile fade. She hadn't wanted to get into this discussion tonight. She'd just wanted to relax and enjoy the celebration. After all the hard work that Miles had put in, he deserved to enjoy tonight. They both did. "I'm thinking about selling my mom's house in the new year, regardless of whether we win the contest."

Miles frowned. "I thought you were determined to keep your mom's house?"

"I was." She shrugged. "Then another contractor came collecting on a bill this morning, and the dishwasher broke. It needs replacing. And after you leave," she said on a heavy sigh, "I'll need another tenant for the garage apartment. Otherwise, I'll be right back in the hole again. I guess I've realized that it's too much for one person to keep up with. It always was. I just wasn't ready to let go because doing so felt like I would be losing yet another piece of my mom, you know?" Tears threatened behind her eyes. No one told her she'd miss her mom so much. It was a pain that kept renewing, finding new ways to ache inside her heart.

Miles reached for her hand. His palm against hers felt so reassuring. It was welcome. She needed his touch. She needed him to hold her and be there for her tonight. "Lucy, this isn't just your mom's house. It's yours now. It's a part of you."

"It's just a house," she said, trying to convince herself as much as him. Yes, this was the house where she'd grown up with her parents. Where she'd learned to crawl, walk, and run. Where she'd sat in her room dreaming of Miles, and then where she'd first nursed a broken heart, no thanks to him.

"No, this house is your home, and I'm not going to let you lose it," he said with determination, his gentle hand clenching into a strong fist. "Not on my watch."

Lucy blinked through her tears, his words striking her in all the wrong places. "Excuse me?"

"I have a little bit of money saved. I'll pay off the new bill and fix the dishwasher."

Lucy blinked again, feeling the tears cling to her lashes. Hadn't he heard her? "But that money is the down payment for the house you just told me you were buying."

"There'll be other houses," he said as if his decision was already made. "I can pass on this one."

"You said you loved it. You can picture yourself spending time on the creek out back," she reminded him.

"I'd give it up for you. You and me. We can fix this."

Lucy folded her arms over her chest, applying pressure over her rapidly beating heart. She supposed she should feel appreciative but instead heat flared behind her solar plexus. There'd been this ache there all day that was now replaced by a growing flame of anger. This wasn't a competition to win. This wasn't a game to play. "This is all on me. I'm solo in this."

He reached for her hand. "But you don't have to be. That's what I'm telling you. I want to be here for you, just like with the lawn decorating contest. We're the winning team, right?"

She let out a laugh but there was nothing funny about any of this. "A team? Where were you when my dad died, huh? You promised to be by my side forever, but you weren't there on that pew with me while I cried my eyes out. Where were you when I got my first job? When I lost it? When my first patient lost her baby and it gutted me and I cried all weekend long all by myself? Were you there? Were you part of my winning team, Miles?"

She choked back a sob as grief and sorrow and all the lonely years crashed over her like a tidal wave. "You can't just put a ring on someone's finger with flippant *forevers* and take it back, then waltz into their lives ten years later and expect to be a winning team."

Miles looked stunned. His mouth opened but no words came out. That was probably for the best because she would have shot them down right now.

"Where were you last fall when I came home and my mother was sick and dying, and I needed someone to hold me and tell me that everything was going to be okay? That's all I needed, but no one said it, and it didn't happen. She died and left me all alone in this huge house." Lucy lifted a quivering chin, her cheeks wet with a thousand tears. Through the blur in her eyes, she could see that Miles's eyes were shiny too. "We aren't a team, Miles, because you left me a long time ago."

"Lucy," he finally said, his voice quiet, "I'm sorry. I can't change the past but I want to be here for you now."

It was really the only right thing he could say. And it still felt wrong. Everything felt wrong suddenly. "No, you can't change the past. No matter how much you might want to." She struggled to take in a full breath.

"But I'm here now. Doesn't that count for something?"

"Maybe that's too little too late, Miles."

"You don't mean that. You're just upset about the house right now."

"Possibly." She nodded. "Or maybe I've realized that there's no revisiting the past."

∞

Miles headed over to the garage and climbed the stairs with heavy feet and a heavier heart. He wasn't sure what had just happened. It was just a fight. Right? They could work this out. Right? But it felt like the issues that had come up between them were as towering as the mountains that rolled along the border of Somerset Lake.

Miles let himself into the garage apartment. He walked over to the sink to get a glass of water and then carried it to the far window that faced the street. While he drank it, he watched the steady stream of vehicles as his thoughts blurred along with the headlights and lighted outdoor decorations.

Maybe he'd been too quick to try to rescue Lucy when all she'd needed was a listening ear. But that's how he was wired. He couldn't stand by and watch Lucy hurting and do nothing. Except she was right. That's what he'd done too often in the years since their breakup. There'd been an awkwardness. An assumption that she was better off without him. A hesitation on his part.

He'd gone to her parents' funerals but he hadn't sat beside her, holding her hand. That wasn't his place. At least that's what he'd told himself.

He drained the rest of the liquid in the glass and turned away from the window, regret settling over him for all the things that had been said tonight. They'd both said hurtful things. Lucy was already emotional because this was the first Christmas since her mom passed. This was one of those times she needed him beside her and once again, he wasn't there.

Miles pulled out his phone, debating whether to send her a text to make sure she was okay. All he wanted was to wrap his arms around her right now.

They'd lost far too much time already. In his mind, that was justification for not losing any more. In hers, apparently, it might be reason to stay apart.

∞

Early the next morning, Miles woke, dressed, and walked outside on his way to Lucy's front door before realizing that her car was gone. That wasn't unusual. She sometimes left in the middle of the night to tend to her clients and deliver babies.

He walked around the back side of the house, got the hideaway key, and opened the door. Then he grabbed Bella's leash and fastened it to her collar. They could both use a walk. He'd slept restlessly last night, replaying his conversation with Lucy. The more he played it, the more he wondered if they'd broken up. Couples disagreed. It was normal and healthy even.

He and Bella circled back to the pink house. He left the little dog inside and went next door to the garage apartment. It was the Sunday before Christmas. His mom would be heading to church right about now. If he hurried, he could join her. Maybe she'd have a little motherly advice on what to do now to smooth over his situation with Lucy.

Miles jogged up the steps and let himself into the tiny apartment. He quickly tugged on his favorite leather jacket and a knit hat. The late-December cold would be biting at the outdoor church service he and his family had been attending for years. Grabbing his keys, he walked out to his truck, got in, and drove to the Point.

"Hey, Mom," Miles said as he walked up to where she was sitting on a cement bench.

His mom looked up with surprise. "Miles. I thought you'd be working this morning."

"I have the day off," he told her. "I thought I'd sit with you, if that's all right."

"Well, this is the best present you could've gotten me." She scooted over to let him share her space. Miles didn't often think about his dad anymore. But Lucy's comments made him think about his parents' situation. His father wasn't just responsible for that moment in time when he'd bailed. He was responsible for all the lonely years his mom had been alone since. "I got you a real present too," Miles told her. "But you'll have to wait until Christmas to get it."

She clucked her tongue. "A gift isn't necessary. You know I don't care about material things." She patted his arm tenderly. "I cherish time with the people I love. Speaking of which, where's Lucy?"

Miles let his gaze wander over the gathering crowd. "She was gone when I woke up this morning. I'm guessing she had a client call."

His mom had that look on her face. The one that made him think she could read his mind and knew exactly what was going on behind the scenes of his life. "Did you two win the Merriest Lawn Contest last night?"

"I don't know that either. We'll hear the results today. The head of the homeowner's association will call the winner and put a sign out in that person's yard. Hopefully it'll be Lucy's."

"I see. Well, what *do* you know this morning?" his mom asked teasingly.

"That it's borderline freezing out here." He bumped his shoulder against hers. "And that I'm happy to be sitting next to you."

She patted him again. "I'll make you soup after the service to warm you up. How's that?"

"Sounds good."

An hour and a half later, Miles thawed at his childhood home over a bowl of warm vegetable soup. While they ate, he told her all about last night's fight with Lucy.

"She got upset about me offering to help her save the pink house."

His mom set her spoon down and looked at him. "No woman wants to feel like she's a burden to the man she loves."

Miles looked up from his bowl of soup. "Lucy isn't a burden. And I didn't make her feel that way. I think the real issue is that she's missing her family and feeling all alone."

"She has you," his mom pointed out.

Miles shrugged. "I'm not sure she wants me anymore. I thought we'd moved on from the past but I guess not."

His mom reached for a piece of corn bread that she'd laid out on a dish in the table's center. "The only way to move on from the past is to face it honestly. Both of you. You can't pretend it never happened."

"We did. I did," Miles said, feeling a bit defensive. He'd told Lucy everything. He'd even told her about Mrs. Hannigan coming to see him all those years ago.

His mom gave him a wary look that told him she wasn't buying his story.

"I told her that her mom came to see me. And that

Mrs. Hannigan convinced me that I couldn't support a wife and a kid. She was right though. I couldn't even support myself at the time. Sometimes love isn't enough. It wouldn't have worked between me and Lucy back then. We would have struggled."

His mom gave him a knowing look that gave Miles pause. What did she know that he didn't?

He sat there a moment, searching his brain, his heart, his mom's face. "This was never about Lucy's mom or whether she thought I was good enough for her daughter," he finally said. "It was about me and whether I thought I was good enough for Lucy." He felt like he'd been sucker-punched by the truth. If he hadn't already thought the same thing, Mrs. Hannigan wouldn't have been able to convince him he wasn't good for Lucy. "It wasn't about her mom," he said. "It was about *my* dad, and *my* fear that I'd let down the people I love just like he did."

His mom smiled warmly. She reached for her glass of tea and took a sip. Something about the gesture said, *My work here is done.*

He reached for his tea as well. She was right. He hadn't fully resolved the past. He was still that kid who was afraid of becoming his dad. That's why he'd wanted a house. That's why he hadn't dated seriously all these years.

"Miles?"

He looked up at his mom, bracing for more revelations. "Yeah?"

"If you are anything like your father, it's the best parts of him, not the ones that drove him to leave us. You don't have to worry that you'll ever let me, or anyone you love, down. That's just not who you are. You are selfless and giving because you've got a heart that won't allow you to be anything less."

Tears burned his eyes. He'd needed to hear that. He looked down into his soup bowl for a long moment, collecting himself. "So what do I do about Lucy?" he finally asked.

"I know this isn't what you want to hear, but sometimes a woman needs a little time and space."

No, that wasn't what he wanted to hear. His instinct was to go see Lucy right now. Even if he did though, he didn't know what he'd do or say to make things right. So maybe he also needed a little time and space to figure that out.

Chapter Twenty-Three

Lucy's heart sank as she watched the homeowner's association drive the stake of the big blue ribbon cut-out into the ground across the street. She and Miles hadn't won the annual Merriest Lawn Contest. All their efforts had been for nothing. All of Lucy's work this year to pay off her mother's bills were futile. There was one she couldn't pay, and now that she'd lost the contest, she had no good way to pay her debt in the HOA's timeline. They'd contact a lawyer like they'd threatened, which would only rack up more bills for Lucy.

What was the point?

Lucy turned from the window, sat down right where she stood, and let her tears fall. She'd thought she'd be all cried out by this point, but apparently not. She was pretty sure she'd broken up with Miles last night. And maybe that was for the best. The only reason they'd been able to move on was because they were older now. Wiser. But they were still the same people.

She sucked in a ragged breath and startled when Bella lapped her sandpapery tongue along her cheek to wipe away her tears. Lucy petted the dog and whispered quietly to her. "Maybe all a woman really needs is her dog."

Bella looked adoringly into Lucy's eyes and then whined a little.

Lucy didn't think she was whining because she was worried about Lucy crying. "Oh, I didn't feed you today, did I?" She blew out a breath. Her crying session could wait a moment while she got Bella something to eat. She stood and walked into the kitchen where she kept the dog food. Her mom had kept a year's supply of canned dog food in the bottom cabinet, which was odd. A lot of her mother's behaviors during her last two years of life were strange and unexplainable.

Lucy bent to grab a can of dog food from the cabinet, reaching to the back to find one. When she did, her hand found something different. She pulled it out and looked at it. A brand-new box of silverware. She reached into the cabinet again and pulled out another. And another. And a fourth box. Why on earth did her mom need four boxes of new silverware?

Lucy shook her head, placing the silverware on the kitchen counter. Bella's soft whine reminded her of her mission. She grabbed a can of dog food and opened it, pouring it into a dog bowl and placing it on the mat where Bella was typically fed. Then Lucy's gaze trailed back to the silverware. Was her mom planning on having huge dinner parties before she'd gotten sick? Was she just lonely? Lucy only worked an hour away. She had come home often enough to visit. She hadn't seen anything unusual during those visits to cause concern.

Wiping away the last of her tears, Lucy pulled on her heavy coat and hat. Then she grabbed her keys and purse and headed to her car. She planned to drive over to the cemetery and have a few words with her mom's headstone. When her mother was alive, Lucy had rarely gotten a word in edgewise when they'd argued. This afternoon would be different. Lucy had a lot of questions. A lot of anger. And a lot of pain. She didn't want to carry it around anymore. She wanted to let it go, once and for all.

The air bordered on freezing as she crossed the cemetery twenty minutes later, heading toward a shaded area in the back. The cold was even more biting without the sun shining directly on her. Snow was forecast in the next couple days, and the temperatures would only drop with the coming hours. That was fine by Lucy. She'd always loved a white Christmas. So had her mother.

Tears collected at the back of Lucy's throat as she hugged her heavy coat around her, carrying two arrangements of pine needles that she'd gotten from the florist on the way here. They were wrapped in huge red velvet bows. Her mom would have gone on and on about how lovely they were and how Lucy shouldn't have, even though the huge smile on her face would have told Lucy otherwise.

Lucy's nose began to run as she approached her parents' gravesite. She placed one arrangement on her father's grave. "Hi, Dad," she said, wiping a gloved hand over his name engraved in the granite headstone. Then she stood and walked over to her mother's site. She set the second arrangement down and stood back for a moment, taking in the two marbled headstones. "Merry Christmas," she said, her words coming in frosty breaths.

Her parents had always loved the holidays. The season brought them together as they decorated the house and sang festive tunes. They were a happy family, and that's the way Lucy would always remember them.

"Mom, I know what you told Miles." And it had hurt when Miles had told her the truth, even if she could almost imagine her mother taking it upon herself to fix what she perceived was wrong with Lucy's life. In the last week, Lucy had slowly come to terms with what her mom had done. One, because it was a long time ago. And two, because Lucy kind of understood where her mom was coming from. Lucy just wished it hadn't cost her so much time with Miles.

She also understood that he was responsible for his choices. It wasn't all on her mom.

Lucy shivered against a rush of wind as she stood there, alone in the cemetery on this cold winter's day. "Don't worry, Mom. I'm not here to argue like we used to in the good ol' days." She smiled to herself. "What I wouldn't give to have those days back, by the way. I'd take our worst day together over a day without you in it." She pressed her lips tightly together, rebelling against the tears she was fervently resisting crying. Their fights hadn't been all that bad anyway. They were just the typical mother-daughter squabbles, most of which had probably been Lucy's fault. They'd laughed a lot more than they'd ever fought. Lucy's friends often commented that they wished their mom was more like Mrs. Hannigan, who took Lucy on spa dates and frequent movie nights. They actually talked, which Lucy learned some of her friends didn't do with their moms.

Lucy sighed as her gaze fixed to the granite headstone. There was a thread of pink and gold in the stone that she thought her mom would appreciate. "I know you were just looking out for me—like always. You were a good mom. I hope you knew that. I hope I told you enough. If you're listening, I want you to know that I love you and I miss you. And I forgive you." Life was too short not to. Her mother's quick illness had taught her that. Hug the people you love tighter while you can. Tell them how you feel while they're around. Because tomorrow wasn't promised.

Lucy sat in front of her mother's grave, hugging her knees to her body until her nose was probably as red as Rudolph's. She felt her mom with her as she let her mind linger through memories. Not because she was here at her gravesite. She felt her mom because she was her mother's daughter. She had the same red-toned hair and rosy cheeks. The same green eyes and determined spirit. She felt her mother because they'd shared a lifetime together that she was so very thankful for. Nothing could take those memories or that closeness away. Not death and certainly not selling the pink house.

Lucy got up and trekked back to her car, resolution settling within her with each step. The last year had been like treading water trying to stay afloat among her grief and her mother's bills. If she sold the house, then *poof!* All the debt would disappear. She could start fresh. No more scrounging, worrying, or being resourceful. A fresh start was exactly what she needed going into the new year. Out with the old. In with the new.

Her heart ached with the thought because Miles was part of the old. Did she need to let go of him too?

∞

Miles knew as soon as Lucy stepped out of her car that their differences hadn't magically disappeared overnight. She wasn't smiling or running toward him. Or apologizing for her role in their argument.

She headed up the steps and faced him. "Guess you saw." She gestured at the blue ribbon in the yard across the street.

"I'm sorry, Luce," he said quietly, hoping that was all she was upset about. Somehow he didn't think that was the case. "We gave it our best shot."

"Yes, we did." She gave him a meaningful look before pulling her gaze to look at the decorations in the yard. "It doesn't matter. I'm selling the house. The money will help me finish paying off Mom's bills and allow me to get a fresh start."

Miles narrowed his eyes. "A fresh start? Where?"

She still wasn't making eye contact with him. He thought he saw a little tremble on her lower lip. "I'm considering moving back to Rose County. Maybe I just needed to resolve things here before I could find happiness there."

Miles swallowed. "What are you talking about? This is your home. Somerset Lake is your home. And what about us? We have a second chance here. Yeah, we have some things to work on, but I'm not giving up on us. Not this time," he said.

"Miles..." She paused for a long moment, visibly trying to steel her emotions. "It was never going to work between us. You can't go back, no matter how much you think you want to. And sometimes you realize that things weren't as rosy as you thought. Sometimes you remember things in this idyllic way that isn't completely true."

"Maybe, but not in our case," he argued. "And you can't just leave. You have friends here." She had him too.

"I can always come back to visit my friends. Just like I did before. And I don't really think I'll be able to move on in this town." She gave him a look that told him he was the reason that was true. Even still, she didn't say she wanted to work things out.

Miles knew his mom advised him to give Lucy time, but all of a sudden, he felt like he was running out of time with her. She was thinking about leaving town, and if she did, he'd lose her completely. "Luce, I was an idiot last night. I've realized that I am solely responsible for our breakup. It was never about your mom. It was about me and my fear. I own it, and I'm so sorry. I can't stand that I allowed you to spend one second feeling like you were alone in the world when you should have had me by your side. But I want you to know that I always wanted to be there. I want to be there now, in whatever way you need me to be."

Tears filled Lucy's eyes. "Do you mean that?" she asked, voice shaking.

He nodded. "More than anything, with all my heart."

She pressed her lips together for a long moment. "I'll be talking to Della soon about putting this place up on the market," she said. "It's probably best if you find a place to live sooner rather than later in the new year."

Miles felt emotionally stunned. He was laying his heart on the line, talking about their relationship. And she was talking about the house and his living situation. Maybe there was no relationship between them anymore. He swallowed painfully. "I can, uh, probably stay with my mom until I find a permanent place."

"You don't have to move out this week or anything. It's Christmas."

He nodded. If they weren't going to be together, it would be far too difficult to live here on the same property.

"Miles," she said in almost a whisper.

He lifted his brows, hoping she'd change her mind. Instead, she reached into her pocket and pulled out the penny he'd once buried in Lost Love Cemetery.

"Here." Her hand shook as she handed it to him, placing it in his open palm.

He closed his fingers around the penny, throat tight. It almost felt equivalent to when she'd handed back the engagement ring so many years ago. "Goodbye, Lucy."

Chapter Twenty-Four

Miles couldn't stay here. This garage apartment was too close to Lucy. If they weren't going to be together, he wouldn't torture himself by seeing her day in and out.

Lucy had said he didn't need to move this week but he disagreed. Tomorrow, he'd pack his stuff and get out.

Purrball leaped onto his chest, at the exact place that his heart hurt, and purred loudly. Miles absently lifted a hand and ran it over her silky coat. He had planned to have taken her to the shelter by now but he liked having her around. He'd never thought of himself as a cat person but sometimes people discovered things about themselves they hadn't realized.

Miles had learned things in the last month that he hadn't been able to see before. He knew his father's abandonment had hurt, but Miles was holding himself back in life in an attempt to avoid becoming like his dad. It wasn't healthy or rational.

Miles blew out an audible breath that got Purrball's attention. She blinked her yellow eyes at him. Unable to sleep, Miles finally sat up. He'd never really unpacked his stuff, so it would be easy enough to move out. He walked over to the wall of boxes and grabbed one to carry down to his truck. He repeated the process until everything just barely fit in the back of his truck. Then he got behind the wheel and drove to his mom's house. She was a night owl so he was certain she'd still be awake.

Her brows lifted as she opened the door to him. "A little late for visiting, isn't it?"

"Yeah. I'm sorry, but can I stay on your couch tonight?" he asked.

She furrowed her brow but she didn't ask any questions. "Sure. Anytime."

"Can my cat stay too?" It was the first time Miles had claimed ownership, but yeah, Purrball was his.

His mom looked at the feline in his arms, reaching a hand out to pet its head. She'd never kept a pet when Miles and his sister were growing up, mainly because she'd never owned her own place. There were always rental agreements that barred animals. His mom finally had her own home though. She was free to make the rules. "Of course. She can even count as your plus-two at dinner for the guest challenge."

"Purrball will be my plus-one-and-only, I think," Miles said regretfully.

His mother gave him a knowing look. "I'm sorry to hear that. I'll get some blankets to make a bed on the couch for you."

"Thanks. I have to work in the morning so I'll be gone before you wake," he told her. "Purrball is self-sufficient. You won't even know she's here."

She gave him an uncertain look. "Okay. We'll catch up tomorrow night at dinner? You can tell me all about what brought you to my door."

Miles nodded. Maybe by then he'd know exactly what had happened to lead him here.

She broke into a yawn. "But right now, I'm tired. And I suspect you're not up to talking."

"You know me so well." Miles leaned in and kissed his mother's forehead.

After helping his mom prepare the couch, Miles climbed under the covers. Purrball leaped back onto the achy spot on his chest, her purr vibrating all the way down to his heart and lulling him to sleep.

ꝏ

The next day, Miles headed out early for work. He walked into the station and waved at Latoya.

"There's coffee in the pot," she said. "You're going to need it."

Miles turned, waiting for an explanation that didn't come. "Okay, I'll bite. Why am I going to need it?"

Her smile grew wider. "Because the Christmas Crankster has struck again."

Miles folded his arms over his chest. "I caught the bah-humbugger. We made a deal to fix the damage and return the taken items."

"Well," Latoya said, "all I know is your first stop today is to investigate another lawn jacking. You know that Blue Ribbon Winner in The Village?"

"Yeah?" Miles said, drawing out the last syllable.

"Destroyed. Santa and his reindeer are all missing. And the blue ribbon sign was stolen too."

Miles hadn't noticed anything last night when he'd packed up and moved after dark. It must have happened after that. "First coffee and then I'll head over there."

"Told ya you'd need it," Latoya called after him.

Ten minutes later, Miles was on the road and sipping the world's worst cup of coffee. He didn't think Charlie or his sister had anything to do with this crime. Charlie's sister had never given up her friends though. The obvious motive for destroying the winner's yard was jealousy but the original culprits were a bunch of teens. Did one of them live in The Village?

Miles pulled onto Christmas Lane and drove slowly as he tried to piece together the clues of this Christmas crime spree. His gaze trailed over the festive decorations on the houses as he slowed toward the address where he'd been living this past month. He hadn't intended to come back here for a while, but he wasn't going to Lucy's house. Just the house right across the street.

Miles slowed and pulled into the driveway of the winner of this year's Merriest Lawn Contest. Whoever had come here in the middle of the night really had a bone to pick. Everything was strewn about on the lawn. Most were spray-painted in the same telltale blue paint. And the sign declaring the lawn a winner was MIA.

"Oh, Deputy Bruno. I'm so glad you're here." Mrs. Newsome walked out in a flowery housecoat and boots. "Look at my yard. Can you believe this?"

Miles tugged the opening of his coat shut to bar the chilly air. "If you remember, your neighbor over there," Miles pointed at Lucy's house, "was hit a couple nights ago. Unfortunately, her home was hit before the judging."

Mrs. Newsome looked past him at Lucy's house. "Oh, I know. That's where you live too, isn't it?"

Miles cleared his throat. "I was staying there temporarily, yes, but I'm no longer living in the garage apartment." He glanced around the lawn. "Did you hear anything last night? See anything?" He pulled his pen out of his coat pocket and opened his notepad.

Mrs. Newsome shook her head vigorously. "No. I sleep pretty hard though. I use ear plugs," she confided.

"I see. Well, do you mind if I walk around and see if whoever did this left footprints behind?"

Mrs. Newsome furrowed her brow. "There's no snow on the ground yet, Deputy Bruno. The ground is dry as a bone."

"I didn't mean literal footprints," he said. "I was referring to clues."

"Oh." She giggled nervously. "I see. Well, yes, please do walk around. I have family coming over. This lawn was my pride and joy. I was looking forward to showing it off," she said, her disappointment thick in her voice and expression.

"I'm sorry about that," Miles said. "But the joy of Christmas comes from within, right?"

She gave him a confused look.

"I'll, uh, just go look around." Miles walked all over the lawn looking for something that might help him locate the culprit. The only way he was going to do that, though, was to visit Charlie and his sister again. Miles doubted Brittney had participated in this vandalizing spree but Miles was willing to bet she knew who had.

"I'll let you know if I find out anything," Miles told Mrs. Newsome a half hour later.

She was still wearing her flowery housecoat. "Please do."

Miles turned and started to walk to his cruiser. He had no intention of looking across the street. None at all. But his body and his heart had a mind of their own. He lifted his gaze just in time to catch Lucy watching him from the porch. As soon as he caught her watching, she turned and headed back inside without even a wave.

So much for second chances.

Miles sat in his vehicle, cranked the engine, and reversed out of the driveway. Next stop: Charlie and Brittney's house. Maybe he wouldn't find love this Christmas, but he was determined to catch the town's Christmas Crankster.

Lucy stepped away from the window and leaned against the door. When she'd woken this morning, she'd found a text from Miles telling her he'd moved out in the middle of the night and the garage apartment was now vacant.

Yeah, she'd told him to move out, but not within twenty-four hours and under the cover of darkness.

Pain seared the left side of her chest. She felt breathless and sad, even though this was her doing. It would only hurt more if this happened later. Best she take her blows now and get them over with. This year was about clearing baggage. Her mom's debt. Her grief. And future heartbreaks she couldn't afford. Next year, she was determined to start fresh in every sense of the word.

Bella whined softly at Lucy's socked feet.

"It's okay, girl. I'm okay." Lucy scratched behind the dog's ears for a moment. Then she got up. She was just going to get dressed, drink coffee, and visit her very pregnant clients. She'd put one foot in front of the other today, tomorrow, and the day after that. Eventually she'd forget all about Miles Bruno. It was a good thing that he'd moved so quickly. Out of sight, out of mind.

At least that's what she was hoping.

❧

An hour later, Lucy walked into Sweetie's Bake Shop and ordered a coffee and a bagel. Moira was meeting her here any minute after her emergency dispatch shift. Tess couldn't make it today because she was inventorying the bookstore.

"Rough night?" Darla asked from behind the counter.

"Yep."

"I hear that the winner of the Merriest Lawn was hit by that vandal," Darla said. "It was on Reva's blog."

"Bad news travels fast." Lucy handed over her debit card. Darla swiped it, gave it back, and slid her coffee and bagel across the counter. "So does good news. I hear you and Miles are getting along just like old times."

Lucy didn't feel like correcting that hearsay. People would be saying otherwise soon enough. Lucy gestured to the table in the back corner. "I'll be over there waiting for Moira."

"All right, sweetheart. I'll go ahead and prepare Moira's breakfast so you don't have to wait on her for too long."

"Thanks." Lucy walked to the back table, took a seat, and unwrapped her bagel with a heavy sigh. Darla's food usually turned a bad mood around but she somehow doubted it would today. The only thing that might put a dent in Lucy's spirits was delivering a baby. Seeing that there was no imminent due date for any of Lucy's patients, that was unlikely.

The bell on the door jingled, and Lucy exhaled at the thought that Moira was finally here. When she looked up, she blinked Miles into focus. He was dressed in his uniform, the consummate picture of good looks and nobility.

"Hey. I, uh, didn't know you were in here," he said, looking just as surprised to see her. "I didn't see your car."

"I parked by Tess's bookstore and walked. I needed some fresh air."

He nodded. "I was just going to get a coffee. The one I had earlier at the station was awful."

"Don't let me stop you." Lucy felt hurt all over again at the memory of his last text. He hadn't even waited to move out until daylight. "I saw you at Mrs. Newsome's house. Is she very upset?"

"You could say so," he said.

"I don't understand. I thought you caught the person who was doing all the Christmas vandalizing."

"Apparently not. Charlie's sister, Brittney, is protecting someone else who really isn't in the Christmas spirit this year."

"I can relate," Lucy muttered without thinking.

Miles narrowed his dark eyes. "Maybe you're the Christmas Crankster," he said, voice completely serious. "You had motive. You wanted to win, and some might say you were even obsessed."

Lucy smiled half-heartedly. "You were the one who was obsessed. Maybe it was you."

They both stared at each other for a moment. Then the door behind Miles opened, and Moira walked in.

"Oh hey, you two," Moira said. She gave Lucy a questioning look. "Miles, are you joining us this morning? You can if you want. I don't mind."

"No." He shook his head. "I need to get back to work. I'm in the middle of an investigation."

"The Christmas Crankster?" Moira asked. "I read all about it on Reva's blog."

Miles shook his head. "Reva seems to know everything around here. Maybe I should have a talk with her and see if she can fill me in on who I need to be talking to."

"Not a bad idea," Moira said.

Lucy couldn't say anything. Her heart hurt so much right now, and she wasn't even sure which part hurt the most. It was the whole of it all mixed with how much she was missing her mom. And the realization that she was going to have to give up the pink house. And that she'd pushed Miles away for a reason that didn't even make sense in her own mind.

"Enjoy your breakfast," Miles told them both, his gaze sticking on Lucy for a beat longer than it had on Moira.

By the time Lucy had returned the sentiment, Miles had already walked up to the counter to order his coffee.

Moira slid into the seat across from her. "That was kind of awkward."

"It was, wasn't it?" Lucy took another sip of her coffee.

"Classic first post-breakup conversation," Moira agreed. "Nothing a little mistletoe and a kiss can't fix."

"I don't think mistletoe can fix this," Lucy said.

"Only because you're being stubborn." Moira paused for a beat. "You can spend Christmas with me and my mom on Friday, by the way. We'd love to have you."

"Thank you. Maybe I will." Some part of Lucy just wanted to be alone though. The other part, with Miles. She was a wishy-washy mess, which was why she'd been avoiding any conversation with him. Part of her wanted nothing more than to kiss and make up. Another part knew it wouldn't work because their issues would still be there, festering beneath the surface. Until she could sort out her emotions, she was putting one foot in front of the other, taking one breath at a time, and hoping by some Christmas miracle that she'd figure her life out one piece at a time.

After breakfast, Lucy headed out to see Ashley and Allen Herring. Their yard was a winter wonderland as Lucy approached the front door. She rang the bell, shivering as she waited. Snow was forecast for tonight. In her experience, a snowstorm sometimes brought on labor.

"Nurse Hannigan," Allen said, "come in. You've got to be freezing out there."

"Just a little bit of frostbite on my toes and nose," Lucy joked. "How's Ashley?"

"She's napping right now." He lowered his voice. "Physically, she's fine. She was a bit disappointed about the babymoon thing not working out though," he said. "I wish it would've. She's restless, and we can't see our family this year because they live so far away. Ashley can't travel that distance in her condition."

"I was disappointed at the lack of options in this area too. There were several bed and breakfasts within driving distance, but unfortunately, they were all booked up for the holidays. A getaway would have been nice for both of you. In my experience, the father-to-be needs just as much pampering as the mom-to-be," Lucy said.

"We may have to make do with a hotel getaway. Our heat is on the fritz, and it's going to snow tonight. The guy I called to repair it is going to try to come but no promises on getting here today."

Lucy grimaced. "That's terrible." As soon as she said the words, an idea came to mind. "You know what? I have a huge house in The Village. The entire upstairs is nothing but guest rooms that I never even use. You and Ashley are welcome to come stay in one of them. It'll be better than a hotel."

"Wow. That's a really nice offer." He seemed to think on the idea for a moment. "You're sure you don't mind? I don't want to impose. You probably have family coming over for the holidays."

Lucy's throat tightened at that remark. "Actually, I don't. And I'd be right there if Ashley went into labor. You'd have your very own private nurse."

Excitement glinted in Allen's eyes. "Ashley is going to be thrilled. She loves that neighborhood. We've driven through to look at all the lights several times this year. A night or two there would be magical."

Lucy certainly thought so. She loved living in The Village. Saying goodbye to her childhood home would be devastating. She didn't want to think about that right now though. She wanted to help her clients experience a little staycation, a home away from home.

She looked at Allen. "Then come stay. Have your babymoon at my house."

⁂

Miles pulled into the Bateses' driveway and cut the engine. He'd been here just last week and had made a deal with Charlie and Brittney. If Brittney wasn't going to give up her accomplices, she would have to clean up all their messes.

Miles got out of his vehicle and headed to the front door. It opened before he got a chance to ring the bell. Brittney walked out and closed the door behind her.

"Hey, Brittney. You're just the person I wanted to see," he said.

She pulled her jacket around her and headed down the porch steps. "I don't want my mom to overhear."

"I was actually going to have a talk with both of you. It's time that you told me who is destroying all the Christmas displays."

Brittney turned to face him and hugged her arms around her body. "I told him to stop," she said sheepishly, "but he won't listen. He thinks it's funny."

"He?... Well, he's wrong. People work hard on their decorations. It's not funny. Is this guy your boyfriend?" Miles asked.

Brittney chewed at her lower lip. "He'll break up with me if I tell you."

"Maybe that's for the best," Miles said. "This guy sounds like a loser, if you ask me." Miles caught himself sounding like Lucy's mom, who'd thought he was a loser too. But Miles hadn't been a delinquent of any type growing up. He'd just been down on his luck.

"He's a really good guy," Brittney protested. "He's just had a tough year. Like me." Her pale skin was growing red under the cold.

"Is that why he's messing up the decorations?"

"He says Christmas isn't for dysfunctional families like his." Brittney looked down at her boots. "He and his friend are the ones doing it. I was just riding along with them because I liked him." She looked up, tears glistening in her eyes. "I can help clean up that other house. Charlie won't mind helping me again."

"Not this time. I'm going to need your boyfriend's name. And his friend's name."

"He'll get mad at me," she objected, more tears flooding her eyes.

Miles resisted telling her, if that was true, she didn't need that guy. "If he likes you, he'll understand. If he truly is the good guy you think he is, he'll stay with you." Miles swallowed, making the comparison between him and Lucy. Lucy was right. He could have stayed with her. He could have ignored her mom's opinion of him. He could've fought harder for what they had when they were eighteen.

"Brittney? If you don't tell me, I'm going to need to go inside the house and talk to your mom about this."

"No." Brittney shook her head quickly. "No, please. She's having a hard enough time."

"Then do the right thing. Tell me who did this so that person can be the one to undo the damage he or she has done."

She sucked in a shuddery breath. Then finally she whispered, "Brandon Newsome."

Miles took a moment to compute that information. "Mrs. Newsome's grandson?" The boy lived at Mrs. Newsome's house with her. "Why would he destroy his own grandmother's yard? He helped her put up those decorations." Miles had watched him through the garage apartment window, thinking to himself what a great teen the kid was to volunteer so much of his time to his grandmother's cause.

Brittney shrugged. "Only because she made him. His grandmother said that she'd give him half the money if they won the contest."

And they had won. Miles supposed the boy thought he'd get the prize and the added bonus of getting back at his grandmother. Miles patted Brittney's shoulder gently. "All right, Brittney. Go back inside where it's warm."

"Is he going to jail?" she asked nervously.

"Don't worry about your boyfriend. Everything will be okay," Miles assured her.

Her expression crinkled with worry. Miles hoped for the girl's sake that Brandon was as good a guy as she thought he was. "Okay. Thank you, Deputy Bruno."

"Thank you. You did the right thing, Brittney." Miles walked back to his cruiser and got in. Then he headed back to Christmas Lane where he'd started his workday. This time he wasn't paying Mrs. Newsome a visit. He was going to have a chat with her grandson.

Chapter Twenty-Five

Miles couldn't help glancing over at Lucy's place as he pulled up to the Newsome house and turned in. Lucy's car wasn't parked in her driveway. She was probably visiting one of her clients right now. It was just as well that she not see him across the street again. She might start to think he was coming to the Newsome house on purpose, just to see her.

Miles looked out on the Newsome lawn again before stepping out. It was a huge mess. Mrs. Newsome wasn't going to be happy to know her grandson was the culprit.

He pushed open his car door and followed the sidewalk toward the porch. Then he rang the doorbell and waited.

Mrs. Newsome appeared, still in her flowery house-coat. "Oh, Deputy Bruno. Did you find out more information on what happened to my lawn?"

An uneasiness settled in Miles's stomach. He really didn't want to inform the older lady of the truth, which would undoubtedly hurt her feelings. "Mind if I come inside this time?" he asked.

"Of course. I was just about to pull some cookies out of the oven. Would you like one?"

Miles grinned. "I've never met a cookie I didn't like," he told her. He followed her into her home and back to the kitchen where she directed him to a stool.

"How about some apple cider too? It goes so good with these cookies."

"Sure." Miles waited patiently as she prepared him a small plate of goodies. He didn't see or hear any evidence of her grandson being home. "Is Brandon here by chance?" he asked.

"Oh no. He's off with one of his friends. Maybe his girlfriend." She chuckled softly. "He's such a good boy."

Miles's stomach rolled again. "His girlfriend is Brittney Bates, correct?"

Mrs. Newsome turned to him. "You really keep an eye on your citizens, don't you?"

"Well, I was at the Bateses' home earlier today, talking to Brittney."

Mrs. Newsome headed toward the table and set a plate of cookies in front of him, along with a cup of cider. She sat in the neighboring chair. "Oh?" she asked. "Has Brittney caused some sort of trouble? You know, I wouldn't be surprised."

"Why is that?" Miles asked.

"Oh, her family has had a lot of trouble this year. They're struggling. Kids act out."

"That's right. It sounds like your grandson might be acting out too."

Mrs. Newsome pulled back. "Why would you say that? Did that Brittney girl blame him for something?"

Miles folded his arms across his chest. He hated being the bearer of bad news. "Where was your grandson last night, Mrs. Newsome?"

"In his bed sleeping, of course."

"Are you sure he didn't step outside?"

Mrs. Newsome's mouth fell open. "To do what?" She gasped as if the thought finally occurred to her. "To mess up my lawn? Why would he do that?"

Miles sighed. "Maybe he's not really feeling the Christmas spirit this year. Brittney doesn't drive. She's only fifteen. She was home this time but she helped Brandon the other times. With Lucy's lawn."

Mrs. Newsome's eyes widened. "No. Are you sure?"

"I would like to talk to Brandon to be certain," Miles said. "But I don't think Brittney was lying to me. She's very concerned that Brandon will be upset with her."

Mrs. Newsome looked down at her hands. "He knows how much the lawn decorations mean to me. His mom is coming to town for the holiday. I wanted to make things special for her because she's been gone for so long." Mrs. Newsome's expression shifted. "And she left Brandon here with me. I knew he was upset with her and his father but I didn't think he'd take it out on others. You think he did all the destruction to the other homes too?"

Miles reached for his glass of cider. "We'll need to ask him. When will he be home?"

"Anytime now," Mrs. Newsome said.

"Mind if I just stick around a while?"

"Not at all. I have more cookies and cider. Stay as long as you need to." She glanced out the window. "If he is responsible for this destruction, my lawn doesn't deserve that award. The second-place winner should move to first place."

"Let's take one thing at a time." Miles glanced past

Mrs. Newsome to the sound of the front door opening. He set his cup of cider down and stood to greet the town's real Christmas Crankster.

∞

Mission accomplished. Lucy barely had time to dwell on her breakup with Miles since she'd arrived home this afternoon. She was too busy preparing her guest room upstairs for tonight's babymoon visitors.

She was so excited she could hardly stand it. The upstairs would make a great little getaway for the couple. A couple of her other clients still had weeks to go before delivering. Maybe if this worked out well, Lucy could do the same for them. There was an attached bathroom to each of the three upstairs bedrooms to ensure privacy. There was a huge back porch that had a view of the rolling mountains. And the neighborhood was wonderful for long walks. What more could a pregnant couple want? Oh, right. Their very own midwife.

Lucy buzzed around washing linens and dusting the rooms. She placed a basket of snacks and water bottles in the room for the guests. At almost five o'clock, the doorbell rang. Lucy hurried downstairs to invite her guests inside, expecting to find Ashley and Allen on her stoop. Instead, she came face-to-face with Olivia. "Oh. Hi, Olivia. This is an unexpected visit."

Lucy's mind raced through all the possible reasons that Olivia might be here. She had until the new year to pay the bill, so Olivia wouldn't be here for that just yet. Not that Lucy would be prepared to pay the bill when that time came. "What brings you here?"

"Can I come in?" Olivia asked.

Lucy stepped back and gestured into the living room. "Yes, come on in. I'm just preparing for some overnight guests."

"Oh, how nice," Olivia said. "For the holidays?"

"You could say that." Lucy led Olivia to the couch that she'd hid behind just last month when she'd thought someone was breaking into her home. So much had happened since that time. They both sat, and Olivia angled toward Lucy.

"Your lawn came in second place for the Merriest Lawn Contest."

Lucy's lips parted. She and Miles had come close to their goal. "Wow. That's nice to know." It wouldn't help her pay the HOA bill though.

"And I'm sure you saw Mrs. Newsome's lawn this morning." Olivia grimaced. "It's quite the sight."

"But that happened after the judging. You can't take away her title."

Olivia waved a hand. "Oh no, of course not. Not unless she insisted on giving it up. Which she has."

Lucy's mouth fell open. "What? Why?"

Olivia looked sheepish. "It seems her grandson is to blame for all the destruction, including yours. Mrs. Newsome just didn't feel right about keeping the title or the prize money given that someone in her own home was the vandal."

Lucy's eyes widened. "I see."

"So your second place has now become a first place. We're having a new sign made up for your yard as we speak." Olivia reached into her purse and pulled out a check. "And here is the cash prize."

"Oh, wow." Lucy looked down at the rectangular piece of paper that could solve one of her problems.

"Well, we had an agreement. If I won, that money stays with the homeowner's association. It pays off the unpaid dues in full."

"And then some." Olivia dropped the check back inside her purse. "You'll be starting next year with a clean slate. Assuming you're staying here."

Lucy couldn't believe this turn of events. "For the time being at least. My guests tonight are actually some midwife clients of mine. I'm giving them a babymoon of sorts. This house is kind of perfect for entertaining guests. Kind of like a B and B." Lucy inwardly cringed, wondering if Olivia and the HOA might have some objections. "I mean, not a real B and B, of course."

Olivia gave her a strange look. "No? For a second there I thought you might have decided to adopt your mom's dream of turning this place into one."

Lucy blinked. "What are you talking about?"

"She didn't tell you?"

Lucy shook her head slowly, as the pieces began to fall into place faster than Olivia could reveal them. "Tell me what?"

"Your mom wanted to turn this place into a B and B," Olivia said as if it were so obvious. "She did all the groundwork to have the neighborhood rezoned, which the HOA frowned on at first."

"That's why she hired so many contractors," Lucy said. "To fix the roof. To clear the trees in the backyard."

"For parking," Olivia confirmed. "The HOA spoke to your mother extensively about not allowing guests to park on the street."

Lucy nodded as she continued to process everything. "The hot tub was for guests," she said quietly. All of the decorating and renovations too. How had Lucy not seen this until now?

Olivia clasped her hands in her lap. "You know, there's no reason you can't open a B and B here if you want. Your mom has already done everything. It's something to think about, at least."

"Yes, it is." Lucy felt her excitement grow to proportions of a child on Christmas Eve. She wasn't even sure why. A moment ago, moving back to Rose County was still within her realm of possibilities.

"Lots of exciting things for you in the new year, hmm?" Olivia collected her bag and stood.

Lucy stood as well, following her neighbor to the door to see her out. There were so many exciting things ahead. Or there could be. But there was only one person she wanted to share all the wonderful news and possibilities with, and he wasn't here.

∞

Miles pulled up behind Della's car in the driveway of the white house on Mallard Creek. She was leaning against her hood. "Hey, Della," he said as he stepped out.

"Oh hey, Miles."

"You sure you don't mind meeting me here? We could've waited."

Della waved a hand. "A real estate agent is always working. The boys are having a blast on the creek back there. This is a find. It will be swept up fairly quickly if you don't act on it. Do you think you might make an offer?"

Miles looked at the place again. "I just wanted to go in one more time to do a gut check."

"Well, let's go." Della headed toward the front door and unlocked it. "I'll just wait on the back porch and watch the boys. I need to make sure they're not causing trouble." She turned back. "I hear you caught the Christmas Crankster."

"Yep."

"I'm guessing the young man will be doing community service all next year?"

Miles laughed. "Starting this morning. I had him ride along with me and help me deliver some holiday meals for folks in our community."

"You're one of the nice guys, Miles. Lucy is lucky you haven't been snapped up by now. You're lucky too. You two need to just get over whatever is keeping you apart and be happy." She waved a hand. "And done. I'll do my best not to poke any more into your personal life this afternoon."

"Thanks," Miles said. He knew why he was still single. Part of him was always still waiting for Lucy. The other part was waiting to tick off his list of requirements for settling down. Buying this white house would complete that list.

He walked from room to room, going over in his mind where his things would go. He walked the route from his imaginary bed to the bathroom to the counter where he'd get his coffee. While he waited for it to brew, he could look out of this kitchen window at the creek. It was beautiful and peaceful. He could see himself being happy here.

He couldn't see Lucy here though. She belonged in that big pink house on Christmas Lane in The Village with a garage full of Christmas decorations and a jar of rainwater on the back porch. He tried to envision himself here again, but without Lucy, it didn't feel peaceful or happy. It just felt empty.

Della finally stepped into the kitchen. "Well? What do you think?"

"I'm not really sure," Miles said.

"Don't offer if you're not one hundred percent. This is a commitment. You're either all in or all out." She gave him a knowing look that told him she wasn't just talking about the house. She was also talking about her friend.

"Right," he said. "Have you, uh, talked to Lucy?"

"Just this morning."

"How is she?"

"Pretty good. She's committing herself to a few new things that you might find interesting. You should call her."

Miles hedged. "In case you haven't heard, she broke up with me."

Della Rose pulled her coat around her. "She told us. I'm sorry, Miles. I really thought you two had a second chance."

"Me too," he said on a sigh.

She turned her attention to the white house. "It's got a lot of potential."

"It does," he said, but he was still hesitating for a reason he didn't quite understand. He always thought having his own house would mean he was ready to settle down. That he'd finally reached a status that meant he had his life together enough to take a chance on love. But the only person he wanted to share his life with didn't want to share her life with him. "I don't think this house is the one after all," Miles finally told Della.

She looked at him again. “No?”

He shook his head. “I’m sorry.”

“Don’t be. Do you want to look at some other places?” she asked. “I have the time.”

He shook his head again. “Not right now.” Something told him he wouldn’t find *the one* anytime soon. He’d already found her, and she’d slipped through his fingers.

Chapter Twenty-Six

Lucy pulled on her snow boots and winter coat and then headed out the front door, admiring her lawn for just a moment. She appreciated the large wooden cut-out of a blue ribbon as well. She and Miles had done it. They'd won the Merriest Lawn Contest.

She had considered calling him a dozen times since Olivia's visit but she'd stopped herself. They'd both said things to each other, done things, that couldn't be swept under the rug with a blue ribbon cut-out on her front lawn.

She also wanted to tell him about her ideas to turn this pink house into a babymoon B&B. Allen and Ashley had stayed two nights this week, and it had been amazing. Lucy could balance her midwifery caseload with hosting couples at the house. They'd have a key and could come and go as they pleased. Olivia had even offered to be a secondary contact on the house if Lucy was unavailable and guests had pressing needs. Darla had offered to do food deliveries for guests.

The B&B would only be for expectant or new parents, so there likely wouldn't be a huge demand. Just enough to keep the house full and lively, the way it was meant to be and bring in a little extra income to cover the home's expenses—like the HOA bill.

There was still a lot to be done and planned but Lucy had high hopes for the new year.

She stepped inside her car, cranked the engine, and waited for a few minutes while it warmed. Then she backed out and drove downtown. It was Christmas Eve, and she needed to complete one last-minute shopping run. She'd been invited to several houses tomorrow but she'd yet to commit to any. If she went anywhere though, she didn't want to go empty-handed.

The one place she really wanted to be tomorrow was with Miles, but that was the least likely to happen. He hadn't called or texted since he'd moved out. She hadn't called or texted him either. She kept picking up her phone and then falling short of words. The fact remained that they had a past that she still resented him for. It still hurt. Maybe it always would. How could a couple truly move on with those feelings always bubbling to the surface?

She parked in the lot for Hannigan's Market, walked inside, and pushed a cart through the aisles, greeting familiar faces with a cheeriness that didn't fully ring true. But next year, along with all the big plans she was making, she'd find happiness again. Maybe she'd even start dating.

"Oh, Lucy. It's so good to see you," Reva Dawson said, heading in her direction.

Lucy wished she could return the sentiment but all her defenses went up whenever she was around the infamous blogger. "Hi, Reva. Merry *almost* Christmas."

"Yes, indeed."

"I'm glad you're back in town, Reva," Lucy said.

"Ah, yes. I went to visit my son in Magnolia Falls for a little bit. I was cut off from the happenings here in Somerset Lake though. I had absolutely nothing to write about on my blog."

"What a shame," Lucy said, her tone of voice less than sincere.

"The blog keeps me going. It's good to have a passion." She beamed. "And I have good news to broadcast tomorrow," Reva added. "About you."

"Me?" Dread knotted in Lucy's stomach.

"Yes, you. I hear you're the new winner of the Merriest Lawn Contest in The Village. Congratulations."

"Oh. Right. Thank you." Lucy felt a sincere smile curl at the corners of her lips.

"Your mom and dad would have been so proud of you. They loved competing in that contest, didn't they?"

"They did," Lucy said, remembering what Miles had told her. Her mom had felt stuck in her marriage to Lucy's father. She'd only married him out of obligation because she'd found herself pregnant with Lucy. When they'd participated in the decorating for Christmas though, Lucy could see that they enjoyed each other's company. They'd laughed and worked together. They'd been a winning team. That's how she wanted to remember them.

"You and Miles reminded me of your parents when you were decorating your yard this year. I drove by several times and saw you two out there making merry. It did my heart good to see two young people falling in love." Her expression wilted. "I hope you'll get past whatever argument you had."

Lucy could tell the older woman was fishing for

information, probably so that she could broadcast it on her blog. Well, if she wanted information, she'd have to get it elsewhere. As much as Lucy liked the older woman, she didn't want her love life, or loveless life, to be the top headline on Reva's list of happenings.

"He's one of the good ones. Don't let him slip away," Reva advised.

"Advice noted," Lucy said, at a loss for anything better.

"Since I'm your elder, and you're too polite to tell me to buzz off, let me give you another nugget of Reva wisdom."

"Okay?"

Reva lowered her voice as if offering up a well-kept secret. "I consider myself to be an outsider looking in most of the time. I don't mind. But I've watched you growing up. You lost your grandparents. Your dad. Last year, you lost your mom. It's easy to see how you might be afraid of losing anyone that comes into your life now. Sometimes, for people like us who've lost a lot, staying alone feels like the safest choice. There's risks involved in getting too close, and we can sell ourselves all kinds of lies and excuses to keep our hearts protected."

Lucy couldn't speak for a moment. Being compared to Reva was a bit of a shock. Also shocking was that Reva seemed to understand Lucy better than Lucy understood herself. Was that what this was about? Was she protecting herself because she'd lost so many loved ones in her life? Losing her mother last Christmas was the hardest loss of all. She wasn't sure she could stand any more heartbreak. "I mean, I have friends. That's enough, right?"

Reva didn't agree. "Friends won't snuggle with you at nighttime. And for this outsider looking in, it seems to me that the only thing holding you back from Miles is yourself, dear. If you lose him, it's your choice. And, if you don't mind me saying so..." Reva said, trailing off.

Lucy was surprised that Reva would even ask permission to say what was on her mind. She usually did so without a moment's hesitation. "Say it."

"Well," Reva said, "it's a stupid choice."

Lucy's jaw dropped. What Reva said wasn't wrong though. She could feel it. She was being stupid and stubborn. "Reva? Do you think you can do me a favor?"

"Well, of course I can." Reva looked absolutely giddy to have the chance.

Lucy had never, ever wanted to be one of Reva's bullet points on her blog. Ever. But since words were failing her these days, maybe Reva could help.

∞

Miles didn't mind working on Christmas Eve day. He did mind the fact that he had to drink bad coffee on a holiday, though, as he walked through the station toward the lounge, wishing he'd stopped at Sweetie's before coming in this morning.

"Hey, Miles," Latoya said, passing him on her way out of the lounge. She looked like the cat that had swallowed the canary, all wide-eyed and grinning.

Miles smiled back. "Let me guess. You have something on that list of yours that will have me investigating something absolutely ridiculous?" Nothing made

Latoya giddier. "A toilet papering of someone's lawn? An egging of another golf cart?"

"No, no. Not this morning. All I've done this morning is read Reva's blog." Her brows lifted, and then she went on her merry way back toward her desk at the front of the building.

Miles stood there for a confused second and then continued his mission for bad coffee from the lounge. Miles had just finished pouring himself a full cup when Sheriff Mills walked in, also wearing a wide grin.

"Morning, Miles," he said in a singsong voice that grabbed Miles's attention and held it.

Miles lifted his cup of coffee to his mouth and sipped, the bitter liquid hitting his tongue as his mind worked to figure out this little pre-Christmas mystery. "Something's up? You and Latoya are acting strange."

Sheriff Mills chuckled. "Maybe we're just feeling the Christmas spirit now that our Crankster has been stopped, thanks to you."

"Is that it?" Miles asked.

Sheriff Mills gave a half shrug and headed toward the coffee pot. "I also read Reva's blog this morning. Did you by chance get to look at it yet?"

Miles took another sip of his coffee. "I don't make a habit of checking it before I've had my morning coffee."

"You'll want to this morning. I'd hate for you to be late."

"For what?" Miles asked.

The sheriff poured a cup of coffee before turning. "You get off at five today?"

Miles nodded. "Yeah."

"Feel free to leave a bit early if you need to."

"Why would I need to take off early?" Miles asked.

Sheriff Mills got that grin again, sipped his coffee, and headed out of the lounge, calling behind him. "Read the blog! Merry Christmas, Deputy!"

Miles pulled his cell phone out of his pocket. He already knew he was going to be the subject of one of Reva's bullet points today. His chest felt tight as he pulled up her site and waited for it to load, which seemed to take forever. He sipped his coffee nervously, not even tasting it now.

Merry Eve of Christmas, Somerseters!

Here's your daily dose of Reva:

- Candy Cane Chocolate Squares are on sale at Choco-Lovers! Stocking Stuffers anyone?
- Have you heard the rumor that Lucy Hannigan might turn her home into a part-time B&B for parents-to-be? Now there's an interesting idea. Votes needed: Hannigan House? Or the Babymoon Bed and Breakfast?
- Deputy Miles Bruno, are you reading this? If you are, Lucy Hannigan would like to invite you to meet her at the Penguin Wonderland tonight, six p.m., don't be late. (She didn't say this, this is all Reva, but bring mistletoe! That'll solve your quarrel ;)
- Somerseters, Lucy and Miles's relationship is none of our business. Wink-wink. We absolutely should not drive by the pink house on Christmas Lane at six p.m. to look at the Penguin Wonderland display. Wink-wink. Lucy and Miles deserve privacy. Cough. Wink. (See you tonight. Bring popcorn.)

Miles stared at his phone. Lucy wanted to meet. She wanted to talk about their relationship—finally. The question was, did she want to end things or try again? He knew what he wanted. What he'd always wanted.

Latoya was back in the lounge doorway. "It doesn't matter what she wants to say when she meets with you. Fight for her. That's what every woman wants." She held up a finger. "Correction. That's what every woman wants from the man they love. And we all know that Lucy loves you and you love her, so fight. Like your heart depends on it."

Miles blinked his friend and co-worker into focus. "I wouldn't have pegged you as a romantic, Latoya."

"We all are, somewhere deep inside, aren't we?"

∞

Lucy was bundled up in her heavy coat with a scarf around her neck and a knit hat. She had on boots too. The snow had started falling an hour ago—the longest hour of her life. Was Miles going to show? One thing she could pretty much count on: The rest of Somerset Lake would be arriving shortly, no thanks to Reva.

Lucy should have known that the lovable blogger would have issued a blanket non-invitation that felt like the opposite to come watch what would either be a reunion or the last goodbye.

Or...

Lucy stared out her window as the seconds ticked down to the six o'clock hour. Or her being stood up.

She wouldn't blame Miles, of course. She'd asked him to move out. She'd clung to the past when he'd offered her the future. What could she say? She'd been a mess this past week between thinking she might have to sell the house she loved and missing her mom so much she thought her heart might break in half.

Lucy glanced down at her phone. 5:56.

On a breath, she walked to the door, opened it, and stepped outside. The cold air hit her face and made her eyes burn. Her breath puffed in a white cloud in front of her as she pulled the door shut, leaving Bella inside where it was warm. There were two cars parked on the curb across the street. Lucy wondered if they were here for the "show." Undoubtedly they were.

She sighed and ignored them. She didn't care. All she cared about was Miles. Was he coming? She looked at her phone as she stepped off the porch and into her Penguin Wonderland lit up with bright pink lights. 5:58.

A car came down the street, driving slowly. It wasn't Miles's vehicle so Lucy turned and pretended to adjust a penguin's hat. Snow had accumulated on it, making it droop. Tomorrow her whole yard would be covered in a soft white blanket, just in time for Christmas. A white Christmas! She didn't want to spend it alone. She wanted to spend it with the man she loved. She wanted to spend every Christmas forevermore with him.

5:59.

As soon as she looked at the time on her phone, it changed to 6:00. Her breath caught, and her heart sped up. She looked down the street where three more cars were driving up slowly. None of them were Miles's truck. *Thanks a lot, Reva.*

6:01. That minute late was the longest minute Lucy thought she'd ever experienced. Then she heard a siren coming down the street, growing louder as it grew closer. Lucy hugged herself as she stood beside Frosty the Snow Penguin, shivering, heart hammering, watching the street. A deputy cruiser drove slowly with its lights on and sirens blaring. It turned into her driveway a moment later at exactly 6:03 p.m. Lucy immediately saw that Miles was sitting behind the wheel. He cut the siren but not the lights. The lights stayed on, dancing over the hot pink ones on her lawn, clashing horribly.

"Hi," he said as he stepped out and approached.

"Making a scene?" she asked.

"Well, I like to put on a good show." He glanced at what were now five parked cars on the curb.

Lucy smiled when he met her eyes again. "Not my best idea, asking Reva for help winning you back."

Miles took a few steps toward her. "Oh, is that what you're doing? Winning me back? Because I was fully prepared to win tonight." He was standing right in front of her.

She shoved his chest playfully, the touch zinging through her. "You always have to be the winner, don't you?" She shook her head and then tipped her face back to look up at him.

"No. I am fully prepared to lose to you from now on. You win every match, every play, every game, my heart, forever," he said quietly, his voice low and easy.

She swallowed. That was maybe the most romantic thing anyone had ever said to her. "You're making this way too easy, Miles Bruno. You should make me grovel. I pushed you away. I made you move out of your apartment," she reminded him. "The week before Christmas at that."

"Yeah. You cost us a week." He gave her a lopsided

grin. "By my calculations, I cost us about ten years." He reached for her hands, rubbing his thumbs against the backs. They ignored the sound of someone honking from the roadside.

"Kiss her!" someone yelled in the distance.

Lucy pretended not to hear that too.

"One thing I can promise you," Miles said, "is that as long as my heart is beating, I'm never going to leave your side again." He gave her a sheepish look. "Unless you tell me to get lost. Because I am learning to listen."

She smiled up at him. "We just found each other again. I don't want you to get lost."

He squeezed her hands. "So we're making up?"

"If you want to."

"There's nothing I want more this Christmas."

Lucy felt the exact same way.

"Kiss her!" someone yelled again. *Was that Reva?*

"And since we're getting good at asking for what we need, I could use something from you too," Miles said.

"Oh? What's that?" Lucy was willing to give Miles anything. Everything. Her whole world.

"I kind of need a place to live," Miles said, leaning in with every word.

"But I thought you were buying the white house."

"My dream home is actually anywhere that you are." He shrugged. "And I kind of think pink is more my color these days."

"Kiss her!"

Lucy blinked through her tears. "I happen to have a room for rent above my garage for as long as you need it. Do you still have our lucky penny?"

He narrowed his eyes. "Check my coat pocket."

She embraced him and reached her hands into both pockets simultaneously, her gaze locking with his. "What's this?" she asked, pulling out the penny in one hand and a wooden box in the other. She audibly gasped. "Is this what I think it is?"

She remembered this box from the first time he'd proposed. It had held his great-grandmother's diamond. She'd thought she'd never see it again but here it was in her cold, shaking hand.

Miles gestured at the penny in her right hand. "Heads, you say yes. Tails..."

"I still say yes," she whispered as tears streamed down her cheeks.

"Yeah?" he asked.

"Yeah. I will always say yes to you, Miles Bruno." She leaned into him again, pressing her body to his, going up on her toes and...

"Kiss her!"

Lucy laughed. "We're going to have a very disappointed village on our hands if we don't kiss and make up soon."

"Well, I'm ready if you are."

She couldn't wait another second. She pressed her lips to his, wrapping her arms around his neck and feeling like her world was finally pieced back together again.

Then they pulled back, and Miles took the box from her hand. He lifted the lid and revealed the ring that had once been hers. "Warning, once I put this ring on your finger, it's never coming off again. You'll be stuck with me every Christmas from here on out, from now until forever."

Lucy beamed. "That sounds absolutely perfect to me."

"To me too," he said, slipping the ring on her finger.

Then they shared the first of many Christmas kisses against the backdrop of nosy well-meaning well-wishers and the brightest, merriest, most magical of winter penguin wonderlands.

Epilogue

Merry Christmas, Somerseters!

Here's your daily dose of Reva:

- The opossum has struck again! Don't worry, he made a mess of Mrs. Newsome's trash, but nothing that couldn't be cleaned up with the help of her grandson Brandon.
- This coming weekend, be there or be square! Trisha Langly and Jake Fletcher are getting hitched on New Year's Day. Which one of you lucky ladies is going to catch the bouquet?
- Lucy Hannigan doesn't need to get in line for bouquet-catching because guess who's wearing a ring on her finger? That's right. Lucy and Miles are getting hitched! Did y'all see that diamond?
- The white house at the end of Mallard Creek Lane has sold! RIP Mr. Romaine, but I think he'd be thrilled to know that our very own River Harrison has decided to purchase the place!
- There's a new flavor of fudge at Sweetie's Bake Shop! Pomegranate Perfection is only being offered until

mid-January. Get yourself a sample. You can start that New Year's diet in February.

- There's a sale at Lakeside Books. Tess is clearing out the old stuff to make room for the new. Stop in and tell her Reva sent you. I get a discount.

Stay tuned for tomorrow's news, y'all,
Reva

∞

While everyone was commenting on how beautiful the bride looked tonight, Miles only had eyes for one particular bridesmaid.

He pulled at his bow tie, loosening it just a touch as he entered the reception area, looking for Lucy. The ceremony had been nice, and he was happy for his buddy Jake. It still surprised Miles a bit that Jake had asked him to be a groomsman, but it was an honor, and Miles hoped the happy couple would enjoy a lifetime of love that compounded year after year.

The band in the corner of the room was playing something slow and romantic, which made Miles think of Lucy. Then again, he'd been thinking of nothing but her for the last two months. Where was she?

He turned, scanning the crowd and coming face-to-face with Gil, who'd also been a groomsman for the couple of the hour.

"Have you seen Lucy?" Miles asked Gil.

"She's with Tess and Moira." Gil pointed toward a table of refreshments where a line of women in blush-colored dresses were helping themselves to chocolate truffles of every kind. "Don't let me keep you. I know you'd rather be over there with Lucy than hanging out with me."

Miles patted Gil's arm. "And I know you'd rather be talking to Moira. C'mon."

They headed over to where the women were, and Miles stepped in front of Lucy. She held up a chocolate-covered strawberry catered from Choco-Lovers. Miles dutifully took a bite.

"Good, right?" Lucy asked, watching him.

"Mm-hmm," he agreed.

"We were all just talking about how beautiful the wedding was," she told him. "And how handsome the groomsmen are," she added with a wink.

Miles dipped to give her a kiss.

"Hey, you two." Della walked over to say hello. "I wanted to introduce you to Roman Everson."

Miles had heard Lucy talk about Della's new boyfriend. She'd met him on an airplane a couple weeks ago, and they'd shared a road trip.

He stuck out his hand. "Nice to meet you."

"Likewise," Roman said.

"This is quite a way to meet the town," Lucy said.

"There is no way I will ever remember anyone's names," Roman agreed.

"Well, I haven't told you mine yet. I'm Lucy." She shook his hand as well. Then she patted Miles's arm. "And this is Miles." Gil was standing close by, so she pulled him closer. "This is Mayor Gil Ryan."

"The mayor?" Roman asked. "My brother, Brian, is the mayor of Sweetwater Springs."

"I've heard of him," Gil said with a nod.

Lucy stepped over and laid a hand on Moira's shoulder, continuing with introductions. "This is my best friend Moira." She pointed at Tess who was pulling a book out of her purse. "And Tess, who owns Lakeside Books. There'll be a quiz at the end of this reception," she told Roman.

The poor guy looked defeated.

Della Rose leaned in and kissed his cheek. "Don't worry. I'll help you with it."

They all laughed. Then Miles gestured at Tess.

"Are you really going to stand there and read a book at a wedding reception?" he asked.

Tess looked up. "Why not?"

"Because you should be dancing," he said.

She smiled warmly. "In a minute, you will be twirling Lucy. Roman will be holding Della Rose. If Gil is lucky, maybe he'll get a dance with Moira." She lifted her book. "This is why I brought something to read."

Miles looked around the room, spotting River at a table by himself. "Do you know River Harrison?"

Tess frowned and looked back at him. "You know that I do."

Oh. Yeah. Miles really hadn't remembered. Tess's late husband had served in the marines with River. They'd been best friends until River had publicly objected to her wedding at the ceremony. "Why don't you ask him to dance? He's alone. You two could be alone together."

Tess's frown deepened, telling Miles that wasn't going to happen. Lucy reached for his hand and squeezed it.

"Care to dance with me?" she asked.

He turned his gaze to meet her sparkling green eyes, falling in love a little deeper every single time he did. There had to be a limit to how deep one could fall. He couldn't keep going deeper. Could he? "I thought you'd never ask."

One corner of her mouth turned up. She grabbed his hand and tugged, pulling him toward the dance floor where other couples were swaying to a gentle beat.

Lucy glanced over, where Tess leaned against the wall with her book after all. Moira was beside her. Either Gil hadn't asked or she'd turned him down. Both were equally likely.

"Why doesn't Moira like Gil?" Miles asked, lowering his voice as he turned his face back to Lucy.

"I think the opposite is true. I think she does like him."

"She has a funny way of showing it."

Lucy grinned. "The only couple I'm interested in tonight is us." She grimaced. "Okay, and the wedding couple. As part of the wedding party, it's my duty to care about them too."

Miles tightened his hold on Lucy, loving how she felt in his arms. Amazed that he got to hold her for the rest of his life. "Remember that movie you made me watch back at Thanksgiving?"

Lucy tipped her head back, the skin between her eyes pinching softly. "*When Harry Met Sally*?"

"Yeah. I know you told me how it ended but I finally watched the last scene the other night. It takes place on New Year's Eve."

"I remember."

"I liked that part where Harry burst into the party, and he searches the crowd looking for Meg Ryan's character."

"Sally," Lucy said, smiling up at him, seeming to enjoy the replay of her favorite part.

Miles gave a small head nod. "Yeah. Then he finds her, their eyes lock, and he walks up to her and tells her everything he should have told her a million times before now."

"It's the best part of the whole movie," Lucy agreed.

Miles could almost feel her sigh against his chest. "Personally, I liked the next part even better."

The pinch between Lucy's eyes deepened. "What next part? The kiss?"

Miles shook his head. "The fast-forward to when Harry and Sally were old and still in love. I liked knowing they got their happy ever after. That it worked out for them in the end."

Lucy placed a hand on his chest. "Such a romantic, Miles Bruno."

"When it comes to you, I am," he said.

The lights came on in the room, and the DJ's voice announced, "All right, ladies. Time for the lovely bride to toss her bouquet!"

Miles's adrenaline surged. He couldn't help it. A little friendly competition always got him going. He looked at Lucy. "All right, Luce. You got this!"

∞

Lucy lifted a brow. "Really? Competitive over a bridal bouquet? You know what that means, don't you? If I catch it."

Miles leaned in and kissed her lips. Then he pulled back and gave her a meaningful look. "Yes, I do. And I still say, go win that bouquet for the team."

Lucy laughed as her heart gave a little kick against her ribs. "You're hopeless. I'll do my best." She headed toward where the women were gathering. It was a strange tradition if you asked her. Gathering around to rush a flying bouquet in hopes that you'd be next to walk down the aisle. It didn't even mean you would be. She linked arms with Tess and Moira as she walked by.

"Hey. I don't want to catch it," Moira said, even though she didn't resist coming along.

Tess didn't resist either. "I've already married once. That's enough for me."

"Shh. It's tradition, and it's Trisha's wedding. As her friends, we owe it to her to be here for all the festivities tonight." Lucy knocked her elbow against Moira. "Grab Della Rose as we pass by," she said.

Moira dutifully nabbed Della. "You're coming with us."

"I'm supposed to catch this thing," Lucy warned the ladies as Trisha turned her back to the small crowd of women. "Miles will be disappointed if I don't."

"Oh, yeah? But he already gave you his great-grandmother's ring," Tess pointed out. "You're already planning on getting married."

Lucy fanned her fingers in front of her, looking at the diamond. She still couldn't believe that she and Miles were back together, planning a future, and this time it was going to last. She wasn't going to be lonely Lucy ever again. "I know, but Miles is hopeless," Lucy said with a head shake and a laugh.

"Ready, girls?" Trisha called behind her.

Everyone shifted around, preparing to fling their arms in the air. Somewhere behind her, Lucy heard Miles's voice call, "Team Lucy and Miles!"

Lucy turned to glare at him just as Trisha tossed the bouquet backward. All arms went up but Lucy wasn't prepared. She whirled too late, arms flying into the air only after the bouquet was caught.

Lucy turned and looked at a wide-eyed Tess.

Tess pushed the bouquet as far from her body as she could. She shook her head quickly. "Oh no. I didn't mean to catch this. Here. It's yours." She held it out to Lucy, eyes desperate.

Lucy took a small step back, grinning. "No, you caught it fair and square. Like you said. I already have a ring on my finger. My happy ever after is pretty much a sure thing."

Tess whirled the bouquet toward Moira who nearly stumbled in her heels to get out of the way.

"Watch where you point that thing, will you?" Moira said.

Trisha stepped up to them, radiant in her gown. "Tess! You caught it!"

Tess frowned.

Lucy laughed and wrapped an arm around her friend's shoulders. "It's okay, Tess. We'll be here for you at book club when you meet this guy who sweeps you off your feet."

"That's a promise," Trisha agreed.

"Can't wait," Moira said.

"This is going to be the best year yet," Della chimed in.

Lucy looked down at the ring on her finger, felt the love pulling in her heart, and turned to search the room for the man who'd stolen it this holiday season. Della was right. This year held all the promise in the world, and she planned to enjoy it, day by day, hour by hour, minute by minute.

The lights dimmed again, and a slow song began to

play. Lucy broke away from her friends and crossed the room toward Miles.

"I'm sorry," she said when she was standing in front of him. "But if you hadn't called out, I wouldn't have gotten so distracted."

"So it's my fault?" he said, a smile lifting at the corners of his mouth.

"We can try again next wedding. You'll stay quiet, and I'll elbow all the women to catch the flowers."

Miles wrapped his arms around her waist, holding her close. He positioned his mouth beside her ear, his voice a low whisper. "Next wedding, you'll be the one tossing the bouquet, Lucy Hannigan."

Acknowledgments

First, as always, I want to thank my family. With every book, I have a greater understanding of my own family's sacrifice to help me bring these books to the shelves, but especially with this one. I love every second of writing, but this book gave me a run for my money and made me so much more certain that I have the most understanding family in the whole world. Thank you, Sonny, Ralphie, Doc, and Lydia for allowing me to take the time to polish and make these books the best that I can.

Secondly, a huge thank you goes out to my brilliant editor at Forever, Alex Logan, who has the creative insight to make my work a thousand times better than it would be otherwise. Thank you to the entire publishing team at Grand Central Forever, especially Estelle, Mari, Daniela, and Shelley Paventy.

Thank you to my super-agent Sarah Younger. I could not do any of this without you by my side. You are amazing! Let's stay together, okay?

Thank you to Rachel Lacey, Tif Marcelo, April Hunt, and Sidney Halston (Jeanette Escudero). You ladies mean the world to me. You're my writing sisters, my friends, and my much-needed support system. Thank you for bouncing ideas about this book, especially the two nurses in our group, April and Tif! Muah! Xoxo!

Last, but never least, I want to thank my readers for reading and loving my stories. That's something I've been dreaming about since I was six years old. So, from the bottom of my heart, thank you for making my dream come true; you're dream makers. You matter and make a difference to me and to so many others, I'm sure. May this holiday season be merry for all of you and your families!

About the Author

Annie Rains is a *USA Today* bestselling contemporary romance author who writes small-town love stories set in fictional places in her home state of North Carolina. When Annie isn't writing, she's living out her own happily ever after with her husband and three children.

Learn more at:

AnnieRains.com
Twitter @AnnieRainsBooks
Facebook.com/AnnieRainsBooks
Instagram @annierainsbooks

Can't get enough of that small-town charm? Forever has you covered with these heartwarming contemporary romances!

AT HOME ON MARIGOLD LANE
by Debbie Mason

For family and marriage therapist Brianna MacLeod, moving back home to Highland Falls after a disastrous divorce feels downright embarrassing. Bri blames herself for missing the red flags in her relationship and thus worries she's no longer qualified to do the job she loves. But helping others is second nature to Bri, and she soon finds herself counseling her roommate and her neighbor's daughter. Bri just wasn't expecting them to reunite her with her first love…

Find more great reads on Instagram with @ReadForeverPub

THE BEACHSIDE BED AND BREAKFAST

by Hope Ramsay

Ashley Howland Scott has no time for romance as she grieves the loss of her husband, cares for her young son, and runs Magnolia Harbor's only bed and breakfast. Ashley never imagined she'd notice—let alone have feelings for—another man after her husband was killed in Afghanistan. But slowly, softly, Rev. Micah St. Pierre has become a friend . . . and now maybe something more. Which is all the more reason to steer clear of him.

RETURN TO CHERRY BLOSSOM WAY

by Jeannie Chin

Han Leung always does the responsible thing, which is why he put aside his dreams of opening his own restaurant to run his family's business in Blue Cedar Falls, North Carolina. But when May Wu re-enters his life, he can no longer ignore his own wants and desires. Garden gnomes are stolen, old haunts are visited, and sparks fly between the pair, just as they always have. Han and May broke up because they wanted vastly different lives, and that hasn't changed—or has it?

Connect with us at
Facebook.com/ReadForeverPub

THE CHRISTMAS VILLAGE
by Annie Rains
As the competition heats up in the Merriest Lawn decorating contest, Lucy Hannigan can't help feeling like a Scrooge. Her mom had won the contest every year, but Lucy isn't sure she has it in her to deck the halls this first Christmas without her mother. But when Miles Bruno, her ex-fiancé, shows up with tons of tinsel, dozens of decorations, and lots and lots of lights, Lucy begins to wonder if maybe the spirit of the season can finally mend her broken heart.

DREAMING OF A HEART LAKE CHRISTMAS
by Sarah Robinson
To raise enough money to start her own business, Nola Bennett needs to sell "the Castle," her beloved grandmother's historic house, and get back to the city. But Heart Lake's most eligible bachelor, Tanner Dean, rudely objects. He may be the hottest, grumpiest man she's ever met, and Nola has no time to pine over her high school crush. But sizzling attraction flares the more time he spends convincing her the potential buyers are greedy developers. Will Nora finally realize that this is exactly where she belongs?

Discover bonus content and more on read-forever.com

SUGARPLUM WAY
by Debbie Mason
Aidan's only priority is to be the best single dad ever, and this year he plans to make the holidays magical for his young daughter. But visions of stolen kisses under the mistletoe keep dancing in his head, and when he finds out Julia Landon has written him into her latest novel, he can't help imagining a future together. Little does he know that Julia has been keeping a secret that threatens all their dreams. Luckily, 'tis the season for a little Christmas magic.

A LITTLE BIT OF LUCK (2-IN-1 EDITION)
by Jill Shalvis
Enjoy a visit to Lucky Harbor in these two dazzling novels! In *It Had to Be You*, a woman's only shot at clearing her tarnished name is with the help of a sexy police detective. Is the chemistry between them a sizzling fling…or the start of something bigger? In *Always on My Mind*, a little white lie pulls two longtime friends into a fake relationship. But pretending to be hot and heavy starts bringing out feelings for each other that are all too real.